# What the critics are saying...

### Heather's Gift *Men of August 3*

"Lora Leigh proves herself once again in the third book in this series. Heather's Gift is clearly as well done as the first. She easily takes an unorthodox situation and shows the love radiating in the characters of her book." - *Angel, The Romance Studio*

"In Book 3 of The Men of August series, wounded heroes, fantastic sexual appetites and group sex make this story quite electrifying and highly erotic. With characters this real, readers may forget that they are reading fantasies. Leigh has penned another very powerfully written sexual suspense." - *Cindy Whitesel, Romantic Times*

"Heather's Gift is a book you'll not want to put down. The searing intrigue of this novel most certainly makes it a page turner. As the secrets of the past are revealed, the pain and the passion rise to unbelievable heights for this family." - *Robin Taylor, In The Library Review*

"I applaud Ms. Leigh on her wonderful creativity and courage to go beyond the everyday norm. Heather's Gift will make you laugh, cry, and sigh before it's over with." - *Reva Moore, Just Erotic Romance Reviews*

### B.O.B.'s Fall *with Victoria Chadwick*

"I greatly enjoyed the creativity and imagination wielded by Ms. Leigh and Ms. Chadwick. Their tale of advanced technology in a futuristic world is one I will enjoy reading repeatedly. I highly recommend B.O.B.s Fall to anyone looking for a unique and refreshing story to read!" - *Susan White, Coffee Time Romance*

"B.O.B.'s FALL is an irresistible blend of humor, action, and love. The sparks fly when Mac and Ilyiana are together. Lora Leigh and Veronica Chadwick certainly know how to create a powerful story of the meaning of love while keeping the scenes hot and captivating." - *Nicole Hulst, eCataRomance* Reviews

"B.O.B.'s Fall is a tantalizingly stimulating read. I anxiously await Amarenth's and Tael's story. If you, like me, have fallen under the "The MacDougal's" family spell that Ms. Chadwick and Ms. Leigh have created then this book is a must read. You will not be disappointed." - *Dianne Nogueras, eCataRomance*

## Soul Deep *Coyote Breeds 1*

"This sizzler was so good that I finished it in one night. Great read and a great job! " - *Kelly, Soul Deep, Sizzling Romances*

"First time Lora Leigh readers and long-time fans will want to read this story of a Coyote Breed, his mate, and their path to a lifetime of love and commitment that is soul deep. Bravo, Ms. Leigh, you have once again written a winner." - *Nicole, Romance Junkies*

"Lora Leigh is a very talented and prolific writer. She has the ingenious ability to enrapture her reader with two characters that so real that you can almost reach out and touch them. The deep emotion of the characters in this book caught me from the start and kept me riveted. I have loved all of Ms. Leigh's books but this one by far has to be one of my favorites. If are a fan of Ms. Leigh's, then this book is a must read. You will not be disappointed." - *Dianne Nogueras, eCata Romance*

# HEATHER'S GIFT

## By Lora Leigh

Heather's Gift
An Ellora's Cave Publication, January 2005

Ellora's Cave Publishing, Inc.
1337 Commerce Drive
Stow, Ohio 44224

ISBN # 1-4199-5048-7

Heather's Gift©2003 Lora Leigh
Other available formats: ISBN MS Reader (LIT), Adobe (PDF),
Rocketbook (RB), Mobipocket (PRC) & HTML

Edited by: Sue-Ellen Gower
Cover art by: Syneca

# Warning:

The following material contains graphic sexual content meant for mature readers. *Heather's Gift* has been rated E-*rotic* by a minimum of three independent reviewers.

Ellora's Cave Publishing offers three levels of Romantica™ reading entertainment: S (S-ensuous), E (E-rotic), and X (X-treme).

S-*ensuous* love scenes are explicit and leave nothing to the imagination.

E-*rotic* love scenes are explicit, leave nothing to the imagination, and are high in volume per the overall word count. In addition, some E-rated titles might contain fantasy material that some readers find objectionable, such as bondage, submission, same sex encounters, forced seductions, etc. E-rated titles are the most graphic titles we carry; it is common, for instance, for an author to use words such as "fucking", "cock", "pussy", etc., within their work of literature.

X-*treme* titles differ from E-rated titles only in plot premise and storyline execution. Unlike E-rated titles, stories designated with the letter X tend to contain controversial subject matter not for the faint of heart.

# Look for these other exciting books from Lora Leigh!

# HEATHER'S GIFT

## By Lora Leigh

# Prologue

The night was soft. A gentle, early summer night, thick with the scent of honeysuckle and the rain that had passed hours before. The glow of the full moon shadowed the land, leaving secrets hidden, scars unseen and the gentle mystery of the land left to soothe the soul.

Sam slid through the shadows cast by the stables and the thick brush that led to a sheltered grove. He was adept at hiding in the darkness, at using the shadows to slip and hide and make his way to whatever destination he had chosen. He had been doing it since he was ten. Finding adventure, finding peace within the open land he called home. There had been times when it had saved his sanity, that peace, the wide-open freedom, the smell of juniper, honeysuckle and a cleansing rain.

He wasn't a kid now, or a tormented young man. He was an adult, and though he fought the shadows in his own mind, he knew the demons weren't far behind. He hid behind careless laughter, teased his brothers, played childish pranks. Even at the age of thirty-one, he made certain to find a way as often as possible to break the bleak sadness that filled Cade and Brock.

The sadness was lifting a bit now, and Sam found as their happiness began to bloom, the darkness within himself began to grow. Marly helped. Bright and filled with laughter and a compassion and acceptance he would never fully understand, she lightened the hell they all lived within.

He paused beneath the spreading limbs of a thickly leafed oak and glanced back at the house. She would be sleeping now, held close by Cade, and possibly even Brock, unless he had headed back to town and Sarah, while Sam was showering.

Marly wasn't the first they had shared, but she was the most important. She was Cade's soul. She was his and Brock's heart. They had helped raise her since she was twelve, had endured her teenage years as she flirted and rubbed against them like a frisky foal, and they now shared in the passionate, heated love she had for Cade.

"Bad Sam, sneaking out of the house like that." He jumped as the amused, feminine voice brought him out of his thoughts.

He turned quickly, watching as a dark form separated itself from a nearby tree. His lips quirked in humor. Heather March was going to break his heart. He couldn't help the thought as he watched the petite redhead stroll slowly toward him.

Slender, as graceful as a doe and as sexy as sin itself, she moved as light as the wind, as soft as a shadow toward him. She made his dick come to instant attention and his body tense with a hunger he had never known with another woman.

"You're following me again." He tried to sound disapproving, stern, but it was hard when she made him feel so damned light inside.

"It's my job, Sammy." He winced at the nickname she had stuck on him. Marly's mother used to call him Sammy. He didn't like it then, and he didn't like it now. "I'm supposed to follow your bad ass."

A soft ray of moonlight speared through the trees, glistening in her red hair, glowing against the soft creamy skin of her pretty face. Her green eyes reminded him of a cat, softly tilted, inquisitive. Her pert nose was just too cute for words, but her pouty little mouth was a work of art. The curves glistened with moisture and made his cock thicken and harden beneath his jeans with abrupt need.

As she came close he reached out, jerking her against his chest as she gasped in surprise. He held her close, letting her feel the erection straining beneath his jeans.

"Sam," he reminded her softly, inhaling the soft scent she wore. It was romantic and soft, and undeniably hot. "Not

Sammy, Heather. I'm going to get you for that nickname you're trying to pin to my ass."

A grin stretched her lips as her body softened against his. "My sister catches you holding me captive like this and she'll kick your ass," she snickered. "Better let me go."

He turned until he could back her against the tree, holding her there with easy strength. "Your sister just likes to think she's all bad," he whispered, the fingers of one hand playing with the long braid that fell down her back. "I'm not scared of her."

Her hands smoothed up his chest and he fought himself, fighting for breath and for control. Damn, he shouldn't be this horny, this hot. Not after the hour he had spent with Marly, her lips wrapped first around his thick cock, then the tight, velvet heat of her ass gripping him. But Heather could make him hot when no one else could. She was soft and sweet, and so damned smart-mouthed she could make him crazier than hell.

"You better be scared of her. She's mean." Her hands paused at his heart, and he knew she could feel the hard throb of his excitement there as easily as she could feel his hard-on pressing against her abdomen.

Silence lengthened between them then as sexual tension thickened in the air.

"You were with Marly tonight," she finally whispered softly. "Tara cleared us away from the house. She always does."

He wanted to look away from her, but he could see the questions in her eyes. Why did he go to his brother's woman, when he could have her? And he could have her. He knew she got just as wet for him, as his cock got hard for her.

His finger ran over her cheek gently. "Would you want to watch?" The thought of it was almost enough to make him crazy with arousal.

"I don't think so, big boy," she sniped with a fierce frown. "You're a real interestin' man, Sammy. But watching you fuck another woman wouldn't be the highlight of my day." Jealousy shimmered in her voice along with a thread of anger.

He sighed deeply. "It's not like that, Heather." He moved away from her, shaking his head as he crossed the short distance back to the stables.

She was silent, but he was aware of her following him, keeping up with his longer stride until they entered the dimly lit haven of the building. The horses were all in the pastures, and the building smelled of sweetly scented hay and leather saddles.

"You shouldn't be sneaking out like this, Sam," she said as she closed the door behind her. "With the stalker's return, it's hard telling..."

"I wish he would come after me." He turned to her, rage surging through his body. "Son of a bitch thinks he can get away with attacking our women and trying to destroy our lives. He's a fucking coward, Heather, and one day, one of us will get our hands on him."

"If he doesn't kill you first," she snorted, watching him with that bright, sharp gaze that sometimes seemed to pierce his soul. "You need to be more careful. All of you do."

She leaned against one of the stalls, her arms crossing under her breasts as she watched him with that militant look in her eye.

"Keep looking at me like that, and one day I'll take you up on the fight you seem to be wanting," he told her softly, unable to keep from going to her again.

His hands settled on her hips, and he marveled at how small she was, how delicate her bones seemed. But she was tough as hell. He had watched her practice her martial arts moves with Tara, as well as Rick, and he knew she was a hell of a lot tougher than she looked.

"If you have the energy left, you mean?" She arched a fiery brow mockingly.

He sighed deeply. "Do you want to know, Heather, why I haven't taken you? Why I haven't come after you with every weapon I can think of to get you into my bed?"

"Because you know I can kick your ass?" Her hands ran up his arms until they lay against his shoulders. Soft, graceful fingers that he was dying to feel on his bare flesh.

He shook his head. She was good, damned good, but he wasn't the least bit intimidated by her. He could take her, eventually.

"Because I know that sooner or later, I would need to see you beneath my brothers as well," he told her softly, warningly. "We survived hell together, Heather. A hell unlike anything you could imagine if you hadn't lived through it. And I don't think you're ready to consider the thought of being part of that."

"And how does the sharing help you, Sam?" She tilted her head, frustration lighting her eyes. "How can sharing something that should belong solely to you heal any part of that?"

He shook his head, wondering how to explain. It was complicated, difficult. At times he couldn't make sense of it himself, so he struggled with how to make her understand.

"We gave our souls for each other in that hellhole." He fought the blinding pain that the thought of it, the shadowed memories of it, brought. "We were forced to betray each other, to brutalize each other, Heather. And we swore we wouldn't let it break us. It changed us though. It forged a bond that can never be broken, but it destroyed another part of us in the process. A part that kept us together as brothers, the love that was between us as brothers, he destroyed that. Destroyed it, Heather. It's gone. Now we fall back on the only thing we had before it happened. It's not just a desire, or a need. It's a bonding that reaffirms we didn't lose everything to that bastard's cruelty."

"Sam, it's unnatural." She shook her head, and though her voice was gentle, it lacked any understanding. "You love each other more than you love those women."

"That's not true." Shock filled his system, traveled through his body. "Heather, that's not the way it is, baby. It's not. It's because of our love for them, don't you see? The fear that one of us alone can't protect them, can't care for them. We know our limits; we know the horrors out there and the monsters who live to destroy. We know how easily one of us can be destroyed. It's our love for those women, our need to see them always protected, always cared for, always loved, Heather. It's to prove to each other that we trust the other to do this. And Heather, the heat…" He broke off, his cock throbbing, thinking of her sharing in that, screaming out in the pleasure. "The heat and pleasure is like nothing you've known. Marly connects us again, she reaffirms that we're alive and that we can still function and love. That we're not alone."

She stared up at him, a frown darkening her brow. "But Sam, you aren't alone," she stressed. "You shouldn't need to share your lovers to reaffirm this."

"No, we shouldn't." He sighed heavily, hearing his own doubts, his own guilt in her words. "But it's always been that way, Heather," he whispered, knowing it was true. "Cade glories in Marly's pleasure. You can see it in his eyes, in his love for her. Her pleasure and her happiness are everything to him. He gives her in return the only thing he knows how. More love. More pleasure. His brothers. And it will be the same for Brock and Sarah, if she agrees to come to the ranch. It's all their love, Heather. All our love."

He watched as she licked her lips nervously, nibbled on the lower one as she thought, then she sighed deeply, regretfully.

"And if the woman you eventually love can't accept it?" she asked him softly. "What if she can't bear your touching another woman, or one of your brothers touching her?"

He was quiet for long moments, sadness filling his soul, because he had a feeling he held the woman who would very well hold his heart. The woman who would refuse.

"Then she would hold only half a man," he whispered painfully. "I worry, Heather, and I agonize that we're hurting Marly, that we'll hurt Sarah. The guilt eats at me in ways you could never understand. But I also know if I didn't have it, or one day share in it, then a part of me would be lost forever. A very important, very vital part of me."

"Or," she whispered. "A part of you would be healed..."

\* \* \* \* \*

It was a question Sam couldn't answer. As one week turned into two, and the attraction progressed, thickened, Sam couldn't reconcile his needs with those he felt were Heather's. A kiss progressed to two. He tasted her breasts, brought her to climax with his mouth and felt the overwhelming pleasure of her mouth enveloping his cock.

When he learned she was a virgin, he pulled back. What he needed from her a virgin could never accept, he told himself. But the attraction wouldn't die, the needs wouldn't extinguish. Then she left for a brief time, returning to her home. When she came back, he went to her. Went to her because he couldn't resist her laughter, her smart mouth or touch. And he began to hope. Began to believe that perhaps one day she would understand...

And then the stalker struck again. They found Heather bound, her slender legs spread, the soft mound of her cunt sliced by a madman's scalpel. Sam knew that, no matter how much he loved her, and he did love her, no matter his need for her, he couldn't have her. The past was rising, swift and sure, and it could very well destroy him as it hadn't during those bleak, dark days of captivity. So he fought...

# Chapter One
*Two months later*

He was out there. Sam could feel it. The knowledge throbbed in the scars on his abdomen, in the dark nightmares that were suddenly surfacing even while he was awake. The bastard was watching them, waiting, perfecting his timing before he struck again.

He stared into the night through the bulletproof balcony doors of his bedroom and wondered when the stalker would strike again. Who was he, and why was he intent on revenge for the destruction of a madman? Jedediah Marcelle had been a monster. A creature of such evil, such black, all-consuming perversions, that he was every nightmare come to life.

Sometimes Sam wondered if the bastard's ghost wasn't stalking them, threatening to steal from them everything they held dear. And those women were held dear.

Marly, Sarah and Heather. His jaw clenched at the thought of the pain each of them had already endured. Especially Heather. The bastard had cut her, stripped her of her clothes, spread her legs, and sliced into the soft, velvety flesh of her mound.

The razor thin cuts had been just deep enough to ensure that scars remained, but not so deep as to maim. Barely visible now, but easily felt. He ran his hand over his abdomen, feeling the roughness of the flesh there, the scars he carried himself. If he went further, he would feel those on his cock.

He closed his eyes then, fighting the sick rolling of his stomach, the guilt and shame and never-ending knowledge that his violent refusal of Marcelle's advances had resulted in months of horror for not just himself, but his brothers as well. A refusal that had changed all their lives forever.

He propped his elbow on the doorframe and rubbed his forehead over his arm. Thinking of the past sickened him. The smell of blood, semen and tears drifted through his memories as agony pierced his soul. He clenched his teeth, fighting the dark visions that drifted through his mind.

For the most part, he had blocked the memories. Unlike Cade and Brock, he had somehow managed to dim the brutal clarity of what had happened. For a time. Now they seemed to be returning with a vengeance, and not just in the form of nightmares. In the form of bloody flashbacks and twisted expressions of death.

He shook his head, feeling the moisture that chilled his flesh as a cold sweat enveloped his body. He raised his head, blinking as he stared out at the moon-shadowed landscape of the ranch and fought for answers.

"Where are you?" he whispered bleakly. "And what the hell do you have planned now?"

"I'm sure he'll let us know soon." The soft, feminine voice had him jerking the curtains closed and turning to the connecting door.

She stood there, framed by the soft light from the room, red hair gleaming from the backlight, her expression shadowed.

"What the hell are you doing up here?" He frowned as he checked to be certain the curtains were closed securely and that there was no chance prying eyes could see her. She had been attacked because of his attraction to her, his affection for her. He couldn't take the chance that the violence against her would escalate.

"Cade didn't tell you?" She stepped farther into the room, her slender body moving languidly in the dim light. "He thought it would be safer for me to sleep up here rather than downstairs. Personally, I think I'm starting to cramp family time down there."

She smiled as she said the words, but he heard the vein of hurt in her voice. She knew...knew he had been with Sarah and Marly, knew he had gone to them when he continued to refuse to go to her.

"I won't make excuses..."

"Do I ask you for excuses, Sam?" She tilted her head as she watched him. "You explained it to me pretty clearly the first time. I don't have a hold on you, so it's none of my business..." She paused. "Right?"

Sam watched her broodingly. If only she knew. Unfortunately, telling her would only add to his problems.

"Yeah. Right," he grunted as he turned away from her. "Fine, you're in the room beside me. Keep the door closed, ignore my snoring and we'll get along fine."

Now he could only pray she could ignore the nightmares. Somehow he had a feeling that was wishful thinking at its height.

"So you snore?" She walked farther into the room, as though she owned the place, Sam thought.

"Loudly." He tried to ignore the fact that she plopped on his bed and watched him expectantly as he stared back at her.

"Fine." She shrugged. "I'll ignore your snoring, you ignore my vibrator buzzing."

He blinked. His heart damned near shot out of his chest, it thundered so hard, and his cock was fully erect and throbbing no sooner than the words were out of her mouth. Damn her, she didn't play fair.

"Son of a bitch!" He raked his fingers roughly through his hair as he stared at her in amazement. "You're a virgin."

"So?" She was laughing at him. He could hear the amusement in her voice, the mockery. "Even virgins get horny, Sammy."

She scooted back on the bed, crossing her legs like a damned pretzel as she propped her chin on her fist and watched him.

"Aren't you on duty or something?" If she didn't get out of his damned bed he wasn't going to be responsible for his actions. The thought of that vibrator was killing him.

"Nope. I just came off duty. Everything's quiet and calm for now so I thought I'd come see if you needed to be tucked into bed or something."

Or something, definitely, he thought heatedly. Less than two hours ago he had climaxed until he wanted to scream with the pleasure, and now he was dying to touch Heather, to take her, to hear her cries echoing around him. To possess her in a way she could never imagine. A way he knew she could never accept.

Then he stopped. Had she heard? Did she know it was her name he cried out as he pumped his semen deep inside Sarah's body?

"Where were you earlier?" He couldn't stop the question. Couldn't stop the need to know.

"I wasn't watching, if that's what you want to know." The amusement was gone from her voice. "I was tucked nice and safe in the camper, hon, so you don't have to worry."

He heard the hurt, the lingering question in her voice, and fought to ignore it.

"Who was worried?" Hell, he almost came in his jeans just thinking about her watching.

"Sam." Her voice warned him that he was treading dangerous ground. A subject she didn't want to discuss, one she refused to understand.

"Fine, Heather." He breathed out roughly. "Now go tuck yourself into bed and I'll play nice and stay in the house tonight. How's that? But get your ass off my bed and out of my bedroom before I forget why you were attacked, and why I can't have you. Because God's truth, I'm within minutes of fucking you until you can't move."

"Amazing." Her voice was mocking. "I'm convinced the August men stole testosterone and stamina at birth. You three are like bunnies."

"Keep it up and you'll find out," he grunted, fighting not to touch her as she moved slowly from the bed.

"Fine, I need to sleep anyway." She shrugged, though he could feel the hurt echoing in the air around him. "More damned shopping tomorrow. As though either of those women need more dresses. Rick's going to have to give this up soon."

Sam stilled, watching her closely as she leaned against the tall poster of the bed.

"He's still trying to draw the stalker out?" It would make the fourth venture into town.

Rick was convinced that the stalker had to be living close, in a position to hear the gossip concerning the August men and to sneak in and out of the ranch unnoticed.

"We have to do something, Sam. We can't just wait on him to strike." She shook her head, sighing roughly. "No one will be safe until he's stopped."

"Putting the three of you in danger isn't the answer." He turned away from her, rage ricocheting through him. "Goddammit. The bastard isn't sane." He shuddered as dark memories twisted inside him. "Heather, you don't know. You don't know what he could do to you."

But Sam knew. He knew the pain and the horror, the bleak evil that could infect such men's minds.

"We aren't in danger, Sam." She came to him, moving easily, comfortably into his arms as he opened them for her.

He needed to hold her. Just hold her. To feel her soft and warm against him, to feel, that for a moment, he was keeping her safe, keeping her sheltered. It was all he could allow himself for now.

"You're all in danger." He lowered his head, inhaling the clean, delicate scent of her.

"Rick will take care of us, and we'll be surrounded by the bodyguards." She moved back from him a second after he felt her tight nipples pressing into his chest through their shirts, though he kept her in the circle of his arms. "I just hate the shopping part." The wry amusement in her voice was designed to distract him. He knew that, and for the moment allowed her to believe she had succeeded.

"Buy a dress," he whispered, bending down to nuzzle her ear as she shivered sensually. "Something short and light. Something to show off those pretty legs of yours."

"I don't think so." He could hear the breathless quality of her voice. "I've seen what happens to the women in this house when they wear dresses. I'll just keep my jeans for now, thank you." She pressed against his chest, an indication of her need for escape.

"Heather." His arms contracted around her, loath to release her. "If the danger weren't so high, the situation so desperate, I'd show you in a way you could understand. Explain everything in such sensual actions that you would never forget. I'd love you, baby, in ways you can't even imagine."

"Sounds good, Sammy." Her voice was soft, sad. "Let me know when you run out of excuses, okay? I might be willing to try then."

She moved away from him, glancing over her shoulder as she turned her back on him. For a moment, from the light of the other bedroom, he thought he saw a sheen of tears. But then she turned away and stepped slowly into her own room, closing the door behind her. The darkness enveloped him, inside and out.

"Son of a bitch," he cursed the situation, cursed the throbbing desperation of his hard cock. He couldn't be around her, couldn't think about her, without growing spike hard.

Being with Sarah or Marly didn't help. It eased the demons, but not the emotional and physical demands that Heather inspired. He grimaced as he undressed for bed, throwing the clothes carelessly on the floor. The bed was big, wide enough for three, and too damned lonely. He lay atop the blankets, staring up at the ceiling bleakly, then to the door that separated the two rooms as his eyes narrowed in intent.

Jerking a tube of lubrication from the beside table drawer, he squeezed a healthy amount into the palm of his hand then stroked it over his straining cock as he imagined her. Imagined her coming to him, her soft body naked, hot, taking him, needing him.

His fingers tightened around the throbbing shaft as the images of Heather, naked, wet and wild, drifted through his mind. She would be tight. So damned tight. He stifled his groan as he stroked his straining cock, his fingers moving slowly over the scarred flesh as they tightened with the thought of Heather's tight, soft cunt.

She would grip him, sear him. His hips flexed, his cock pulsing to the imagined sensation as his fingers stroked over the bulging flesh. The pace of his hand increased as he imagined her cries, her expression going slack with pleasure, her pussy tightening, spasming. He couldn't stop the strangled groan as his cock exploded, spewing his creamy release over his hard abdomen as the pleasure tingled up his spine.

"Now that wasn't fair." His eyes snapped open as Heather stared at him from the doorway. And she was pissed. "Don't use my fucking name, Sam, unless it's me you're actually fucking."

She turned and slammed the door as she left again, leaving him surprised, a shade embarrassed, and so damned hard again he could do nothing but growl in misery.

# Chapter Two

"Heather, you'll be with Marly and Sarah shopping," Tara told her firmly the next morning as the group of bodyguards met in the bunkhouse for a final briefing. "Helena and Calvin's team will be moving into place soon in the shops along the street while Rick and his team set up to watch the street from the café across the street. We'll keep it simple and short and see what happens."

"Nothing's happened yet." Raider, a big, rawboned ex-mercenary shifted dangerously in his seat. "And it won't until Sam makes his move. What you're dealing with here is someone too smart to mess up until you make him mad. I say we make him mad."

Heather glanced over at the big man, frowning. Raider wasn't his real name, and he hadn't been with the team long enough for her to get to know him very well. His black eyes were cold; his expression, more often than not, devoid of emotion or feeling. But sometimes, like now, she caught a lingering glimpse of humor in the corners of his lips when he watched Tara.

"What do you suggest, Raider, an August orgy in the center of town?" Tara sneered coldly.

"Only if Heather's in the center of it." He shrugged. "But it seems like overkill to me, Tara. The stalker's got a line on that house somehow. He'll know if she's fucking him."

Heather flushed and cursed the flare of arousal that lit, fast and furious, in her body at the thought of Sam. He had carefully avoided the "family times," as Tara had labeled them, several months before, until the past night. But in walking away from them, it seemed that he only grew darker, edgier, more dangerous.

"My sister isn't being pimped out for this assignment," Tara snapped furiously.

"That's enough, Tara," Heather said softly as she turned to her sister. "The bad part is, he's right. These little outings aren't doing anything but wearing on those women's nerves, and mine." She was tired of shopping, tired of the tension and fear that marked Heather and Sarah's gazes while they were out.

She looked at Raider, and for a second, caught an edge of savage mercilessness in his eyes. Only Rick and Tara seemed to know the other man very well. There were times he flat terrified her.

"Until we come up with something better, this is it," Tara informed them both ruthlessly. "If you don't like following orders, Raider, you can pack up and head out anytime. No one forces you to stay here."

The tension thickened instantly. Raider drew slowly to his feet as the other six agents in the room watched warily.

"Yeah, someone does, Tara," he growled, his voice deadly. "But I'll take that up with her when the time's right. Let me know when you're ready to leave."

He stalked from the room. He didn't move fast, he didn't stomp. You never heard a footfall, he was so damned quiet. And it was all the more terrifying for the complete silence. The door clicked quietly behind him before all eyes turned to Tara.

"He'll live." She shrugged as though unconcerned, but Heather saw the worry that lit her light green eyes.

"That boy's going to slip his leash one day. When he does, there'll be hell to pay." Bret Austin, the August employee who had joined the group months before, shook his head warily. "I'd watch that one."

"Don't you have cattle to watch?" Tara frowned, her voice reproving.

A careless grin tipped the cowboy's face as his hazel eyes lit up with laughter. "Hell, cows ain't this much fun. Can't I stay around and watch some more?"

"Show's over," Tara grunted. "You're here on house detail. Make sure you keep those damned men here at the house, Bret. It defeats the purpose if they follow us."

Bret grimaced. "Damned good thing Rick promised me work when Cade fires me. 'Cause by damned, he will eventually. Keep him home," he snorted. "That's like ordering me to keep a momma bear in her den while you torture her cubs."

Tara rolled her eyes. "At least warn me if they head out. They made the deal. One more trip out. Don't let them screw us over without warning."

"Will do." He nodded shortly, though Heather doubted seriously that he would go against Cade August if push came to shove. Hell, even Rick hesitated before going up against the oldest brother.

"And you," Tara snapped as the men filed from the room. "Stay the hell out of Sam August's bedroom."

Heather arched her brow slowly. "You're not my keeper, Tara."

"No, I'm your sister, and I'm telling you that the August men are more than you can handle. Stop playing with fire and concentrate on your job."

"Sam August is my job," she said softly. "I won't pretend I don't care for him. Even for you."

She understood Tara's worry, knew the dark experiences from her sister's past that fueled her concern.

"God, Heather, haven't you learned how dangerous this is yet?" Tara demanded. "You're scarred forever. Dead lasts just as long. You were lucky the first time, now pull back."

"Stop, Tara." Heather faced her sister slowly, tucking her hands in her jeans pockets to still the need to wrap her arms around the other woman. She could see Tara's pain, the ghosts that haunted her. "You can't protect me from this, and you can't order me away from him as though I were a child."

"I can fire you," she snapped angrily.

"Then fire me." Heather shrugged. "I won't leave, and I won't stay any further away from Sam than he keeps me pushed back, anyway."

Her sister's expression tightened, her lips thinning out to a cold, ruthless line.

"He wants to share you, Heather," Tara said tightly. "Do you want to know what that's like? Do you really want to know just how loveless that is? You think you love him. You think he loves you. But he doesn't. Love isn't packaged like that. It's sex. It's lust. Period."

It was Tara's lifestyle. She had lived it with her husband before Rick had pulled her out. She had lain between the man she hated and the man who pitied her, and Heather knew it had nearly destroyed her. And yet, now that there was no chance of emotion, no chance of caring, the sexual lifestyle was one she embraced rather than denied.

Heather knew the destruction that could be waiting for the Augusts. She knew the pain, the betrayal, the loss of self-respect that came from such a relationship. She had watched it with her sister, Rick and his brother, Carl, before Carl's accident and death.

"It's not the same here," she whispered, knowing her sister couldn't see it, couldn't look beyond her own past to see the reality of these men. "I don't know how it's different, Tara, but I know it is. And I won't argue it with you. I don't want to share Sam, and I don't want to be more than a hug and a peck on the cheek to those brothers. But I won't leave him like this. I won't walk away while some bastard wants him destroyed. I won't do it. Not even for you."

Tara's eyes sparked with fury, and Heather knew the explosion was coming. Thankfully, the door swung open at the same time.

"Time to go, wildcat." Raider's dark voice matched the black shadow he cast over the floor. "Rick just called in, everyone's in place. Time to go shopping."

"I need to change." Heather shook her head as she glanced at her sister, seeing the conflicting anger and fear in her face. "Give me half an hour and I'll be back out."

She didn't wait for a comment or a refusal, but turned on her heel and rushed past Raider as he stood carefully aside. She shivered as she glanced in his face. Cold, hard. He watched her with an edge of steel that was almost frightening, but the way he watched Tara should have terrified her. Heather was more than surprised by the fact that it didn't.

* * * * *

The stalker watched the woman, her pretty features filled with humor as she smiled with the other two who were window shopping with her. She was a beauty, just as the others were. Her long red hair flowed down her back like a living flame, almost touching her slender, curved hips. She was petite, almost tiny, delicately made and looked like one of those pretty pixies found in fairy tales.

She was dressed in a light linen sundress that barely covered her thighs. Such scandalous clothing. Evidently the lesson she had received last month hadn't impressed upon her how serious her sins were. She was tempting those men, even more so than Marly and Sarah had.

While with those August men, she would swing her curvy hips, laugh and flirt with them all at all hours. She was a Jezebel, and she knew it. A flame-haired temptation drawing the men further into their perversions. Soon, the final boundary would be breached, and something would have to be done.

She reached back, lifting a dainty foot to adjust the strap of her sandal. So pretty. Her skin was soft, like silk. The sight of it brought to mind the smooth contours of her pretty cunt; the little slit that separated it was incredibly soft. Soft and marked with the proof of her wayward sensuality. She carried the mark of temptation there now, on the very flesh that tempted mortal men past their boundaries of control.

The smooth mound had been striped by the knife, and the scars that were left would never be forgotten. Slender, almost invisible scars that she would wear forever. Scars that any man who touched her would feel, would know, and therefore, know her for the temptress she was.

The other two women were no more than a minor irritation. Marly should have, of course, known better. She was an angel, so sweet and lovely, so tempting and pure before the bastards corrupted her with their depravities. Sarah was older, supposedly wiser, but even she had been impossible to get rid of effectively.

It had been impossible to kill her. But the desire to kill hadn't really been there. No one wanted to listen anymore, was the problem. It was as though the warnings of the past had been completely forgotten, overlooked and ignored. Words of wisdom had been tossed away, and all the dreams destroyed. In one blow-one remorseless, powerful blow-the bastard had taken it all, and it would never return.

But then, an idea began to form. Perhaps the plan was being executed in the wrong way. Punishing innocents for the crimes of the guilty. The punishment should go to the one who committed the crime. The one who refused to understand. Refused to know his place and his crimes. For with every crime comes punishment, and he had committed the ultimate crime.

For the first time in months, a true plan began to form. The women were pure, innocent. They were doing as women should, submitting to who they believed were their rightful masters. They didn't know. Bless their hearts, they weren't aware of the demon defiling them. They were too sweet, their hearts too kind to see or to understand such evil.

The knowledge was clear now. Eyes narrowed, fists clenching as the women walked to the next window, the next shop that displayed their frilly items. They were being corrupted, and it must stop.

A moment of distraction came as a husky brute began to move in on the women. The man, Sarah's ex-husband, was a pitiful excuse of a male. Unable to control his woman or his home.

The man paused. It was obvious that whatever he said was upsetting the women. They moved to walk away, but the bastard reached out, grabbing Sarah's arm, jerking her to him. The little redhead dynamo would have chewed his ass up good with the fist she was ready to let fly, but she wasn't expecting the bastard to kick out at her tender legs. She fell, but she was neither weak-willed, nor willing to give up. She was up again and going for him when another male moved in.

From across the street, the door to a dark, window-tinted truck flew open and a male raced across the street. Sam. He pushed her back, his hand going for Tate's throat as the other man twisted Sarah's arm. Tate let go of her quickly, his hands clawing at Sam's fingers, his eyes bulging from his head as he was thrown against the wall of the building.

The women were crying out, the redhead was pulling at Sam's arm, watching the street nervously as the sound of sirens was heard. The demon refused to listen for long seconds. He said something to Tate, a snarl twisting his lips a second before he tossed him to the sidewalk like the garbage he was. Tate could do no more than scramble away before the sheriff's car rounded the street.

And in watching the spectacle, an idea began to form. It wouldn't be hard to do. Sam was furious, and everyone knew his temper, his possessive instincts. It would work. The Defiler would be destroyed and sent away, and the women would once again be pure and untarnished. The other two men, though just as guilty, would wilt away without the one they fought so hard to protect. Sam was the catalyst, the Defiler, the Demon. And he must be destroyed.

# Chapter Three

"Dammit, Sam, what were you trying to accomplish today?" Heather stalked into Sam's bedroom after finally finding a free moment, to berate him for his violence on a public street. She came to an abrupt stop.

Maybe she should have knocked, she thought then kicked herself. Hell no, that would have been an even bigger mistake. Any chance to catch Sam August in the nude was worth taking. The man was a work of art. That was all there was to it.

Sam turned away from the dresser he had been searching through. Her mouth dried out then watered as she glimpsed the hard, dusky-tanned body. There were no white strips, and she would be damned if there was any indication that he used a tanning bed. He was like an Indian. Dark, hard flesh and even harder muscle beneath. Muscles that rippled and tempted, and made her long to run her hands over them.

Her eyes dropped to his hips. She couldn't help it. She watched him come fully, gloriously erect in a matter of seconds. It was like a hard, thick stalk rising from between his thighs. The head was broad, plum-shaped and tempting, thickly veined and just plain thick. The sight of it made her very aware of her own femininity, the need to feel him pushing inside her, taking her, fucking her with hard, pounding strokes.

"Hell, Heather, why not just barge right in," he growled as he pulled a pair of sweat pants from his dresser and jerked them on over his long, well-muscled legs.

"Do you keep a hard-on?" she asked him, fighting to control her breathing and her regret as he covered the sight of it.

He muttered something under his breath that she couldn't catch, but it sounded smart enough to piss her off. He flashed her a dark look. "What are you chewing my ass about now?"

She slammed the door, propping her hands on her hips as she watched him in irritation.

"I wasn't," she replied caustically, "but now that you mention it…"

"Forget I mentioned it," he grunted, exasperation filling his voice.

"Today? In town?" she reminded him, ignoring the suggestion. "What the hell were you doing, trying to kill that bastard on the street? Do you want to go to jail? You will, you know, if he presses charges."

She watched as his jaw bunched, fury coursing over his expression as his eyes darkened with it.

"Let him," he grunted. "Because when I get out, I'll be in the mood to kill. He'll make a handy subject for the exercise." Her look of disapproval had him shaking his head in irritation. "Don't worry, Heather. Tate doesn't want to mess with me and he knows it."

The tone of voice, the hard expression, showed the man carefully concealed beneath the laughing exterior. Rick and Tara thought Cade was the one to watch out for, but Heather had always known that Sam's lazy, laughing exterior held a core of hard, cold steel.

"Sam, that's not the point." She shook her head furiously. "Dammit to hell, we were there for a reason and you know it. If you keep jumping out of the shadows, we're never going to draw that damned stalker out so our men can get a look at him."

A week of shopping, dressing in the finest clothes and playing debutante was getting on all their nerves. Marly and Sarah were chafing at the constant window shopping, and Cade and Brock were so damned nervous letting them go alone that they were like cats in a roomful of rockers.

"Heather, I will not stand by and let some bastard abuse you, Sarah or Marly. What in the hell makes you think that's ever going to happen?" He turned on her incredulously. "Did you think I was just going to stand there and let him kick the hell out of you?"

What made her think he would do anything sensible at this point? He hadn't in all the time she had known him.

"I would have handled it," she snarled.

"Yeah, I saw that," he snapped. "The bastard kicked you, Heather. Look at the fucking bruise on your leg. Stop chewing my ass for trying to stop him."

She didn't have to look at it; she felt it. But she wasn't a fool. She had known it was coming, and had known how it would appear to anyone who saw it.

"I didn't need your protection," she informed him furiously. "We had a plan, Sam…"

"It was a stupid plan," he growled as he threw himself down on the bed, watching her through heavy lidded, suddenly sensual eyes. What was it about the August men that any kind of confrontation with women produced this reaction? No, she took that back as her heart leaped. They only reacted that way with "their" women.

"Come over here." He patted the mattress. "I'll see if I can't find something else for you to chew on."

She frowned as she glanced at the door, then back to Sam. "I'm on duty. Tara would kick my ass. Besides, I'm tired of playing with you. You're nothing but a tease."

His teasing had her in such a heightened state of arousal that she was about to drive herself and the other bodyguards crazy with her mercurial moods. He might be treating her like his lover now, but she knew damned good and well that he wasn't about to fuck her.

"Lock the door. Let me kiss that boo boo on your leg better." He tempted her with a soft, seductive growl.

Heather bit her lip as she glanced at the door again. Tara was like a damned bear with a sore paw lately. If she caught Heather playing when she should be working there would be hell to pay. And Tara would know if she was playing. Every time Sam touched her, aroused her, only to leave her aching, her temper became so testy that it was becoming a running joke within the group assigned to the ranch.

"Come on, I dare you." Soft, teasing, he urged her to join his naughtiness. "Come here, baby, let me kiss your boo boo all better." The words were childish, the voice and the expression were pure sin. He tempted her when she knew better.

"Not a chance, Sam." She watched him mockingly. "You're all talk, and no action."

The air seemed to thicken with her challenge.

He frowned. "It's not nice to call me a tease, Heather."

She crossed her arms over her breasts. "Are you denying it, Sam?"

He shrugged, his glance brooding, brimming with intensity, both sexual and angry. "I'm trying to protect you, Heather."

She shook her head, a sense of hopelessness spreading over her.

"Find someone else to play with, Sam," she snapped out, seeing the surprise, then the heat that spread over his face. "I'm tired of it. And if you can manage it, next time we're trying to draw that bastard out, let us do our jobs instead of jumping in. I didn't rip Tate's head off for a reason. You should have had enough sense to know that."

She turned and slammed out of the bedroom, anger and arousal mixing inside her system until she felt like a volcano ready to blow. She moved to her own room and slammed the door closed. She twisted the lock furiously then moved to the door that connected to Sam's room. She twisted that lock as well.

It was a Pocket Rocket moment, she thought as she jerked her dresser drawer open and retrieved the small, battery operated clitoral vibrator. Before the arousal drove her crazy, before she begged him to fuck her. She needed relief, weak though it might be without his touch. She needed the strength and heat of his body. And she needed it now.

She removed her panties and the light summer dress before kicking her shoes off by the bed and laying across it as she whimpered in agony. Her pussy was pulsing, clenching. Sam was making her crazy.

She twisted the control on the little external vibrator, moving it slowly over the bare lips of her pussy as her fingers moved to the sensitive opening of her vagina. She was too hot, too desperate to go slowly. She plunged two fingers as deep inside her hot cunt as they would go as she moved the vibrator to the side of her clit.

Her hips jerked, her strangled moan tearing from her throat as she worked her fingers through the thick cream of her juices. She imagined Sam, his fingers working inside her, his tongue on her clit, his breath hot and hard as he licked her, sucked her clit into his mouth or pushed his tongue deep inside her pussy.

Her fingers spread the natural lubrication of her body back, along the puckered opening of her anus. She couldn't stop her moan of need as the third finger gently pierced her anal opening.

She remembered the one time Sam had touched her there. The one time his mouth had moved over her sensitive pussy, his fingers invading it as one hard, long finger pushed into her anus.

Invaded from both ends, her body shook. Her eyes were tightly closed, her body shuddering as she worked her fingers inside her, driving her pleasure higher, deeper. The strong vibration of the powerful little device at her clit made her release come hard and fast.

She bit her lip, moaning, her hips thrusting convulsively on her fingers as the pleasure tore through her, exploding through her clit, her hungry pussy and echoing along her body.

Heather didn't bother to try to breathe through the little explosion. She let it tear through her, carry her along until her clit protested the strong stimulation of the battery-operated device. She eased it from her as she pulled her fingers free of her twin entrances. Her body still tingled, and though the worst of the extreme arousal had eased, she was by no means satisfied.

She stared up at the ceiling, ignoring her tears, and cursed fate and reality. In her dreams it was Sam taking her, yet it seemed the reality of it would never come to pass.

\* \* \* \* \*

Sam stared at the ceiling, arousal and anger moving through his system as he fought to ignore the erection tormenting him. Damn. This wasn't working out. Heather in the house all day, tempting him, her smile and her laughter teasing him in ways that stretched his self-control to its limits.

He remembered finding her the night of the attack. Unconscious, naked, blood staining her thighs from the slashes made across her mound. One had come dangerously close to her tender clitoris. Thin, shallow, but devastating all the same.

His hand lowered, tucking beneath the waistband of his sweatpants, gripping his cock. He could feel his own scars. Razor thin, but even now, twelve years later, easily felt. They crisscrossed the head, the shaft, his scrotum. A madman's brand. A madman's revenge.

He closed his eyes, the misty nightmare visions silhouetting behind the closed lids as his heart rate increased and his stomach tightened with tension. The memories were there, so close…

The jarring ring of the phone beside him jerked him from the forming visions of the past. With a curse on his lips, her rolled over and jerked the phone from its base.

"What?" he snarled.

"You like fucking your brothers, August?" Mark Tate's voice came through the line. Breathless, almost frightened as he spoke. "You have two hours to show up at my place, or I send these pictures I have to every newspaper and law enforcement agency in the country. Interesting pictures of a dead man."

Sam stilled. A haze of pain and white-hot fury swelled in his gut.

"You're a dead man," he whispered.

The line disconnected.

# Chapter Four

There was blood everywhere. Like his worst nightmare come to life. The stench of death was like a blow to his chest, taking his breath, stealing the very air from his lungs. Sam could do nothing but stare in horror. Mark Tate was laid out in the small dingy living room of his mobile home, his body beaten nearly to a bloody pulp. It was Mark, he knew it was, but the features were nearly indistinguishable, his limbs were contorted, bits of flesh and blood splattered walls and furniture alike.

Sam shook his head, fighting for breath. He had seen such brutality before, and felt the violence of it searing his system. He shook, fevered and yet chilled as memory and reality collided, and for a moment, the scene was overlapped by that of another.

*I killed him, Sam,* Cade screamed furiously through his mind, his expression savage, commanding. *Do you hear me? He's dead. I killed him.*

Blood had stained them both, the room in his memories reeking of filth and agony, and the bone-chilling scent of death. Just as it did here.

*I killed him, Sam.* Cade's voice echoed around him again.

But Sam had wanted to kill him. Wanted to kill so bad, even now, twelve years later, he dreamed of it. He felt bones cracking beneath his pummeling fists, blood spraying, a gasp of death in his ears.

He shook his head, blinking. But he couldn't make himself move. All he could do was stand there, the door opened behind him, staring at the bloody body and the mark of a painful death. The horror of this death didn't lay on his conscience, yet the previous one did.

"Sam, back away from the door." The authoritative, cold voice of the sheriff shocked him back to reality.

Sam froze, fear flashing through his mind for a moment. His fists clenched, his mind switching into a primal survival response before he was able to overcome it.

"Sam, I have you covered."

Sam glanced back slowly, feeling his face pale. He hadn't even heard the vehicles drive up, hadn't seen the flashing lights that blinded him now, nor heard any sirens if they had been blaring. But they were there now. Three sheriff's units, five men with weapons aimed at his back.

He turned around slowly, careful to keep his hands in clear view. Son of a bitch, he could feel the panic starting to overwhelm him. There was a dead man in the trailer behind him. A man he had sworn to kill just earlier that day. A man everyone knew he detested. His hands trembled. Damn.

"Josh, I just got here." He swallowed past the tight lump in his throat and fought the insidious voice that warned him no one would believe him. He looked at his hands. They were clean. Scratched but not bloody, and the scratches were already healing. "There's no blood on my hands, Josh. I just got here."

Joshua Martinez stood coldly firm, the police issue pistol aimed at his heart. Sam felt the cold bite of reality and the knowledge that, for now, he could do nothing but sweat it out.

"Step down, Sam," Josh advised him, his voice echoing with menace. "Keep your hands where I can see them."

Sam took a deep, hard breath. God help him, he didn't know if he could let Josh cuff him. He only prayed he wouldn't. He stepped down slowly, fighting a horror he had sworn he would never visit again.

He followed Josh's orders explicitly, leaning against the sheriff's car while they searched him for weapons, answering Josh's short questions in a deceptively calm voice. He was anything but calm.

"I'm not going to cuff you, Sam," Josh said quietly as he backed away. "I have to take you in though. Are you going to come easy?"

Sam swallowed tightly, nodding with a brief movement of his head.

"I'll call Cade…"

"No," Sam ground out, enraged. "I didn't do it, Josh. Don't upset the family. You go in that trailer and all you'll find are my prints at the door and on the light. I just got here. I swear it, man. No sense in upsetting family."

No sense in making the nightmares worse.

Josh opened the door. Sam steeled himself as he glimpsed the steel cage he was being forced to willingly step into. He did so, his mind screaming out at him to run, to hide, to escape the cage. His fists clenched and his breath became strangled. Stepping into the back of the sheriff's cruiser wasn't the hardest decision he had ever made in his life, but it ranked in the top ten.

The door slammed shut behind him. He breathed out roughly, closing his eyes in an attempt to shut out the reality he was being locked into. He shut out the sounds around him, the flashing lights and the knowledge of what could be coming. Instead, he thought of her. Heather.

She would be sleeping peacefully at the ranch house, her long red hair haloed around her head, her soft face flushed and too damned innocent. Was she wearing another of those sexy little nighties he had caught her in the other night, he wondered. Sure she was, he convinced himself. Silk, of course…maybe that green one. The silk and lace teddy that made her look so damned pretty. Her eyes, sparkling like emeralds and tempting him, her smile honeyed, promising the sweetest secrets. Dear God, he should have never left tonight. Should have ignored Tate when he called earlier instead of leaving the house like a fool and charging over here. This wasn't one of the smartest moves he had ever made in his life.

He hadn't been gone long, he assured himself. He had talked to Cade and Rick before leaving the house, though they had been unaware where he was going. He had come straight over here, hadn't stopped anywhere. He wiped his hands over his face, disgusted with the fine, cold sweat he wiped from his forehead.

God, this couldn't be happening.

Heather. Her name was a mantra, whispering through his mind. Silken skin, and hot kisses; something else denied him. He grimaced. Something he denied himself.

"Sam?" Josh opened the driver's seat door and slid into the cruiser. "I've got to take you in, buddy." He turned, staring through the cage, his brown eyes somber. "It's going to take a while to dust for prints and the like. It's an unholy mess in there."

"Josh." Sam flinched at the graveled sound of his own voice. "I didn't do it. Just let me go home. I'll be there if you need me. I promise."

Josh sighed, shaking his head as he pulled his door close. "One of the boys will bring your truck in. We'll have to search it, and let the investigator finish his job. I have to hold you till then, Sam. I don't have a choice."

Hold him. In a cell. He could feel the sweat building on his face, his body. Dammit straight to hell.

"You can call Cade from the office…"

"Goddammit, I don't need Cade," Sam snapped then tightened his body, fighting for control. Control. He wouldn't survive without it. "Sorry, Josh." He pushed his fingers wearily through his hair as Josh watched him, his expression clinical, emotionless. "Not everyday you see something like that."

But it hadn't been the first time he had seen so much blood, either. Not the first broken and mangled body, bones broken, blood flowing. Nausea welled up inside him as scattered images flitted through his mind.

"Hell no, it ain't," Josh grunted, turning around. "Hopefully, they'll have things settled by morning though."

Sam prayed they settled sooner than that.

\* \* \* \* \*

It was a cage. A cell. Bars surrounded him, enclosed him, nightmares twisted at the edge of reality and caused sweat to dampen his body, his clothes. It ran down his face in slow rivulets, despite the air conditioning. A cage. Bars that were locked. He was unable to escape, unable to run from the monster who would slowly destroy them.

Sam shook his head, fighting the nightmare images, the sense of unreality that surrounded him. He clenched his fists. He was older now, stronger, and a hell of a lot meaner than he had been then. Besides, this was the county jail, not the basement of some bastard's mansion. There were windows here.

He stood and paced over to it, trying to ignore the bars there as well. He stared down at the parking lot as he ran his hands through his damp hair. Dammit to hell. He had to get out of here. He could feel his throat closing up on him, and terror roaring at the edges of his mind.

He wiped at his forehead, grimacing at the cold sweat that wet his hands. He could feel it all along his body. His back. His chest. He fought to shake off the fear. Dammit, he wasn't a kid anymore. He could handle this. Sheriff Martinez would check things just like Sam had told him, and he would release him.

But what if the proof didn't show? That insidious thought rocked his mind. His stomach roiled, pitching in terror at the thought. God help him, he couldn't stand it here much longer.

*You ain't goin' nowhere, boy.* The ghost of his nightmares sounded in his brain. *You had a chance, Sam-boy... I offered it to you, and you didn't take it.* Sam shook his head. Memories better left forgotten slipped demonically through the veil that often hid them. He didn't want them to escape, didn't want to remember the dark, agonizing pain of those months he and his brothers had been held captive.

*It's okay, Sam. I killed him. I killed him, Sam. Remember that. Remember, Sam.* Cade's voice was savage, determined. Blood surrounded them, but none of it marred Cade. Sam's hands were stained with blood. His nude body, nearly flayed to the bone, criss-crossed with vicious welts and deep cuts. He hurt. God, he hurt so bad, and there was so much blood.

He shook his head. *It's over, Sam. I killed him. Let it go. It's over.* Cade's voice was insistent as he used the tone that the younger brothers knew brooked no refusal.

He swallowed the bile in his throat. It was over. Years past. In a time as dead as the bastard who had tortured them. The cells were gone, the house destroyed, all of it wiped away as though it had never been. Wiped from everything but their memories.

He collapsed on the cell cot, holding his head in his hands as he fought the lash of memories that were as brutal as the whip that had once been used on them. He didn't remember it all. He never did. The rapes he remembered. The drugged, hallucinogenic hours that they were forced to...

Bile rose in his throat. He had screamed that first time. They all had. And the bastard had laughed. Sneering as he forced them to hurt each other. He swallowed tight, hard. He had destroyed them in ways he could have never imagined. Even his death hadn't stopped the horror.

God, he wished Martinez would hurry. Goddammit, how long did it take to dust the fucking place and check fingerprints? Hell, it should have been pretty damned easy to tell he had just arrived there.

He had no idea how Mark Tate had finally found his just reward, but it was no more than he deserved. Not that Sam wouldn't have killed the bastard if he'd had the chance. He tightened his hands as they dropped to his knees. Opening his eyes, he stared down at his fists as though they belonged to someone else. For just a moment, they were dripping with blood—his and someone else's. Then he shook his head and the blood was gone. All he saw was the faint, thin lines that crossed the backs of his broad, rough hands. They criss-crossed back and forth like a design of horror. A reminder. A signature of evil. The same small, spider-thin scars covered other parts of his body. Tender, sensitive parts.

He breathed in hard and deep. If he didn't get out of here, he was fucking going to go crazy.

"Sam." Sheriff Martinez stepped into the cell area, leaving the main door open as he approached.

Sam raised his head slowly, fighting for control in front of the other man. Josh Martinez had gone to school with the August brothers, knew them all as well as anyone did, Sam guessed. But the other man didn't have a clue the hell he was going through right now.

"Let me outta here, Josh," he said hoarsely. "I didn't kill the bastard. You know I didn't."

"Forensics didn't find any of your prints, and whoever called and reported the murder hasn't come forward. I'm letting you go, but I'd suggest getting a lawyer, man." He unlocked the door, the keys rattling, taunting Sam with the misty memories that wailed in his mind.

Sam fought to keep from shaking as he rose from the cot and left the cell. The air was oppressive in the cell area, thick, menacing.

"I don't need a fucking lawyer," Sam informed him bitterly as he strode quickly for the door. "I told you, I didn't do it."

Not that the bastard didn't deserve to die, Sam thought vengefully. Mark Tate had been a waste of human flesh.

"That's not good enough, Sam." Josh slammed the outer door closed behind them, following Sam through the small sheriff's office as he walked quickly for the exit. He needed air, and by God, he needed it now.

"It will have to be." Sam turned back, ignoring the frustration he glimpsed on the sheriff's face. "I wasn't there, Josh." But he knew he would have killed the bastard if he had the chance.

"It's easier than you think to frame a man," Josh warned him quietly. "Be careful that you don't let someone do it to you. If your prints had been on just one thing in that room, then I would have had to arrest you."

Sam took a deep breath. "Coincidence," he muttered.

Josh shook his head slowly, his brown eyes narrowed, thoughtful.

"I don't think so. I checked it out myself. Someone went to a lot of trouble to make it look like you were there. And a lot of trouble to make the scene as bloody as possible."

Sam's stomach rolled. He remembered the blood, dammit. So much fucking blood.

"Bastard put up a fight, though. No way you could have fought him without at least a bruise. So I'm letting you go. But watch your ass," he warned again. "Next time, you might not be so damned lucky."

Sam nodded shortly before he flung himself out the door. If he didn't get out of the stifling atmosphere of the sheriff's office, he would disgrace himself by vomiting all over the waxed floor in front of the door.

Outside, the sun shone down on him with blistering intensity as he strode quickly for his pickup. Son of a bitch, Sheriff's department had been going through it, he knew. His fists clenched at the thought.

The door was unlocked, his keys hanging in the ignition. Sam jumped into the black, four-door Explorer and twisted the key furiously. The engine caught immediately and he would have torn out of the parking lot then if he hadn't remembered his wallet. Josh still had it, lying on the desk, taken from him just as his keys had been.

He grimaced. Leaving the vehicle running, he jumped out and strode quickly for the door again. Maybe he could get Josh to just toss it to the door. He was starting up the stairs when the explosion rocked the ground, throwing him through the air with a blast of heat that took his breath.

Sam hit the ground hard, his shoulder slamming into the pavement, his head scraping a low wall as the lights went out. His last thought was praying his truck hadn't been damaged too badly. Dammit, he had just bought it.

# Chapter Five

"Sam, at this rate, you're going to top my record of the most hospital stays in a year," Marly teased him as they sat in the back of the limo, heading for the ranch several days later.

The truck was totaled. The explosive had malfunctioned, otherwise… Sam grimaced. Toasted August served up for the pleasure of the bastard who had most likely been watching the whole show.

Sam grinned his normal, reckless grin deliberately. There was nothing to say though. Not even to Marly. Mark Tate was dead, his truck was destroyed, and according to Cade, they had lost more than forty head of stock the night before to some maniac who had picked them off one by one before Rick and his men could do anything to stop him.

Twelve fucking bodyguards and no one could catch the son of a bitch. It just didn't make sense to him.

"Sam, why didn't you call the house while you were in that fucking jail?" It was Cade's voice that drew him out of his thoughts.

The tone was dark, angry. Sam looked into his brother's face and saw the fury reflected there. Sam shrugged. "I'm a big boy now, Cade. I can take care of myself."

Blood covered his hands. He looked down at his hands as the vision flashed before his mind. No blood, just the scars.

"You spent the night in a fucking jail cell and didn't have the good sense to call your family?" Cade demanded roughly. "What the hell's got into you lately?"

Sam could hear the echo of Cade's nightmares in his voice. A cell. The pain, the rage, and a madman's laughter.

"I don't need you to baby-sit me, Cade." Sam almost winced at the sound of his own voice, but a cold, hidden core inside his soul suddenly hardened further, making itself plainly visible.

Cade's eyes flashed silver with his anger. His expression hardened, his large body tensing as Marly watched them both in confusion.

"Sam, we were concerned." Marly's softly spoken chastisement pricked at his conscience.

He wiped his hands over his face, shaking his head as he tried to still the demons fighting inside him.

"I'm sorry." He shook his head at his own anger. "It's been a helluva week."

"Sam." He felt her move, his arms going around her instinctively as she moved into his lap.

Oh God. He trembled, feeling the warmth, the gentle weight cuddling against his chest. He opened his eyes, looking directly into those of his brother. There was no jealousy, no anger that she was in his arms. Cade watched his lover with lust mixed in with his anger at him, for him. A lust Sam felt for her. A lust he felt for Brock's lover, Sarah. Needs and desires both men, he knew, shared for the woman Sam had yet to claim for his own…Heather.

For now, Marly was in his arms, and as always the demons stilled, though his heart ached. Ached for himself, for Cade and Brock, and for Marly. He felt her lips at his neck, as soothing and soft, as hot and sweet as they would be for his brother.

"Marly." He swallowed tightly, his hands tightening on her waist as she moved to straddle his body.

The soundproof window was secured between the back and front of the limo. The special design of each compartment afforded the brothers their privacy from the bodyguards in the front.

"Sam." She clasped his cheeks between her slender hands.

Her blue eyes were wide, bottomless and filled with such love. She knew his needs. She knew of the dark demons, the nightmares, the anger and fear that filled all of them. And he wanted to scream out in agony. It shouldn't be her place to ease his pain. And yet she did. God help him, but it did ease him. It eased his soul.

He laid his head against the back of the seat, feeling her lips move over his neck, her fingers loosening his shirt. His hands tightened on her waist as her tongue stroked over the vein throbbing at his throat. Her teeth scraped it, sending his blood pressure soaring.

Then she was moving lower, her mouth removing the horrifying memories that pounded at his brain, blocking out the horror of his own screams. Her small moans, her warm hands touching him. He looked at Cade as he felt his jeans being loosened.

The other man was watching his lover with swirling gray eyes. The dark rage of his own memories was gone, replaced by lust and love. Sam buried his hands in the thick length of Marly's hair as she opened his jeans, releasing the thick length of his cock.

His body jerked. "Fuck. Marly." Her mouth closed over the throbbing head with heated moisture, suckling pressure.

He saw Cade grimace at the erotic sight. Sam looked down at Marly, seeing her kneeling between his thighs, her mouth working over the dark shaft of his cock. Heat, pressure, moist strokes of incredible sensual pleasure.

"She's killing me," he gasped out to his brother as she tugged at the waist of his jeans. She moaned around his cock, taking the head to her throat before pulling back and going down on him again. Lightning sizzled on his flesh, the stroke of her tongue, the delicate scrape of her teeth, just the way he liked it. And for a moment there was peace.

He lifted his hips, helping her to drag the material down his thighs, her lips never loosening from his cock, though her hand, warm and teasing, began to play sensually with his scrotum.

"She kills us all," Cade whispered.

There was no jealousy, no sense of anger or reluctance. Pleasure swirled around them, heating the interior of the enclosed space, dampening their skin with the heat of passion despite the steady surge of cool air from the air conditioning ducts beneath the seat.

Sam watched as Cade moved then. His hands went to the zipper at the back of her short dress. The rasping sound of its release tightened Sam's muscles. The thought of what was coming nearly destroying his control. His cock jerked, spilling a small measure of his seed into Marly's greedy mouth.

She moaned, her lips stilling, her tongue flickering, probing at the sensitive skin beneath the head of his cock. He shuddered, his hands tightening in her hair as Cade lowered the straps at her shoulders, removing the dress she wore.

"Come here, baby," Cade whispered heatedly as he drew her away from the sensual feast she was making of Sam's cock.

The loss of pleasure was almost a physical pain. He gripped his desperate flesh, stroking it slowly as he watched Cade undress the little vixen. She smiled, a sensual, pleasured smile as the dress was pulled from her body, leaving her clad only in the midnight thong she wore over her bare cunt.

Sam's mouth watered. He didn't wait on Cade, but reached out, pulling the scrap of fabric from her body as Cade held her steady between his thighs, her back arched against his chest. The minute the thong dropped to the floorboard, Sam spread her thighs, going to his knees before her and burying his mouth in her dripping pussy.

Slick, heated honey met his intimate kiss as his tongue plunged inside her. She shuddered, crying out in pleasure as he lifted her legs, positioning them over his shoulders as he and Cade kept her suspended between the two of them.

She was chanting Cade's name, and as Sam looked up, he could see the hard, male fingers that pulled and caressed her long nipples, the hands that cupped the full mounds of her breasts. He licked at her cunt, fucking into it with a rapacious tongue as his hands gripped and separated the cheeks of her ass. She twisted against his mouth as his fingers found the wide base of the lubricated butt plug inserted up her anus. She was ready for them. Had known, had wanted to give him the gift of her passion, the ease that came with it.

"Cade. I can't wait." He was desperate to thrust into her, to feel the heated, tight grip of her hot, forbidden channel.

Only this wiped away the agony of remembered pain. To give in pleasure what had been taken from them in horror.

"Come here, baby." Cade laid back along the limo seat, drawing Marly over him as her legs clasped his hips.

And Sam watched. Watched as the thick cock spearing from the parted material of Cade's jeans kissed the small entrance to Marly's tight, dripping cunt. She was opened for him, like a greedy little mouth, parting for the broad length of his cock head.

Sam was nearly shaking in excitement as he fumbled at the little drawer beneath one of the seats. There, he found the tube of lubricant always kept on hand. Refusing to glance away from the sight of Marly, slowing being taken, inch by inch as she whimpered in pleasure, he fumbled with the flip cap, squeezed the slick gel into his hand and began stroking his raging flesh with it.

He dropped the tube to the drawer then reached out, gripping the base of the plug as Cade pressed the last inch into her stretched pussy. She cried out as he slid the device from her gripping rear. It, too, fell forgotten to the floor as he positioned himself behind her.

He watched…he couldn't help himself. Watched as his cock pressed against the narrow opening of her anus. The head tucked in. He was shaking, the anticipation of the pleasure almost enough to send him careening into his release.

"Sam," she cried out his name as he began to enter her.

Slowly. Oh God, so slow. He watched as his greased cock stretched the tight muscles as he entered her. The pinching heat seared his flesh as the muscles closed on his cock. He trembled at the fiery wash of pleasure, fighting for control. He wanted to take her slow, easy... He groaned in defeat. His cock surged deep and hard inside the silky, lava-hot tunnel of her anus as she screamed out her pleasure/pain.

He heard Cade groan, and knew the cunt gripping his brother's cock had tightened to an almost painful measure. Sweat dripped along his forehead, down his back. He pulled back and began to stroke into the gripping depths of her ass. Below, Cade gripped her hips, his cock thrusting hard and deep inside her pussy, in perfect counterpoint to the shaft stroking her rectum.

Marly was nearly screaming their names now. Twisting between them, begging Cade for the orgasm building inside her.

"Yeah," Sam whispered, his voice harsh. "Come, Marly. Come, baby. Tighten on my cock more."

Sam was almost whimpering, the pleasure was so extreme. He needed her to come. Needed to feel her orgasm rippling through her cunt, tightening her muscles further. He felt Cade's strokes intensify through the thin wall of flesh that separated the invaded channels. He matched the rhythm, feeling her tense, feeling the walls of her anus ripple, tremble. Then with a surge of strength, her muscles clamped down on his pistoning flesh as she screamed out her release. Cade was crying out, slamming deep inside her, holding her close. Then Sam could hold back no longer. He pushed in hard and fast. Again, then again, as blistering waves of heat streaked from his stomach, up his back, and through his cock.

He exploded as he powered inside her. Thrusting hard and fast even as his cock erupted, spewing his semen into the willing, greedy depths of her ass. The added sensations, agonizing in intensity, pushed his release higher as he buried inside her, deep and hard one last time. His body shuddered as she tightened again. She was shaking, crying, holding on to Cade as she fell slowly back to earth.

Fighting for breath, Sam eased out of her, watching as his seed marred the cream and peach perfection of her little hole. Shaking, he removed a small towel from another drawer under the seat and gently cleaned her.

Cade was still buried inside her, his voice soft, soothing, as he calmed her. The intensity of her orgasms when with the brothers often threw her into unconsciousness. She hated that, and could pout for days over it. Thankfully, Cade seemed to have found a cure.

Sam collapsed in his seat again, breathing deeply. Guilt lingered inside him, a fear that he was hurting, rather than loving the petite woman he had known for so long. But he was calm now. That hard, cold core of rage and hatred he often felt growing inside him had thawed, for now.

Marly's soft laughter drew his gaze to the pair once again. Cade had eased up and fixed his jeans, and was now helping Marly to dress once again. He whispered to her gently as she smiled in pleasure, in happiness. His brother, once hard and bitter, steeped in the nightmares of the past, had eased under Marly's loving and her acceptance. As they all had in some ways.

It was the same for Brock. Sarah eased his demons as well. She healed him with love and soothed him with laughter, and though Sam never felt left out, he still felt apart.

# Chapter Six

Heather knew when she saw the trio step from the back of the limo what had happened during the ride from the hospital. She watched Sam's expression carefully, seeing an easing of the tension that had been growing during his hospital stay. His eyes weren't cold and hard, his face wasn't still and dangerous. He looked ready to cause mischief again, until he saw her.

She watched as the animation in his face stilled. Sadness flashed in his eyes, and regret. But no guilt. Of course, there was no reason for guilt. They weren't lovers, they weren't even friends anymore. Despite the sexual heat building between them, he hadn't touched her since before the attack nearly two months earlier. Hadn't touched her, and he appeared in no hurry to do so. But he did touch his brothers' women.

Jealousy raged through her system. Her fingers curled with the need to rage at him. Her chest ached with the tears she refused to shed.

"You can't change him, Heather." Tara stepped behind her, watching as the trio talked after getting out of the limo.

"I didn't say I wanted to, Tara," she said softly. She knew she did though. She wanted him, heart, body and soul, the same way he could have her, if he would accept it.

Tara didn't reply as the three made their way to the porch. They were flanked by the two bodyguards who rode in the limo, their weapons carried in readiness.

"I'm getting sick of this, Tara," Cade snarled as the door closed behind them. "I have a damned ranch to run."

Tara sighed as Heather watched Sam glance around the house. There was little privacy now within the huge ranch house.

"We're working on it, Cade," Tara promised him, her voice firm though not in the least conciliatory. "Rick should be back tonight with the information he went after, so hopefully, we'll have answers soon."

"I'm going upstairs." Sam's voice broke through the beginnings of yet another heated argument over the safeguards in place around the ranch and the August family.

Heather knew they were all beginning to chafe under the restrictions, and the stress of waiting on a damned phantom that struck when they least expected it.

"Not yet, Sam." Heather watched as Tara went to block him.

"Stop." The barely leashed violence in Sam's tone stopped her in her tracks.

Heather watched in surprise as Sam's expression hardened, his eyes turning cold and bleak.

"Sam, I need to know what the hell happened," Tara argued.

"Then call the sheriff," he growled, moving past her. "I need a shower and a fucking nap. Not a bunch of questions that I've answered already."

He stalked past her. As her sister went to stop him again, Heather laid her hand on the other woman's arm warningly. "Let him go, Tara. Now is the wrong time."

Tara turned on them, her gaze going to Cade rather than Heather.

"How the hell am I supposed to protect his ass?" she snarled, throwing her hands up in defeat as she faced him. "He wanders around at all hours of the night, refuses to take the bodyguards with him, and refuses to answer questions. Where does that leave us, Cade?"

They were all worried about Sam. The past months, the dark anger barely glimpsed in his gray blue eyes was growing. He was tenser than ever before, angrier.

Cade turned to Heather, his gray eyes swirling with concern and rage.

"You're the only one who can stop this, Heather."

Heather's eyes widened. How the hell was she supposed to stop any of it?

"Goddammit, Cade," Tara snapped out then, her voice raising. "Don't try to pull her into this mess."

"It's her decision, Tara," he growled furiously. "Stop playing nursemaid to her, it won't help anything."

"And fucking the August men in some glorified orgy will?" Her voice was raising, anger surging through it.

"Dammit, Tara, shut the hell up," Heather snapped out, moving between the two combatants. "It's not up to any of you, it's up to Sam and me, and he doesn't want me here. So the question is not debatable."

Cade's head snapped around, his eyes penetrating, filled with cynical derision. "Are you insane, Heather? There's nothing Sam wants more in this world than he wants you. Don't play the fool at this late date."

Heather took a deep, steadying breath. "He's damned good at denial then. But still, that's beside the point." She looked at Marly, seeing the glimmer of humor in the other woman's eyes, the way she watched Cade and Tara as though they were children, arguing over a prized toy. The woman never ceased to amaze her.

"Heather's right," Marly said firmly, placing her hand on Cade's muscular arm. "Sam has to work this out for himself, and so does Heather. All the arguing in the world won't change that, Cade."

He swiped his fingers through his thick black hair. "Dammit, Marly, he's going to get himself killed."

The dark fear that pulsed in Cade's voice seemed to fill the entire entryway. The bond the men shared went far deeper than that of any sibling relationship that Heather had ever known.

"I'll talk to him, Cade," Heather promised. As Tara went to protest, she held up her hand with a sharp shake of her head. "This isn't any of your business, Tara. It's mine and Sam's."

"Goddammit." Tara turned and stomped through the house then, the sound of her boots a rapping tap on the hardwood floor that had Heather wincing. Tara only did that when she was really pissed.

"Heather, Sam's getting too reckless," Cade bit out, his voice lowered in concern. "No matter what he says, try to stay closer to him. Stop letting him run you off."

"Cade, I can't make Sam do anything," she said firmly as she pushed the fingers of both hands through her hair. "He doesn't want me around."

"But he does, Heather." Marly turned to her then, her blue eyes soft, understanding. "That's the problem. Sam wants you too badly."

Heather snorted. "And you know this how?"

"Because it's your name he cries out while he's coming inside her," Cade growled as Marly rolled her eyes in exasperation. "Dammit, Marly, there's no sense in beating around the damned bush here. If she doesn't know by now then she never will."

"There's no sense in being crude either," Marly snapped back, frowning up at him with an edge of steel that surprised Heather.

Cade grimaced as he pushed his hands in his jeans pockets and looked away for several seconds. When his gaze returned, it was softer, apologetic. "I'm sorry," he sighed. "Marly's right, there's no excuse for that."

"Cade, just because I'm aware of your lifestyle, doesn't mean I agree with it." Heather crossed her arms over her breasts, watching him curiously.

She had been more than aware of the speculation in both Cade's and Brock's expressions the few times she had caught them looking her way. It wasn't lust, not in the normal sense. It was hard to put her finger on it. An emotion swirled in their eyes, affection definitely, but still, an undefined something.

Sexual lust she could have understood. She saw it often when each man looked at his respective lover. But that unnamed emotion was there when they touched, or looked at each other's lovers as well. The emotion Cade felt for Sarah, what Brock felt for Marly, and now, that same look was being shared with Heather. It was confusing, and often kept her awake long into the night as she tried to define it.

"Your approval isn't what we're asking for, Heather." Marly's voice chilled, her head raising proudly. "We're asking you to stay closer to Sam. To attempt to temper his recklessness. Don't pretend you don't want him, just as he can't pretend he doesn't want you. Give him something besides the demons to concentrate on, if you truly love him as much as I suspect you do."

Heather took a deep breath, her lips pressing together in irritation as she confronted Marly. She had rarely seen the other woman anything less than easygoing and smiling. This edge of finely tempered maturity she glimpsed in her was a surprise.

"And if you're wrong, Marly?" she asked her softly, staring directly into the dark blue eyes that regarded her coolly. "What if it's no more than lust? What then?"

Marly smiled, her expression softening, her eyes warming with compassion.

"We know Sam, Heather. He won't be easy, because he cares. I can almost guarantee I'm not wrong."

"Almost." Heather shook her head roughly. "I can't believe I'm about to trust my heart to an almost."

\* \* \* \* \*

Heather knocked on Sam's door softly before turning the knob and opening it slowly. "Sam?" She entered the bedroom, stepping slowly inside as she saw him standing at the window, staring into the distance, his body tense as she stood silently and watched him.

Their gazes met in the bulletproof glass. His hooded and dark, hers quiet and questioning. She wanted to go to him, to touch him, ease him.

"You shouldn't be here," he growled. "Aren't you on duty tonight?"

She bit her lip, fighting the pain his words caused.

"I remember when you used to sneak out and meet me wherever Rick had me stationed," she said quietly, allowing the regret to sound through her voice. "What happened to that, Sam? We were friends. For a little while."

He had always laughed when he found her, because he had managed to slip away from Rick and his men. Then he would tease her, those thickly lashed eyes lowered sensually as he watched her blush and her nipples harden.

"The first time he struck, we thought the stalker was Marly's stepfather," he said quietly. "When Jack Jennings tried to take her, we never questioned his ranting that someone else had contacted him, told him how to get to Marly. We couldn't find Anna, so we'd assumed he finally got to her, and then came for Marly. We thought we were safe, that the past couldn't touch us ever again."

He turned to her then, his hands tucked in the pockets of his jeans, his expression lined with the bitterness of the years.

"We'll find him, Sam," she promised him softly. "There are three different agencies working on this, not to mention the law enforcement officials. We'll catch him."

He took a deep breath. "When Brock went after Sarah, we found out that the stalker hadn't been caught after all," he continued. "But still, we prayed our past wasn't reaching out to dirty those two women any more than it already had. We thought we could survive, that we could catch him." He swallowed tightly. "I thought I had a chance, a right to love, Heather, until he attacked you."

Heather crossed her arms over her breasts and drew in a deep breath. She fought her tears, the blinding pain she felt each time she saw the brutal memories in Sam's eyes.

"Sam, he'll mess up soon…"

He shook his head, cynicism washing over his face, his gaze hardening. "Eventually, he will. When he does, he's a dead man. But what if, Heather, what if he kills you? Or maims you so terribly you can never face life or love the same?"

It was a risk she was taking, and it terrified her. She knew enough of the August history to know what the August brothers had endured. Endless months of pain and brutality. A hell most men would have never survived.

"That's a cop-out, Sam," she whispered sadly. "You know you won't stop him now. It won't matter if you love me or hate me, if you fuck me or you revile me. The bastard will see me as your weakness. I'm still in danger."

He flinched. A hard, sharp movement that tore at her heart as he turned away from her again.

"You don't talk to me anymore," she finally said moments later when he didn't speak again. "I miss that, Sam. Just talking to you."

She moved toward him, watching him watch her, seeing the bittersweet arousal that glittered in his eyes. He was furious. She could see it in every taut line of his body. Furious over the danger to his family, furious over his desire for her. She knew that much. Knew that the heat and fire that tore through her body was matched in his.

"There's nothing to talk about, Heather," he said roughly, jerking the curtains closed over the window before he turned to her. "What the fuck should I say, baby? What do you want me to do? Maybe, just fucking maybe, if I stay the hell away from you, he won't hurt you again." His voice was strangled. "Do you have any fucking idea what it did to me, to see you bleeding like that, and then to see the fucking scars he left on you?"

"Well it wasn't exactly a picnic for me, Sam." The ire in her voice more than matched his, she made sure of it. "But do you think hiding from it is really going to help anything. You're stalking around this damned house like an animal, growling at everyone and ready to fight at any opportunity. How does that help?"

"And what do you suggest instead?" he asked her bitterly. "Do you think fucking you is going to stop it, Heather? That I'll turn into some little tame pussycat that you can stroke and cuddle with when you need to? Goddammit, what kind of freakin' fairy tale are you living in?"

His rage cut through her like a knife, cutting into her soul, wounding her not with his words, but with the pain that creased his expression.

"Definitely not yours," she yelled back. "Because yours is nothing but a damned pity party and a lot of hot, bitter looks. You're going to get yourself killed, Sam. Dead. The bastard will kill you, and he'll kill your family with your death. Is that what you really want?"

He stilled, the muscles in his jaw working furiously as he stared back at her.

"Keeping you safe is not a damned pity party," he growled.

"What about your family?" she snapped back. "You ran out of here the other night and refused to tell anyone you were even leaving, and walked right into a murder. That's not a man whose only thought is protecting his family."

Something flashed in his eyes. There, then gone. A knowledge of something he was clearly keeping hidden. Over the past year Heather had come to know Sam better than he was aware. She knew when he was hiding something, when he was fighting his own desires, and when he was lying. He was hiding something, something important.

"What happened, Sam?" she asked suspiciously. "What did Tate say when he called?"

His look was brooding, intent, as he watched her.

"Sam?"

"He just asked me to meet him." He crossed his arms over his chest, challenging her to prove otherwise.

"You're lying to me, Sam." It tore at her heart, because she had seen him hide from others, but never her. Not until now. "What happened?"

"Heather." The gentleness in his voice had her breath catching in need, in fear.

She watched him silently as he came to her. Tall and broad and so sexy he nearly mesmerized her. And sad. So very sad it tore at her soul. He stopped in front of her, his fingers reaching out to touch her cheek and she watched the small flush of arousal that heated his face.

"Sam, what happened?" He was frightening her, terrifying her with his recklessness.

"Nothing that can hurt you or me, baby. Not anymore," he promised her. "He can't hurt anyone now. And I can't say I'm not glad to see his ass gone. But you're right, it was stupid to run out like that. It won't happen again."

She started to question him further, her suspicions sitting tight and hard in her stomach, when a sharp rap sounded at the door.

"Sam, we need you out here," Tara called impatiently. "And if Heather's with you, tell her she's supposed to be on duty, not entertaining the resident stud."

Sam frowned toward the door. "One day," he sighed. "I'm going to give that woman something to bitch about." He looked down at her again and shook his head. "Well hell, babe, your babysitter just found you. We may as well go."

Heather followed him from the room, but nothing could still the cold chill of premonition. The feeling that whatever he was hiding was more important than even he knew.

\* \* \* \* \*

Several hours later, the house went on alert with the arrival of Rick's helicopter on the August landing pad. The family gathered around the large dining table where the women sat in tense silence, and the men with a brooding anger that set everyone's nerves on edge.

Heather stood propped against the wall across from where Sam sat, watching him closely. His expression was closed, that edge of barely contained violence glittering in his eyes once again.

The investigation into the family of the man who had tortured the three brothers didn't sit well with them. Cade especially was furious over it. The bastard was dead, he had informed them all. There was no sense in trying to resurrect a damned ghost. But Rick, like Tara and Heather, believed it was all connected. The letter Marly had received after the second failed attempt on Sarah's life proved that, even if the brothers didn't want to face it. The poetry style letter worried and concerned her. Her friend Greg had often left her letters written in such a style.

Marly was insistent that Greg would have never tried to hurt her. That he wouldn't have been able to take those pictures while he was at the ranch the year before last, and Sam was inclined to agree. Greg was an intense young man, but he wasn't a stalker, or a killer. To be assured of this, Cade had secretly had his scholarship moved to an Eastern college where one of Rick's men had befriended the boy. He hadn't moved from the area since, which eliminated him as a suspect.

"Okay, boys and girls, we have a lead." Rick stepped into the dining room carrying a thick manila folder in one hand. On his hip, he had strapped his pistol, a precautionary measure all the bodyguards had taken after Mark Tate's death.

"Rick." Cade stood to his feet. "We'll take this into the office."

"Like hell you will." Marly stood, anger vibrating through her voice. "This involves all of us, Cade."

The family was standing now, the women's expressions protesting, angry, the brothers' bleak and savage. Rick faced the group, his face showing his exhaustion, his eyes his sorrow.

"Marly." Heather watched as Sam touched Marly's arm, drawing her attention to him. "Cade will tell you the details later. Let us take care of this, Munchkin, for now."

Heather couldn't see enough of Sam's expression to know what Marly saw there. Her face tightened in pain, and tears came to her eyes. She turned back to Cade. His expression Heather could clearly see. A man tormented, tortured. He couldn't even look his lover in the eye.

"Cade. I love you," Marly whispered deeply, and if Heather had ever doubted the woman's love for the surly rancher, she didn't doubt it anymore. "You can't hide this forever."

Marly's voice was filled with pain, anger, and helplessness. She touched Cade's cheek unselfconsciously, aware that everyone watched the display. When Cade looked down at Marly, Heather's heart clenched in pain for him. His emotions were dark, and so painful it broke her heart. She wondered how Marly bore the pain.

"Not yet." He shook his head, the bitterness of his rage echoing in his voice. "Not yet, Marly."

"Fine." She nodded, her voice lowering, her expression tightening in anger. "When you're ready to trust me, Cade, just let me know. Maybe I'll still be ready to listen."

She ignored the rough protest in his voice as she left the table and rushed from the room. Heather couldn't say she blamed the other woman at all.

"I'll talk to her," Sarah whispered, looking up as Brock leaned to her. His arms went around her in a tight hug, his lips pressing to her forehead as his face twisted with his pain.

"Thanks, babe," Brock whispered so low that Heather barely heard him, despite the fact that she stood only a few feet from him. "I'll be up when we're done."

When he released her, he touched her hair then watched as she turned away and headed for the stairs.

"Can we get started now?" Rick asked, laying the folder down on the table.

"Not yet." Sam took a deep breath. "She goes too." He nodded in Heather's direction.

Her eyes narrowed.

"Heather's part of the security force, Sam," Rick said, his voice cold. "It's information she needs to know to protect your ass."

She crossed her arms over her breasts, staring back at him in challenge.

"I'm nothing to you, remember?" she reminded him of his past inference.

His hands gripped the back of the chair Marly had sat in, nearly turning white from the grip he had on it.

"Doesn't matter," he growled. "She goes, Rick."

"She might go, but it won't make a difference." Rick's voice was firm, his expression icy. "I won't hide this information from her. It affects her, not just due to her job, but due to the fact that her life is now in more danger than any of the rest of you. Would you deny her the information that would help save it?"

The bombshell was dropped with the ease of words, but the echo of the implications resounded throughout the room. Sam paled, but all eyes now turned to Heather.

"Why?" Cade snarled, turning quickly back to Rick.

"Reginald Robert Jennings. He's Jack Jennings full brother, and both men are half brothers to Jedediah Marcelle, the man you killed, Cade. Reginald Robert is Marly's natural father."

Silence, thick and all consuming filled the room for long seconds.

"No." Cade's voice was furious, blistering with his rage.

"Someone went to a lot of trouble to hide the records. There were even false records recorded in the computer system, which is why we were stumped for so long. It took a physical search." Rick opened the file and pushed it toward Cade. "I have birth records, marriage license, divorce record, all of it. Some of it was pretty cleverly hidden. Someone wanted Reginald Robert's name erased from any public files. I think he's the one who was writing to Marly, and I believe he's the one stalking the family now. If that's true, then Heather's life won't be worth shit if he's not caught."

The cold brutal edge of his voice assured her of just how serious he was.

"Thanks, Rick," she expressed mockingly, fear flashing through her now.

Rick sighed roughly.

"He's focused on Sam," he said. "I can't figure that one out. I would expect him to focus on Cade, because of Marly and the fact that Cade was the one who killed his brother. Instead, he blames Sam. I believe it's because his social status, as well as his brother's life, ended because of Marcelle's fixation on Sam."

"Enough." Sam's voice was like broken glass.

Rick glanced away, but when he looked back, his expression was even, cool and impersonal.

"Servants gossip, and it seems there were several who were aware of what was going on in that basement," he continued, ignoring the way the man began to shift dangerously, muscles bunching as though preparing to attack.

"I managed to track one down, and to get him to talk. He was the one who carried the meals down to the room, who injected the drugs…"

"Enough." Cade shook his head, his hands bunching into fists in the pockets of his jeans.

"Reginald went to medical school for a while," Rick continued. "He was especially proficient with a scalpel. The scars Sam carries proves that whoever did the work, knew what they were doing. As do Heather's."

Heather watched Sam. He flinched with each word, denial raging in his expression. She felt her heart breaking for him. She couldn't stand here, knowing that listening to every word out of Rick's mouth was destroying him further because she was hearing it. Because she knew.

"Enough," she whispered, holding a hand up to stop Rick.

Everyone turned to her then.

"Sam," she whispered his name, tears coming to her eyes as she saw the unbearable shame in his expression. "I think I need to go talk to Marly as well. Will you let me know what I need to stay alive?"

She was placing her life in his hands; something she had never dared to do with anyone else. He blinked in surprise, in relief.

"I will." He swallowed tightly.

"Heather." Tara's voice was filled with protest. "I'll fill you in…"

"No." Heather shook her head. "Sam can fill me in. He knows what I need to know and what can wait until he's ready."

She didn't give Sam time to answer, or Tara to protest. She swept from the room, pain echoing through her body; for herself, for Sam, and for his brothers. They stood there, together, yet apart. As though invisible shields separated them, refusing to allow them to draw together, to face the past as a unit.

She was already aware of many of the details. Painful, horrendous. Rick hadn't cut them any slack when he first detailed the dangers they faced. They were three men lucky to be alive, to be able to function in any normal way, and one of them had committed murder.

Men so horrifically abused, that their only connection to each other was the sexual bonds they shared with each other's women. Strong, dependable, decent men whose only faults were their sexual needs and their loyalty to each other. And these men were being stalked, possibly by someone who had aided the monster who tried to destroy them. Wanted to destroy them because Sam had refused the homosexual relationship his abuser had wanted.

The drugs they had been injected with had aided the abuser in forcing them to rape each other. The normal bonds of brotherhood and trust had been destroyed in ways Heather could only imagine.

Her stomach roiled with the sickening realization of what Sam had suffered. The guilt and the pain he lived with was suddenly more real to her than it ever had been. Her feelings for him though, rather than dimming at that knowledge, were only growing. And in growing, she faced the bitter realization that there were now choices she would have to make as well.

# Chapter Seven

"They're going to try to hide from us forever," Marly raged furiously as Heather watched her pace the room.

Her long hair fell in ringlets down her back, swishing against her hips as she stalked the room.

"They can't hide for much longer, Marly." Sarah sat back in the chair she had taken at the side of the room.

"It's not like I'm unaware of what happened," Marly argued, pushing her fingers through her hair, as she seemed to grit her teeth in pain. "Dammit, Sarah, he treats me like I'm still a child."

Not hardly, Heather thought sarcastically. She had been unlucky enough to walk into the kitchen one morning searching out coffee, only to find Cade buried balls deep between his lover's thighs as he bent her over the counter.

"You look like you disagree," Marly snapped as she turned on her.

Heather watched her curiously before shrugging. "He doesn't treat like you a child."

Her eyes narrowed until only a sliver of the brilliant blue could be glimpsed.

"What would you call it?"

"He thinks he's protecting you," Heather pointed out.

"I'm aware of that, Heather," Marly sighed then, sitting down on the bed wearily. "It's the only reason I don't kick his ass now."

Heather fought the grin that wanted to touch her lips at the thought of the petite, delicate Marly attempting to kick big Cade

August's ass. It would be an interesting sight...a lesson in futility, she thought humorously.

"Sam's right, your sense of humor is warped. That wasn't supposed to be funny," Marly accused her with a frown.

Heather could only shake her head.

"Why didn't you stay?" Sarah asked her then. "You could have at least let us know what they were talking about later."

"Do I look like your spy?" Heather grumbled. "I couldn't tell you anything."

"Of course you could," Marly waved her hand carelessly. "You are quite aware that those men are only hurting themselves, Heather. We need to know what's going on."

"I know that having even one of us down there while Rick is dissecting their pride isn't a good idea," she countered. "Until I break Sam of this idea that he has to share me with your lovers, then I'm a weakness to all of them."

"And you think you can do that?" Sarah leaned back in her chair and watched Heather as she sat on the edge of the couch. "Break him of that idea?"

Heather frowned. The other woman wasn't being sarcastic, rather mildly amused, which grated on her nerves.

"Sarah, you two are entirely too accepting of these relationships for comfort," she said warily.

"Of course we accept it." Marly shrugged. "Heather, we have every woman's dream. Three men who live, and I mean live, for our pleasure and our comfort. They love us, completely, accept our moods and enjoy our differences. What isn't there to accept?"

"Marly, your lover fucks another woman." Heather felt as helpless in the face of these two women as she had when Sam had attempted to explain it.

"And mine fucks her," Sarah countered. "Not anyone else, Heather, and only because she's a part of Cade. These men aren't like other brothers, and I know that's hard to accept. But you have to understand; it's who they are. You can't change it. He might stop to please you, because he loves you, but that need will be there, and it will only grow. If you can't accept it, then you need to stay as far away from Sam as possible."

Heather came to her feet in a surge of anger. "I love him, Sarah. And I know he loves me. I can feel it; I can see it."

"And he still comes to me and Marly when he needs us." Her voice was gentle, her expression compassionate. "I can't turn him away any more than I could turn Brock away. I would hurt us all to do so. How do you fit that into your perception of love now?"

Confusion washed over her. She had never discussed their relationships with their men with them, had avoided it every chance she had. Now it was there and impossible to ignore, and she found herself wishing she had stayed downstairs instead.

"He just needs to heal," she whispered desperately.

"No, Heather, he needs to face it," Marly said then. "Sam hasn't faced the past, he doesn't remember it, and refuses to face it. When he does, he'll heal. But he won't change. To a point, Cade and Brock have both faced what happened. It's painful, and sometimes, though rarely, the nightmares are still there. But it hasn't changed that need inside them."

"Men will take what you let them get away with." Heather could feel her body trembling with a rush of nervous energy. "You let them get away with it."

Sarah sighed as she shook her head. "If it were any other man, I would agree with you." She stared up at the ceiling somberly. "Mark was my ex-husband, Heather, and he screwed anything he could get to open its thighs for him. But Brock's not like that." Heather watched as she lowered her head again, her golden brown eyes intent, piercing. "Brock loves me; I'm his heart and soul. But he loves Marly too, and even you, because Cade and Sam do. They aren't separate like other brothers are, Heather. A part of them—a very intrinsic, spiritual part of those men—is so closely bound that you'll never separate them. If you try, you'll hurt them all."

"And they've been hurt enough." Marly's voice carried an edge of warning.

"Or maybe the two of you are just loath to lose the affection and the relationship you have with each of those men." She voiced the suspicion that had filled her for months.

"Heather." Sarah held her hand up when Marly would have spoken. "I understand you're upset, and even angry. I was at one time, too, just as Marly was. Upset because we didn't understand, to the extent that we've grown to understand, these three men. This isn't a life that just any woman could lead. Selfishness and possessiveness won't work here. And you'll see, if you accept Sam for who he is, that there's no need for it. But it's something you have to accept alone."

There was such compassion, such understanding in Sarah's tone that Heather's throat tightened with emotion. She couldn't accuse these two women of not loving their individual men, but she knew they loved each other's, as well as Sam, too. She shook her head, fighting her emotions, her sense of what was right and what was wrong, and found that still, she had no answers.

"Heather, Sam does love you," Marly said softly. "I know he does. I know you're all he wants, all he needs, to ease the pain he carries. Without you, Sarah and I..." She seemed to struggle for words. "It's like needing water, and being given a soda instead. It eases for a moment, but the thirst is still there, and it's soul deep."

"If he loved me, I would be enough," she whispered, fighting her tears as she crossed her arms protectively beneath her heart. "He has to love me enough."

"Or maybe you have to love him enough," Sarah said gently. "I suspect the demons Sam lives with. Marly and I both suspect that it wasn't Cade who killed that bastard, but Sam. If that's true, Heather, then that means Cade and Brock know it, they protect him from it, for a reason. Sam's heart is softer, gentler than the other two. He's the one who brings home stray puppies, even now. The one who plays Santa every Christmas for families in the county who don't have money for their kids. The one who does what's needed to lighten everyone else when the demons are at their worst. You won't change Sam, Heather. But you, and you alone, could very well destroy him."

And how was she supposed to live with that? The emotional pressure, as well as her own feelings, twisted and fought inside her until she felt the raking talons of her own lack of answers. She looked at both women, seeing anger, but also their compassion and understanding. They knew how she struggled, how she fought. She could see it in their eyes, in their acceptance of the men they loved.

"How can you do it?" she whispered. "Walk into a room and know the man you love has just had sex with another woman?"

"Not just another woman, Heather." Marly leaned forward, her expression sincere, kind. "A sister. And I know it's not just lust. He's a part of Brock. His soul is merged so tightly with his brothers that he loves and needs Sarah, not as deeply, but just as true as Brock does. And it's the same for Brock and for Sam."

"We've watched them, Heather," Sarah spoke then. "The closer Sam gets to you, the more instinctive Brock and Cade's attraction to you becomes. It's instinct, because they know each other that well...are that much a part of each other. And nothing you or I or Marly can do will change that. And if you want the truth, that part I wouldn't want to change. Because I love Sam and Cade, too. They are a part of me. Not as deeply as Brock is, but still, a part of me."

Heather looked to Marly. She nodded slowly, her expression showing her agreement, her acceptance of the men and the love she had for all of them.

"I don't think I can do it," she whispered.

"Heather, Sam will lead you through it. You'll know when it's right, and when it's needed. And then, only then, can you really make the decision."

"And don't say you aren't attracted to them all, either," Marly snorted then. "I saw your face when you walked into the kitchen on us. You're attracted, Heather, and be damned thankful you are Sam's life, because that's the only way in hell I'd let you within a mile of Cade."

There was a smile on her face, but Heather knew she meant every word of it.

"This family is insane." She sat back on the couch heavily, leaning her head back, closing her eyes and shaking her head at the impossibility of the situation. "Every damned one of you is certifiable."

\* \* \* \* \*

Heather gave Sam several hours to find her. Long after the meeting with Rick was over, and the other men had retreated to their rooms with the women, Sam still hadn't shown up. The whispered cries of sexual release penetrated the thick walls of their bedrooms, drifting into her room. The men were separate, though. They weren't sharing, weren't turning to each other, and Heather felt a vague warning in that knowledge. An uncomfortable sense of an impending storm with the potential to destroy them all.

The worry became so intense that she finally left her bedroom and went searching for Sam. She knew he hadn't come to his own room. She would have heard him if he had.

"Heather." Rick stepped into the entryway as she descended the stairs.

He was positioned at the front door, watching the night from the long, tinted windows at the side of the door.

"Seen Sam, Rick?" Heather asked softly, hoping Tara wasn't around. Her sister was becoming so overprotective it was beginning to grate on her nerves.

"Game room. Sure you want to go searching for him?" Rick asked her gently. "He's in a dangerous mood, Heather."

She pushed her fingers through her hair, licking her lips nervously.

"He shouldn't be alone."

"He has his family," he argued softly. "He'll go to them when he needs to."

She shook her head and smiled sadly. "Haven't you noticed, Rick? He rarely does anymore. I bet the limo was only the second time he's had sex since I came to stay here. He's dangerous because he's alone."

"Heather." He grimaced tightly. "Tara's worried about this. And so am I. I don't think you're ready to be what Sam needs."

"Maybe not." She shook her head, remembering her earlier conversation with Sarah and Marly. Tears pricked her eyes because it was the one question she couldn't answer. Could she handle it? "But I can't leave him like this either, Rick. It's breaking my heart."

He watched her, his brown eyes dark and intense before he nodded his head abruptly and gave her one of those small, self-conscious smiles that had endeared him to her years ago.

"He's a lucky man then."

"I wish he saw it that way, " she said in resignation. "Thanks, Rick."

She moved away from him, drawing the edges of her long robe together as she made her way through the house to the basement entrance. And there she found Sam, alone, the air of shifting violence that surrounded him stronger than ever before.

"You're worrying your family, you know." Heather stepped into the game room, a large room arrayed with damned near every amusement a man could want.

A regulation-sized pool table dominated the center of the first quarter area of the room. Farther inside the wide area were arcade game machines, a wide screen television, a bar in the far corner, and a few scattered conversational areas made up of curved sectional couches and a chair or two. The furniture was wide and comfortable, the carpet under her feet was thick and luxurious, and in the dim light cast by the two single wall lamps, Sam stood, picking off pool balls with an air of bored contempt.

He was hiding here, she thought. Bare-chested, dressed in a pair of dark blue sweat pants, his feet bare. Sexy as hell and as tempting as sin as he watched her with that narrowed, brooding look that set her blood temperature rising.

He straightened, propping himself against the pool table as he watched her enter the room with narrowed eyes. His strong-boned face was lined with sorrow, his blue-gray eyes dark with exhaustion, and with a shadow of horror that broke her heart. The nightmares were growing worse for him, she knew. She heard him nightly as he came awake with a snarl, death echoing in the sound of his voice.

*Die, you mother fucker!*

She wondered if he knew what he cried out. Did he know the rage, the horror, the unbearable pain that echoed in his voice?

"The family doesn't have anything better to do than worry," he finally shrugged. Muscle rippled beneath his broad shoulders as he turned from her, the tanned flesh glowing beneath the dim light, sleek and tough, tempting her to touch.

"So they may as well worry about you, right?" she asked him softly as she stopped at the edge of the pool table, watching as he replaced the pool stick.

He sighed deeply, still turned from her, staring at the pool sticks as though they held some fascination for him.

"I'm okay," he shrugged, turning back to her, his expression carefully composed, a reckless smile shaping his lips. "They're just worried I'll leave the house again."

"Will you?" She arched a brow questioningly. "Leave the house again?"

A crooked smile tilted his lips, so male and tempting she nearly missed the fact that it didn't reach his eyes.

"I promised I wouldn't." He laid his hand over his heart. "Didn't you hear me?"

Heather snorted. "Actually, you said, and I'll quote, 'Fuck it, Cade, I'll just rot here if that's what you want,' unquote."

He grunted. She wondered if he meant to pass the sound off as a laugh.

"Same thing." He scratched at his chin. "Just different words."

Heather grinned, watching as he picked up a cue ball, then sent it spinning across the table into one of the slots.

"Cade seemed less than appreciative of the words then," she said as she walked past the pool table, heading for one of the wide couches that faced it from the other side.

As she walked, she felt her long robe caressing her bare feet, and she knew Sam was watching her. She could feel his gaze on her, searing in its heat. She curled up on the couch before looking up at him with what she hoped was an innocent expression. It was spoiled by the flush blooming on her cheeks, though. There was no missing the tenting of those sweat pants. Sam was sporting a hard-on long enough to make her mouth water and her heart hammer in cunt-clenching arousal.

Sam cleared his throat, turning from her. "Cade doesn't appreciate a lot of things," he growled as he pushed the pool balls from the table as though it were his life's mission.

He wasn't nervous. She didn't think she had ever seen Sam nervous, but he seemed hesitant around her now, as though in some way, she threatened him more than ever before.

"Is there anything I need to know from that meeting?" she finally asked him.

She watched his jaw bunch, the way his eyelids flickered as though he needed to shut out reality, to hide from the events around them.

"Same ole shit," he finally shrugged. "The bastard wants me because his half brother was a depraved son of a bitch, and because he's not much better. Marly's damned near destroyed because Cade refuses to tell her what's going on. Cade's not talking to any of us because Marly's tears rip his soul apart, at least what's left of it. And here I stand." He held his arms out as though in invitation. "Once again the reason why my brothers are being destroyed."

She wanted to touch him, to hold him, but the look in his eye warned her that he would never allow it. The cold, hard core that worried them all was growing.

"Do you want me to leave, Sam?" she asked him softly as he raised his head to look at her. "Leave the ranch, and you?"

His hands were braced on the pool table, his shaggy hair falling over his forehead rakishly. His eyes were direct, his expression still and quiet.

"I want you to stay," he said softly. "Too much. I'm the wrong person for you to be around, Heather. You should know that by now. The scars that bastard left on you should be enough to convince you of that."

His eyes were a mixture of sadness and lust and brittle fury.

She tilted her head, watching him curiously.

"My pussy isn't ugly anymore, Sam," she told him in irritation. "You don't have to act so strange with those little warnings."

She still remembered the look on his face when he had stalked into her bedroom over a month ago, jerking up her gown, his face paling at the sight of the raw flesh of her cunt. The cuts had still been raw, not requiring stitches, but slow to heal, and extremely tender.

He frowned. "You act as though the sight of them is what bothered me." He watched her bleakly, throwing the last ball across the table. "Dammit, Heather, he cut you. Cut you because of me. You should be terrified to be in the same house with me. Hell, all of them should be."

Anger filled the area, the air thickening with tension, with rage.

"Why, Sam?" she asked him softly. "You weren't the one that cut me."

"He did it because of me." He placed his hands on the table, gripping the edge until she could see his fingers pale with the strength he exerted. "He did it, Heather, because he thinks you matter to me. Do you understand that?"

Heather shrugged. The edge of violence that swirled in the air around him was begging to be deflected. Deflected or freed. She had a feeling if it was freed, then neither of them would come out of it unscathed.

"I think you're just turned off by the scars now." She shrugged. "What's wrong, Sam, afraid someone else is wounded more than you in some way?"

It was a dangerous game she was playing, and Heather knew it. Sam's sexuality was more intense, deeper, rougher than the other men, and the memories of that time always made it flare hotter. The memory of the one time Sam had allowed her close was brutally vivid. She still remembered his hands in her hair, pulling at the strands as he fucked her mouth with long, slow strokes of his thick cock.

The heavily veined, rough flesh of his cock had nearly bruised her lips. The scars were thicker than her own, requiring a rough touch to give him the sensation needed to orgasm. Her teeth had scraped him as he cried out, panting.

*Oh yeah, Heather. Like that, baby. Just like that. God yes!* He had nearly choked her as he sent his cock thrusting past her teeth and stroking her tongue as he exploded in her mouth. His semen had shot down her throat, salty, dark and male. Perhaps he would have returned the favor. Maybe he would have buried his still-hard flesh between her damp thighs if they hadn't been so rudely interrupted then.

"Stop, Heather," he growled.

"Stop what?" She frowned over at him, still lost in the memory of his touch, his taste.

"Stop remembering my cock in your mouth," he bit out furiously. "It's bad enough that I can't forget myself."

And evidently his cock wasn't about to forget either, if the raised material of his sweats was any indication.

"Maybe it would be easier to forget if you had gotten around to returning the favor, rather than worrying about my virginity," she pointed out with mocking calm. "That was rather rude of you, Sam."

He gaped at her, his eyes widening, obviously surprised that she would upbraid him over something he was taking such pains to forget. Not that she would have let him forget.

"Heather, you are aware you were attacked because of your friendship with me. Right?" he snarled, fury filling his voice. "Do you have a death wish I don't know anything about?"

His eyes darkened, his cheekbones flushing with his anger.

Heather leaned back against the couch, her eyes narrowing on him.

"I'm your weakness. Do you think that's going to change, even if you don't touch me, Sam?"

She watched his breathing accelerate, rather from lust or from anger, she wasn't certain.

"I don't have a weakness," he warned her coldly.

"Oh really?" she asked him with a touch of mocking amusement. "I guess that's why your cock is harder than dried oak less than six hours after a little limo sex with your brother and his lover. What happened, Sam, did Cade get greedy on you and not let you have any?"

She was pushing him, and she knew it. But she was getting damned sick of the continual charade playing out between them.

She was as much a prisoner to that damned stalker as he was, and she was getting sick of it.

"Cade doesn't get greedy where his brothers are concerned, Heather." His voice dropped, but there was no disguising the sneer in his tone. "Be careful, or you just might find out how much we do like to share."

"Oh goody, a dare." She grinned as though they weren't talking about her in the middle of an August orgy. "Shall we see which of us is stronger, Sam? Can you make me want to share? Or will I make you greedy instead?"

She watched as he straightened. He did nothing to hide the erection beneath his sweat pants now. It was blatantly obvious.

"Oh baby, greedy will be the least of your problems," he told her then, softly, dangerously.

Her heart sped up in excitement, the blood pounding through her veins as he began to advance on her.

"I'm a very greedy person, Sam. What about you?" She sat still, though the adrenaline racing through her body demanded action.

"I could be." But he didn't sound so sure. He didn't look so sure. "But can you handle what you're inviting, Heather?"

Could she? She sure as hell hoped so, because she knew she wanted it.

"Sam, I can handle anything you want to dish out." Tara had always warned her that the day would come when her mouth would get her into more trouble than she could handle. Heather had a feeling that day had just arrived.

# Chapter Eight

She had no idea how desperately he wanted her, Sam thought as he watched the deliberate provocation in her eyes. She was daring him as though it were a game, as though there would be no casualties, no pain involved. But there was, and he knew it. He faced it daily with Marly and Sarah. The knowledge of what they were doing to those beautiful, loving women destroyed his soul.

Yet, here she sat, daring him, as though the dare could be called back as easily as saying the words. She had been in the August household as a bodyguard long enough to catch the subtle hints of what defiance and a sexual challenge did to them. Sarah and Marly teasingly defied them on a daily level, keeping them focused on the here and now, rather than the past. And the challenges always fired their sexuality, their need to dominate sexually, to reaffirm their sensual control.

He crossed his arms over his chest as he leaned against the end of the pool table and watched her. Her green eyes were dark with arousal, her nipples peaked beneath the silk of the long gown and flimsy robe. He could see them clearly defined, hard little points tempting his hunger.

"Why are you still a virgin?" The question plagued him. He needed an answer, needed to know why she seemed so willing to give him what no other man had ever taken.

She propped her arm on the back of the couch, resting her head on her hand as she watched him curiously.

"I've never been with a man because I haven't found one that could make me half as hot as a good erotica book and an even better toy." It wasn't the answer he expected.

He closed his eyes briefly as though gathering his strength.

"Toy?" he asked softly, his body tightening, his cock jerking beneath his sweatpants as though trying to slice through the fabric to get to her.

"Toys, perhaps." She shrugged, a grin tugging at her mouth. "Are you shocked, Sam? I told you I had a vibrator."

"What kind of toys?" His imagination was killing him now.

She shrugged, her slender shoulders rising, lifting her breasts against the material that covered them as she watched him with more amusement than the fear he thought she should feel.

"All kinds of toys, Sam," she said softly. "I'm technically a virgin, not physically a virgin."

His brows snapped into a frown. "You didn't tell me that before," he growled.

"Would it have made a difference?" she asked him, her voice husky. "What business of it yours, anyway? You made it pretty plain you had no intentions of going to bed with me."

Sam could feel his body nearly trembling with excitement. His imagination was going wild, imagining her spread out on his bed, her legs open to him as she used one of the more unique dildos he could buy for her. Moving it in and out of her bare pussy, stroking herself, moaning...

"Fuck." He drew in a hard breath, staring at her accusingly. "Why are you telling me this now?"

"Because you asked." Her smile was a challenge in itself.

His cock was so hard it hurt. Harder than he could ever remember it being in his life. His hands itched to touch her, his mouth watered with the need to taste her.

"Heather." He closed his eyes, fighting his desires, his sexuality. "I don't want to hurt you."

His sexual appetites were raging now. She had thrown gas on a fire already burning nearly out of control. When she didn't answer him, he opened his eyes. She watched him, equal parts innocence and seductress as he fought for control. Her lashes lowered over her eyes, a sexy, knowing move that broke his resolve.

Before he could convince himself once again how disastrous the consequences could be, he moved to her. He glimpsed the surprise on her face an instant before he flipped her over on the couch, holding her down as he jerked the hem of her gown up over her bare ass.

Dear God. One hand held her shoulders down as he straddled her legs, restraining them. Her hips were raised, the cheeks of her butt clenching, all cream and peach perfection. Well rounded, full globes of beauty.

"Stay still," he growled as she bucked against him once again.

To reinforce the order, his hand landed firmly on one pale cheek, flushing the flesh marginally with a warning tap. She stilled, but he heard the hard catch of her breath, felt her body tremble.

"You have no idea what I want, Heather," he said, his voice dark and dangerous, his hand stroking over the silken flesh of her butt once again. "You think you're ready for me. You think what you've heard about with Marly and Sarah is who I am, what you can expect. You're wrong baby…very, very wrong."

He smacked her ass again, just enough force to flush the other cheek and have her moaning, confused, fighting to separate the pleasure from the pain.

"Sam," she moaned his name, her voice questioning, shocked.

"I want to tie you down," he whispered, coming over her now, tucking his cloth-covered cock into the crack of her ass. "I want to see you stretched out on my bed, leather restraints holding you in place while I show you pleasure you never imagined existed. Helpless. At my mercy. Screaming out for me while I take you places, Heather. Places you've never imagined existed."

She wiggled against him, the cheeks of her rear flexing around the erection separating them.

"Yeah, tighten on me just like that, baby," he whispered in her ear as he caught her wrists in his hand, shackling her to the couch with his strength. "That's how you'll tighten when I bury my cock up your tight little ass. Just like that, Heather, while you scream, because you don't know if it's pleasure or pain."

His free hand moved beneath her hips, forcing its way between her thighs as she bucked against him, panting, but not denying him. Damn her, she should have been screaming out in fear. Instead, heaven help him, his fingers found hot, slick moisture, thick syrupy need that collected in the narrow slit of her cunt.

"Sam, you're a tease," she accused him roughly, heatedly.

He stilled, his hips pressing hard into her.

"A tease?" He couldn't believe she had said that.

"A damned tease," she moaned. "Take those pants off and fuck me or get off me."

He chuckled. "Do you think it's that easy, Heather?" he asked her silkily, his fingers rasping over her swollen clit. She shuddered beneath him, her breath catching.

"Oh, you're close." He grinned at her neck, his teeth scraping the delicate skin there. "Poor baby. Can your toys do this for you, Heather?"

He gripped her clit between his thumb and forefinger, then delicately, with the utmost care, began a gentle milking motion on the sensitive little bud.

"Oh my God." She jerked in his grip, an involuntary shudder so close to orgasm that he knew it would be torturous.

He continued the motion. Just enough pressure to make her crazy, never enough to make her climax. He could feel her juices flowing now, knew her pussy would be spasming in desperation.

"Get ready, baby," he whispered, knowing the climax, though intense and powerful, would only leave her hungry for more.

His fingers rasped her clit, milked, stroked. He felt her tense, her thighs tighten, her syrup flow, then her strangled cry shattered the silence of the game room as she bucked in his arms. Her hips twisted, grinding her clit harder against his fingers as the climax ripped through her body.

She was struggling to breathe, trembling in the after effects of her release as he held her close, his hand cupping the hot mound between her thighs.

"Listen to me," he growled, his voice strained, desperate lust pumping hard and fast through his system. "Listen to me well, Heather. When I take you, I won't make allowances for your innocence, or your need for romance. I'm riding an edge that terrifies the fuck out of me. So there's no way in hell it's going to be easy for you. Stay the hell away from me, baby, or you could very well get hurt."

He jumped away from her, stalking from the room and rushing up the stairs. He prayed she didn't see the wet spot on his pants, the proof of his own climax as she shattered beneath him. Something he had never done before. Something that scared him almost as badly as the nightmares awaiting him.

\* \* \* \* \*

The next morning dawned too bright and too damned early. Dressed in Levi shorts and a tank top that barely skimmed the low waistband of the shorts, Heather descended the stairs. The leather sneakers she wore made no sound on the carpeted steps, so it was easy to hear the sounds coming from the family room. She had learned to be certain she wasn't walking in on an ill-timed moment where that room was concerned.

As she stepped into the entryway, she noticed the door was open and the sounds in the house were in the kitchen. Thankfully it wasn't moans, but rather the low murmur of male voices. Which meant coffee was on. No one made coffee like the August brothers did.

Pushing the door open, she stopped and damned near turned around and left the room again. Sam stood by the counter with Brock and Sarah. Sarah was being held against Brock's chest as Sam's head was rising from what was obviously a lingering kiss.

Cade sat at the table watching them, his gaze sharp, clinical, as he watched Heather now.

"Mornin,' Heather." He lifted his coffee cup in a salute as Sam moved unselfconsciously and lifted a mug from the cabinet. Sarah and Brock moved to the table as Sam filled the mug and handed it to her.

"You guys are up early," she commented, fighting her jealousy as she accepted the cup. "Where's Marly?"

"Still sleeping." Cade's voice was a smooth hum of male satisfaction. Evidently all that moaning and groaning a few hours past had been coming from their room. The August men had too much damned testosterone, that was all there was to it.

"Drink your coffee." Sam handed her the mug as he pressed her toward the table. "I'll get you some sausage and biscuits."

"Don't you guys eat anything else in the mornings?" She frowned, wondering what they had against ham and eggs and gravy, and her stomach pitched in hunger.

"That would require a cook," Cade stated firmly. "I don't want a cook or a housekeeper."

"It would mean good meals," she pointed out. "Something besides sandwiches and soup, or steaks and sausage biscuits."

"We don't have time to cook." Cade shook his head.

Heather looked at Sarah. Why the hell weren't she and Marly cooking?

"Don't look at me, I can barely boil soup. And Marly's worse." She laughed as she sat sideways in her chair, her back braced against Brock's chest.

Brock stared back at her, a gleam of laughter and hunger glowing in his eyes. What as it with these men, she asked herself, not for the first time, that made a woman want to give them whatever they asked of her.

"What do you do when you get tired of soup, sandwiches and steaks?" She shook her head in bemusement. She felt as though she was starving to death.

"We go out." Cade shrugged. "Usually, that is. Remind me to kill that bastard twice for the food we're missing out on."

Death iced his words. Heather turned to him slowly, seeing the cold, hard menace in his voice.

"You won't kill anyone, Cade. We'll catch him, and take him in. That simple."

"Nice dream world you live in, Heather." He leaned his elbows on the table and watched her mockingly. "Do you think I'll let him live after I get my hands on him? He shot Sarah; he scarred you. He'll die for it."

She turned to Sam and saw the same cold purpose in his face, then in Brock's as well.

"That's murder, Cade," she whispered.

"It won't be the first one, Heather," he stated as he stood to his feet. "And you know it."

He moved around the table then paused behind her. Before she could think, before she could jerk away, he leaned close, brushing a kiss across her cheek. "I have to go. I have plenty of work to do." Then he moved to Sarah, repeated the caress and left the room.

Heather caught the other woman's worried glance as she looked to her for a reaction. A reaction she was saved from looking too deeply into as the back door opened.

"Company coming in, boys. Sarah, your brother's on the warpath again."

"Oh hell." Sarah jumped to her feet and glanced at Brock then Sam. "Either one of you hits my brother today and I'll hit you back."

Heather blinked then turned to Sam. "Why would you hit her brother?"

Sam shrugged. "You'll see when you meet him."

\* \* \* \* \*

Dillon Carlyle was gorgeous. With thick, dark brown hair that fell below his neck, and velvet green eyes in a dark complexion that was damned near perfect for a man. A strong jaw line, high cheekbones, and sensually firm lips, she bet he had no end of women falling over themselves to get to him.

At the moment, that gorgeous face was creased into a frown of anger though, and his six-foot plus frame was tense as he faced the August men.

"Dammit, Cade, what the hell is going on? I come back from vacation to find out this stalker shit is still going on and no one thought to call me?" His deep voice boomed through the entryway as the door slammed behind him. "The least you could have done was call me."

Before anyone could stop him, his fist drew back and slammed forcefully into Brock's jaw.

Brock bounced against the wall as Sarah cried out and jumped for her brother, protecting him from the wrath of four bodyguards. The biggest of which was Rick, who looked ready to retaliate rather forcefully.

"Call them off, Cade," she yelled, dangling from Dillon's neck as he tried to pull her loose. "Don't you let them hit him."

"Dammit, Sarah," Dillon cursed. "Get off me so I can kick his ass."

"You moron." She kicked his shin as he stumbled against the opposite wall. "Do you have a suicide wish I don't know anything about?"

"Dammit, Sarah, let him go." Brock was laughing, though the blood on his rapidly swelling lip didn't look too amusing.

He gripped his lover's waist and with Dillon's help lifted her away from his body. Dillon stood ready, his eyes narrowed as he watched the August brothers.

"Pack your stuff, Sarah, you're coming to the house with me, where you'll be safe," he growled aggressively.

"I don't think so, Carlyle," Brock grunted. "Get over yourself and have a drink. Enjoy your visit with Sarah then you can head home. Alone. The same way you showed up."

"Dillon, are you causing trouble again?" Marly entered the fray then, her amused voice drawing eyes as she stepped into the entryway. Dressed in snug jeans and T-shirt, she looked like a mischievous teenager rather than a fully-grown woman.

"Marly, you look pretty as ever," he sighed. Heather noticed most men sighed a bit wistfully when they saw Marly.

"Thank you, Dillon." She stepped into Cade's arms and sent Heather a warning glance.

What? She frowned the question back at her.

Marly looked over her head at Sam. Heather glanced back then moved quickly to place herself in front of him, close. He looked ready to kill. Instantly his arms went around her, and she almost laughed at the instinctive response. If she put aside the whole sharing issue, the August men could be rather endearing. Strange, but endearing.

"I'm not going anywhere, Dillon," Sarah told him with a vein of exasperation. "Now why are you really here, because we both know you knew I wasn't leaving with you."

"Where's that drink I was promised?" He turned and headed into Cade's study after shooting him a veiled look.

"Keep your people out here, Rick," Cade ordered as he headed into the room behind Dillon.

"Cade." Rick stopped him as he moved to pass. "Don't keep information away from me, man. We can't protect you, or catch this stalker if you start hiding things from me."

Cade's eyes narrowed. "My family is my life, Rick," he growled. "You'll have everything you need to know, I promise you that. But some things are just not any of your damned business," he informed him before stalking into the study.

Heather stayed quiet. Sam led her into the room and she didn't balk. Dillon looked like a man on a mission, and evidently, his sister wasn't the entire mission.

"I talked to the sheriff, earlier." Dillon poured himself a stiff drink as the door closed behind Sam and Heather. "I found out about Tate and the explosion from him. But what they don't know, and one of my hands told me, was that Tate had a friend. They aren't certain who. One who knew quite a bit about your family and the situation here. One who promised Tate some interesting information."

"How do you know about this?" Cade asked him, his voice dark, warning.

"Tate liked to talk when he drank, Cade. He told a lot of people he would have some interesting pictures soon. Pictures of the August men..." He paused, his jaw bunching as he glanced at his sister. "Explicit pictures from twelve years ago."

Tension thickened in the room. Heather glanced at the August men, watching the instantly closed expressions, the flash of bleak pain in their eyes before it was quickly covered.

"If he had them, the sheriff would have found them," Cade pointed out logically as he glanced at the others in the room. "Whoever's behind this was using the bastard."

"But he told a lot of men, Cade. Men who wouldn't mind watching you fall. And he hinted that the person with the information was right under your nose."

A pin drop would have echoed in the room, the silence was so thick, as all eyes turned to Heather. She could see the suspicion, feel it swirling around her.

"No." She shook her head, feeling her hair swish against Sam's chest as his arms went around her again. "Rick hand-picked this team. It has to be one of the cowboys."

"It could be anyone," Cade finally murmured.

"Cade, Rick needs to know about this," Heather said firmly, as he watched her intently. "If there's even a chance it could be one of his men, he needs to know."

He drew in a deep, hard breath before nodding abruptly. "You're right. But just Rick, Heather. And you better get ready to spend a hell of a lot more time with Sam than you have been so far."

Oh yeah, that was going to be a hardship, she thought as all eyes turned to her. It was enough to make a woman want to swoon, she thought sarcastically. August heat and hunger should be bottled, it would make millions.

"What kind of pictures, Cade?" Marly asked then, her voice tight, demanding as she turned to stare up at her lover.

It was then Heather saw a glimpse of the hell the men lived through and the division between them and their women. They were fighting to protect them from the truth, while Heather knew both Marly and Sarah were well aware of some of the horrors the men had faced during that long summer, years ago.

The shame and the horror flashed in their eyes. They had dealt with it, survived it, but Heather knew they had never healed from it, and she doubted they ever would.

"The pictures don't matter, Marly." He seemed to draw solace from her, from the need to protect her.

Heather could only watch the play of emotions across his roughly hewn face as his hand smoothed down Marly's long curls, his lips tilting into a comforting smile. It was a battle he waged daily, the one to protect her from the knowledge of the horrors he had faced.

"You know Cade, I'm getting tired of being wrapped in cotton and left to watch the three of you being destroyed." She stared up at him, her gaze narrowed, a pixy challenging the Ogre king, Heather thought as she watched him frown down at the small woman.

"Does anything from the past tie Mark Tate into this?" Heather asked, hoping to diffuse the anger she could feel growing in Marly.

Dammit, she knew better than to challenge Cade, Heather thought furiously. It would end up in a sexual free for all in the living room later, with Marly as the main attraction. And Heather was getting tired of sharing something she hadn't had herself. Namely, Sam.

"Nothing ties Mark in, except for the fact that he was stupid," Brock grunted as Dillon cursed under his breath.

Heather stood silently then, her arms wrapped around her chest as she felt Sam moved behind her. He didn't touch her, but he was close. Close enough for her to smell the earthy, male scent of him, close enough to make her heart ache with the pain she knew they all suffered.

"We'll figure it out," he murmured behind her. "You, Marly and Sarah need to stop worrying."

"Oh yeah, we're going to do that," Marly assured them, the sarcasm in her voice snapping like a whip. "When the three of you get smart and decide to stop protecting us, then let me know. Because I'm getting sick of all the melodrama attached it." She stared at Cade, then Brock and Sam. "I'm not stupid, and neither are Sarah and Heather. You aren't hiding near as much as you think you are."

Heather felt Sam behind her, his tension almost palatable.

"We're not going to get anything done this way." She shook her head at the anger and secrets that thickened the tension around them. "Cade, Rick needs to know about this. He could question Dillon's men and possibly get an idea of who was using Mark Tate."

Cade nodded sharply, his hand buried in Marly's black curls as she moved closer to him.

Brock and Sarah watched, neither saying much. Of the two couples, Heather guessed that their relationship was the strongest. Brock seemed more accepting, less bitter about a past he couldn't change.

"With any luck, we'll have this all wrapped up real soon," she drawled mockingly then. "Personally, I'm getting tired of the melodrama around here, too."

# Chapter Nine

They ran a ranch. Fences needed mending, cattle needed to be moved, horses needed shoeing and stables to be cleaned. Hay was being baled in preparation to stack within the barns and a thousand other details that needed to be taken care of. Days went by with no news, and no report of strangers or otherwise unusual occurrences. Sam was losing patience and control. Heather was with him damned near every second of every day and Rick watched him like a hawk.

The pressure was starting to get to all of them. He was sniping at Cade and Brock, and caught himself just short of sniping at Heather. He needed her too bad. The ache to touch her, taste her, was about to drive him crazy.

Sam knew Cade and Brock were chafing at the restrictions being placed on them within the house as well. They were all damned tired of stalking the confining, if comfortable rooms, and waiting on something that never came. Sam knew if he didn't get away from it, he was going to snap. He needed to be outside where he could feel the breeze, taste freedom. Where he wasn't haunted by nightmares, or Heather's arousing scent.

The nightmares that haunted them all were growing worse for him. He never truly remembered them, but the terror that filled him when he awoke was damned near as sharp as that of the first rape…

He shuddered, pulling on thick leather gloves as he closed his mind to the thought. He gave his head a hard shake, then narrowed his eyes as he realized he was no longer alone in the stables. He turned his head slowly and there she was.

Damn, he'd been praying he could avoid her. At least for today. She was dressed in snug jeans with what was obviously a pair of child's chaps belted around her lean hips, a tan tank top and well-worn boots. He wanted to strip her and fuck her until she couldn't tempt him anymore. He wondered if he could ever take her enough to reach that point.

"Tell Rick to assign someone else," he bit out sharply as she pulled a pair of dainty leather working gloves from her back pocket and started to pull them on.

"Don't worry, cowboy, I know how to saddle my own horse, and how to ride it." She smiled cheekily. "Do I look good in the chaps? I always wanted to wear a pair."

She would look damned good in nothing but the chaps. He narrowed his eyes, imagining it, imagining her, bare except for leather chaps and his cock plowing between her thighs. He clenched his teeth, fighting for control.

"Wear 'em somewhere else," he ordered harshly, tightening the cinch on his horse's saddle. "I don't have time to wait on you, Heather."

"Well you better, big boy." She strolled casually to one of the stalls, loosening the gate and clipping a lead to the horse it contained. "I'm your babysitter today, sweetcakes. Ride out without me, and one of the boys will put a tranquilizer in your ass. Cade's already given them permission, by the way."

He snarled in fury. Like he wasn't well aware of what Cade had fucking done. Goddammit, he wasn't a child any longer to be protected by the other two and he was getting sick of being treated like one. He was two years younger than Cade, not two years old.

He started to speak when he saw her click the small comm link over her head, attaching the tiny speaker to her ear, the mic wand extending to her cheek.

"Two to ride, whose check?" Her voice was low as she tested the device. She glanced at him with a mischievous glitter in her eyes. "Oh boy. Sis is playing watchdog on us. There goes our fun, cowboy."

Sam crossed his arms over his chest, narrowing his eyes as he watched her check her gun, the loaded clip, and the spares that she tucked into her saddlebag. The automatic pistol was tucked back into the holster behind her hip, and still, she was listening to whatever orders were coming through that damned comm link.

"Tell Tara to assign someone else," he said again, his voice louder this time. "Now."

She rolled her eyes as she tightened the saddle and tested it experimentally.

"Give it up, Sam." She shook her head as she looked up at him. "I'm part of this team whether you like it or not."

"Fine, be a part of it somewhere else then." He held his horse's bridle in a tight fist as she mounted her horse.

He felt equal parts lust and rage thundering through his system. She looked like a living flame perched on the back of that damned horse. A ready target for the psycho stalking him.

"I won't ride out with you," he said softly. He wouldn't jeopardize her. He couldn't.

She tilted her head as she stared down at him. Her green eyes were quizzical, her expression curious. "Do you doubt my abilities, Sam?"

Doubt her? He didn't doubt in the least that she was the sweetest, softest thing he had ever touched in his life. That her heat, her passion, wasn't the hardest thing in the world to resist. That he wouldn't destroy her before it was over with. But he would be damned if he would lead her into the hands of a madman.

He didn't answer her. He couldn't answer her. He wanted to scream, to howl out in fury at the injustice of what he faced. He couldn't do either. He glanced out the open stable door, remembering his need to smell freedom. It wasn't worth the possible sacrifice. His stubborn determination had sentenced his brothers to hell; he wouldn't allow the same thing to happen to Heather.

He shook his head wearily as he unsaddled his mount. Poor Rusty. He patted the roan's rump. The stallion had been itching to run, just as Sam had.

"Sam?" Her soft voice questioned him.

"I won't endanger you." He tossed the saddle and blanket atop the saddle rail and led the horse back to its stall.

She sighed impatiently behind him. "Sam, you can't go out alone. You know that. Did you forget what happened the last time you did that?"

His fists clenched as he locked the stall door.

"Yeah, Heather," he snarled, turning to her slowly. "Something real fucking easy to forget…"

The scene surged through his mind, but it wasn't Tate, it was Marcelle. Blood colored his vision as violence surged through his body for one hard, long second. He could feel his muscles tightening, his fists clenching as though to defend himself against the fury of a memory that never fully revealed itself.

"I'm sorry, Sam." She dismounted, her face pale, her eyes wounded as she watched him. "I'll find someone else to ride with you…"

He stopped her. Before he realized it he had gripped her arm, pulling her around until he had her pressed against the stall divider, her slender wrists shackled by his hands and stretched above her head. He stared down at her, breathing roughly, rage and desire burning through his body in equal measure.

"You don't understand," he growled roughly. "Listen to me, Heather. For God's sake, for my sake, listen to me. Stay the fuck away from me. Please. I don't want to hurt you, I don't want to be the cause of your pain."

She wiggled against him, her hips pressing closer, her stomach cushioning the hard-on raging behind the material of his jeans. He fought for his control, his muscles tensing, bunching as she watched him from those knowing, though innocent, eyes.

"How much longer are you going to wallow in self-pity, Sam?" she finally asked him, and the very gentleness of her voice was like acid on an already burning wound. "How much longer will you let him destroy your life?"

He stared down at her unblinking, fighting the overwhelming anger that made him want to hurt, to control.

"As long as it takes, Heather, for the smell of blood and semen mixing to get out of my fucking head," he finally growled. "Take that away, baby, and then we'll talk about it."

He threw himself away from her, knowing if he didn't he might never be able to later. Her eyes were swimming with tears, her face pale with stress and pain as she watched him, and he couldn't bear it. Couldn't bear looking into her eyes, knowing she saw him for who he was, for what he was. Knowing that in one careless moment, in one passion dazed encounter, he could place her at the mercy of a madman once again.

He whipped his hat from his head as the fingers of his other hand pushed violently through his hair. There was nothing he hated worse than this feeling rising inside him. The burning anger and pain. The shame. It never failed to trigger the need to connect, to ease the aching emptiness inside his soul. The need to touch, taste and hear the screams of pleasure. But it wasn't Marly's or Sarah's he needed to hear. It was Heather's.

"Cade, he's headed back in," Heather spoke into her comm link as Sam stalked back to the ranch house. It worried her, the intensity in his blue-gray eyes, the fury that tightened his body.

Anger was riding him hard and it was easy to see that the coming eruption could be more than any of them wanted to face. For all his joviality, the bleak dark core she glimpsed in his soul seemed all the more dangerous.

"Thanks, Heather. We'll take care of him." His voice was darkly brooding, anger and concern mixing in a haunting brew that tore at her heart. Three men, each scarred in different ways and fighting for survival. It terrified her, wondering if they would be able to fight their way clear of this one.

And it hurt her. She knew how such episodes ended. The blistering heat of the female cries as the August brothers joined in an orgy of sexual intensity with them. Though Sam didn't seem to be taking part as often as he had in the past, she knew he had at least taken part in that damned limo. The danger surrounding them only increased the edge of lust that glittered in the men's eyes on a constant basis.

They were highly sexed, and more than a little dominant. And though Sam seemed more playful than forceful, she could see the core of that dark sexuality becoming more apparent. The closer the danger came, the more that edge seemed to intensify.

The stalker shadowing their every move was getting closer. Several attempts had been made to breach the house. Each one had gone unnoticed by any of the investigators until long after it had been too late to catch sight of him. The bastard knew the ranch too well to suit any of them.

She clicked the link back to the open channel, listening with only distant attention to the chatter between the investigators as she unsaddled her horse and led him back to the stall. She stroked the animal's long face, staring into the quiet brown eyes as sadness filled her.

"He's getting worse." Brock stepped into the stables, his eyes so like Sam's, were quiet, sad, as Heather clipped the stall door closed and turned to him.

Heather watched as he moved deeper into the cool, shadowed interior. He watched her closely, his eyes contemplative, the way he held his body suggesting that he was a man on a mission that he wasn't entirely certain of.

"We can't allow him to go riding off by himself, Brock." Heather shook her head, knowing Sam needed the solitude of the open land to help still the demons raging inside him. A solitude that could be fatal now.

She remembered before, when they were called out the first time to protect Marly. Sam had often slipped from the house, hiking or riding several miles away to a sheltering, tree-shaded pond where he would often sit and just stare into the water. He hadn't been able to do that lately, and being confined seemed to only spur his temper.

"I agree with you on that, Heather," he sighed roughly, tucking his hands into the pockets of his jeans as he watched her with a questioning expression. "I'm not asking anyone to allow it."

He looked too much like Sam to suit her. The sharp, almost savage planes of his face reflected a quiet acceptance of the world though, rather than the careful joviality or alternate enraged grief that Sam's could. Of all the men, Brock seemed more accepting of the past, more accepting of who they all were.

She wished she could find a measure of the confidence he carried on his shoulders. At the moment she felt lost, uncertain. She was fighting not just for her life, but for the life of a man who didn't want to love her, even though he did.

"What?" Heather asked with a frown. Brock obviously had something on his mind, and yet was hesitant to broach the subject, whatever it might be. She had a feeling she didn't exactly want to hear it either.

"Why hasn't he come to you yet?" he asked her softly, his head tilting as he regarded her with a quizzical expression.

"For what?" She had a feeling she knew exactly for what, but she wasn't about to let this man poke his nose in her business without a fight.

He seemed to know that, too. He watched her knowingly. "You know what," he growled. "He wants to fuck you so bad it heats the air around both of you, Heather. Don't pretend you don't know that."

Heather felt a curious flutter of nerves in the pit of her stomach. There was no heavy lust in his eyes as there was in Sam's, but there was a sense of anticipation, of waiting. He was asking about Sam, but they were both well aware of what they all expected once Sam took her.

"That's none of your business, Brock." She shook her head. She didn't need the other two brothers complicating her life at this point. Her life, or her heart.

He blew out a rough breath, his head turning as he stared into the shadows of the stables. His arms crossed over his chest, his hard body stiffly erect, as he seemed to be weighing what he should say. His expression was brooding, concerned, as he seemed to chose his words carefully.

"It concerns us all, Heather," he finally said softly. "Not just me and Cade, but Marly and Sarah as well. We all love him. Seeing him like this is…" He paused reluctantly. "It's very hard on us all."

She could see that. Had seen it constantly. The relationship between the men was a curious one. A complete sharing, whether it was work, play or pleasure. Yet never together. For a while, she had wondered if the strange relationship they shared with their women was due to tendencies or desires to be with each other sexually. But as she watched, dissecting events and interactions, she knew that wasn't the case.

Heather believed they would have been inclined to the relationships they now shared. The horrors and nightmares of the past had forced the need for that closer bond, despite moral convictions. The abuse and their fight to survive together had made them closer than even they knew at this point. It was a closeness that went far beyond any sense of sibling jealousy. It had forced such emotions aside, which further enabled them to the sexual extremes they now practiced.

"And I'm supposed to fix this?" she asked him finally, exasperated, just a little irritated. Suddenly, everyone was looking to her to fix the problems this family dealt with. She couldn't see a fix in sight anywhere.

He shifted nervously, spearing her with a look that had her taking a step back. Intense, heated, filled with conviction.

"He loves you, Heather. I know he does. And you know what that implies."

His voice carried a hard, knowing edge. He wasn't about to let her skirt around the involvement with the family should she accept the relationship with Sam. Damned men. The Augusts had to be the most contrary, stubborn, hard to get along with males it had ever been her misfortune to meet up with.

"So you're what, going to try to get your piece of ass now?" she bit out, frowning back at him. These men tried her patience in more ways than one, but this one, on the heels of his twin, was too much for even her normally strong nerves.

He grimaced impatiently.

"Don't be a fool, Heather," he growled, disgust marking his voice, surprising her by the vehemence in his tone. "This isn't about getting a piece of anything. It's about Sam. It's about stilling the anger growing inside him before it destroys him."

"Dammit, Brock, only Sam can do that." Heather shook her head, surprised, and not for the first time, over the brothers' insistence on stilling Sam's anger, and in the process, the healing. "He has a right to be angry. A right to hate everything that has happened and is happening now. You can't expect him to joke his way through this."

"Listen to me, dammit," he growled, his own anger surfacing then, surprising her. She had rarely seen Brock angry. "You don't want Sam like this, Heather. None of us do. It won't solve anything. It will do nothing but destroy him."

Taken aback by the surprising display, Heather could only watch, her eyes narrowed, suspicion beating a warning tattoo within her chest.

"Or heal him," she offered quietly. "Why don't you want Sam upset, Brock? Aren't you upset? Are you taking this stalker thing without a worry or a shred of anger?"

His lips thinned, the muscle at the side of his cheek throbbing as he obviously fought his own sense of helpless frustration.

"Listen to me, Heather. There are things you don't understand here. Things you don't want to understand and you sure as hell don't want Sam thinking about."

"And I'm supposed to stop him, how?" She shook her head, spreading her hands out before him as she watched him with angry frustration. "Am I supposed to fuck him to keep him from thinking?"

"If you have to," he growled, then more softly. "If you love him, Heather, like I think you do, then whatever it takes should be all that matters."

The welling sense of fear rising inside her couldn't be ignored.

"What are you not telling me, Brock?" She crossed her arms over her breasts, watching him impatiently, angrily.

He looked away, and Heather could have sworn she caught a flash of guilt in his gaze.

"Nothing that would help you," he finally sighed.

"Right now, anything would help. Sam doesn't want what I have to offer…"

"That's bullshit." His hand sliced through the air impatiently. "Sam wants you until he can't walk for the hard-on he's packin'. This has nothing to do with lust, Heather, and everything to do with his feelings toward you."

"I can't make him come to my bed, Brock," she sighed wearily. "And I'll be damned if I'll try."

"Even knowing he loves you?" he asked. "And we both know you have to be aware of that Heather. You couldn't touch Sam's emotions if he didn't care for you. And he sure as hell wouldn't be driving himself crazy over you."

She knew that. She hated admitting it, but she knew it. Unfortunately, she couldn't make herself accept the definition of love the three of these men used.

"Brock, enough." The lengthening shadow of Sam's broad form entered the stable entrance.

Heather's head whipped to the side, her eyes widening at the hard, cold edge to Sam's voice. Brock whipped around, his body suddenly defensive, prepared.

"Sam." Brock shook his head again.

"I don't need your protection any more than I need Cade's." Sam's voice was low, thick, with a white-hot throb of rage. "Nor do I need you pimping for me."

Heather winced. "Takes a whore for a pimp to work, Sam. You're not just insulting your brother here."

His gaze speared toward her, and though she couldn't see his eyes for the piercing sunlight behind him, she could feel the intensity in them. For a moment she regretted drawing his attention to her.

"Get serious," he growled, though the restraint in his voice caused her to wince.

"We're worried, Sam…" Brock began.

"Brock, let it rest…" Heather interrupted him, knowing he would try to smooth the event over, to ease Sam's anger.

"Goddammit, I'm not a fucking bone for you two to fight over," he snarled, moving into the barn. "What do you want, Brock? A nice little joke, how about another prank? Let's pretend the world is fine when we fucking know better."

Throttled rage, agony, need. They all reflected in his voice. Heather's heart broke as she watched him and as she glanced at Brock, she knew his was as well. Sam's expression was dark, his face lined with both his fury and his pain. And Heather had a terrible, wrenching feeling that when it all spewed to the surface, none of them would be left unscathed.

Brock raked his fingers through his hair as he glanced at her. Heather could only shake her head. She wasn't about to help him. Sooner or later they would have to realize that Sam no longer needed their protection, all he needed was their support.

"I'll leave you two alone." She headed for the entrance.

"Fuck that. Who do you think I came back for?" Sam caught her arm as she made to move past him. "You, Heather, not my interfering brother."

"Sam." Brock stepped forward as though in protection.

Heather watched as Sam's head whipped around, his expression harsh, defined by the years of pain they had all suffered.

"You're upset. You should calm down…"

The smile that crossed Sam's face did little to still the nervous tremor that fluttered through Heather's body.

"Do you think I would hurt her, Brock?" His voice was silky smooth, but they all heard the undercurrent that ripped beneath it. He was pushing his brother, and Heather wondered why.

"Would you, Sam?" Brock asked him quietly.

Sam shook his head. As Heather watched, the anger drained away and bleak sadness replaced it. She could see the sense of betrayal in his expression, his knowledge that for some reason, he wasn't trusted.

"I've never put so much as a bruise on Marly and Sarah, Brock. Never. Why the hell would you think I would hurt Heather?"

# Chapter Ten

"Fuck." Brock's face twisted with his own pain, the curse slipping past his lips with a tone laced heavily with self-disgust. "Hell, Sam, I know you won't hurt her physically. It's not her body I'm worried about. Dammit, you shouldn't make her cry either. That's just as bad."

Sam watched his brother, seeing the truth, the fact that Brock knew he would never truly hurt Heather. For a moment, everything in his body had twisted in agony, and he smelled the blood, the death, and he wondered... He shook his head, trying to shake away the dark pain along with it. The women were all that mattered. Their laughter, their happiness. Their happiness fed Cade's and Brock's, and in a way, his own. Their tears made the demons rise, snapping with hungry jaws and rapacious teeth in the form of nightmares that none of them could escape.

He drew in a deep breath, ignoring Heather's incredulous expression at Brock's explanation. She didn't understand, and he wondered how Marly and Sarah could.

"Sarah's looking for you," Sam finally sighed, weary to the bone, filled with such a mix of emotions that making heads or tails of them was impossible right now.

His twin shifted, glancing at Heather as though trying to convey a message. Pacify Sam. Protect Sam. He knew it by heart, and it grated at his pride now, as it never had before.

"Go, Brock." He shook his head wearily. "Don't piss me off any more than I am already.."

Brock cursed. A mumbled sound, all the more violent for the fact that it was so quiet. He stalked from the barn, much as Sam knew he had done himself earlier, leaving him alone with Heather.

He turned to her, watching her quietly as she stood beneath his narrowed stare. She gazed back at him directly, never flinching. Her green eyes were dark with sadness...sadness for him. He breathed in roughly. As much as he wanted her laughter and her happiness, he'd be damned if it wouldn't make him feel like a fraud right now.

Cade and Brock needed it. To see Sarah and Marly truly happy made them happy. It lifted their hearts, and in some degree eased the shadows that haunted their gazes. For Sam, he had eased his demons in the happiness of his brothers, and for a very brief time had thought he could reach for his own with this woman.

"Have they always been so overprotective?" she finally asked him quietly, tucking her hands nervously into her back pockets.

The shirt stretched across the full mounds of her breasts, making his hands itch to touch them. The hard-on he had had earlier hadn't even had time to abate when he'd heard Brock was headed for the stables and he had to go back. Now, it pounded beneath his jeans with an imperative demand that made him damned near crazy.

"Yeah," he finally answered her, fighting for control.

"Hard to deal with, isn't it?" She tilted her head watching him, trying to understand him.

Damn her, he didn't want or need her understanding.

"Are you coming back to the house?" he finally asked, ignoring her question.

She leaned back against the frame of a stall, regarding him with that look. The one that said she knew, that she cared. Damn her to hell, he didn't want this.

"The house is too crowded sometimes." She finally shrugged. "I've been sneaking out a bit myself, as a matter of fact." She grinned at him, as though the secret mattered. It did matter, but he'd be damned if he'd tell her that.

"Why?" he finally asked when she said nothing more.

Her gaze never left his. "Because, I can't bear listening to the others together. Terrified you'll go to one of them again, instead of me."

He wanted to hit something. His fists clenched at the naked vulnerability in her gaze, the need, sweet and hot that glittered in her eyes. Need that he knew was leaving a searing sweet cream along her cunt lips. His mouth watered. He wanted, no, he needed to taste her. To feel the soft juice that ran from her pussy onto his tongue, rather than his fingers.

"You don't take warnings very well do you, baby?" he growled, wondering what it would take to scare her off, to make her see just how dangerous he could be for her. Hell, a madman's scalpel hadn't done it, what the hell was left?

Her lips lifted in a grin. A sad little knowing grin.

"If your cock wasn't trying to burrow out of your jeans, I might pay more attention to your protestations, Sam."

He crossed his arms over his chest, his eyes narrowing on her.

"What the hell made you so damned forward?" he asked, exasperated. "What happened to the sweet little blushes you used to get a year ago?"

She lifted a brow. Just like that, a single brow, much as Marly did when she knew something they didn't and wasn't about to tell.

She shrugged, the gesture reminding him of a dare.

"You make me wetter than the toys." Her answer floored him.

Sam clenched his teeth, fighting for control.

"But I won't throw myself at you again, Sam. I'm not a whore, and I'm damned sure not willing to pamper your feelings like everyone seems to want to do."

"Pamper my feelings?" he snarled, knowing that was what they did, but he hated admitting it.

"Yes, they pamper your feelings," she said softly. "They pet on you, make you laugh, encourage your pranks and your jokes while they try to let you pretend that nothing's wrong inside. And you try to go along with it. Because it makes them smile. Because it eases their pain."

"Armchair psychology," he snorted. "Just what I need, a wannabe psychologist."

"Doesn't take a psychologist, Sam." She shook her head slowly. "I've been a part of your life for a year now. We were friends before you ever touched me. But once you touched me, I was yours, and you knew it. You knew it, Sam, and you walked away."

"You're a virgin," he ground out, forcing himself to keep distance between them, not to touch her. "Goddammit, Heather, what I want to do to you is illegal in every state in the country and you're bitching because I won't do it."

"Bullshit." Her voice deepened then, her own anger coming through. "I'm not arguing this with you, Sam. You're a coward, that's your problem. Terrified of caring for anyone or anything that might touch you too deeply. Too scared of what I make you feel to reach out for what you want."

"You want me to reach out, Heather?" His control snapped. Her accusation, his need, the truth of her statement, all hitting him where it hurt. His heart. His soul.

He moved before he really intended to. Beside her, an empty stall waited, and it was there he dragged her. He slammed the half-door shut, pushing her against the partition, watching the excited gleam that filled her eyes.

One hand gripped the back of her head as his lips slammed down on hers. He made no allowances for any innocence she might have. Made no concessions for the needy whimper that escaped her throat. His tongue forced its way into her mouth, licking over silken lips, groaning in hunger at the taste of her.

His other hand tore at the buttons of his jeans. His cock was raging, the blood pumping hard and fast through sensitive tissue until he was harder than he could remember being in his life. Heather was arched to him, her head bent back, her lips opening to his, her tongue tangling with his. And he couldn't help but remember. Remember the feel of that hot mouth sucking his cock, her teeth and tongue torturing, tormenting him.

"You're killing me," he panted as he nipped at her lips, his erection straining in his hand as he fought the impulses flooding his body.

It would take him hours, days, by God, weeks to take her in as many ways as he wanted to. As he needed to. And he couldn't wait. Couldn't bear the pressure exploding in his mind, ripping through his body.

"I'm sorry." He hated himself. Hated the needs that tore through him, made him no more than an animal in rut. And yet he still couldn't stop himself. Couldn't halt the demands, the need for release, not just of the sperm building in his nuts, but the agony in his soul.

"Sam." Her longing cry shattered his senses.

He gripped the braid at the back of her head, his eyes staring into hers as he applied pressure, pulling her down as he gripped the thick stalk of his cock in his hand.

"I need to fuck you," he whispered desperately as he watched her go to her knees. "I need to fuck you, Heather, until you're screaming out for me to stop."

"Never." Her voice was strangled. Then she licked her lips. A slow, longing sweep of her tongue that moistened the silken curves, preparing them for him, for his cock.

She didn't wait for him to press the bulging head of his cock to her lips. They opened, but it was her tongue, a hot lash of white-hot heat searing his flesh that had him crying out as it probed at the underside of the thick head, stroking ultra-sensitive, unscarred flesh with the moist fire of her tongue.

He watched her, watched the pink flesh touch him an instant before her lips touched the bulging head, then slowly,

God help him, so slowly enveloped the head as her teeth raked the engorged tip.

Sam gripped the braid at the back of her head, pulling her close, watching her, staring down at her as her eyes nearly closed in pleasure. Pleasure? He trembled. This wasn't his brother's woman, taking him because of her love for another man. This was his. His woman, taking his cock into her mouth, and loving it.

He pressed his flesh deeper, watching her lips stretch, her pouting little mouth envelop him as he felt her groan against the pulsing head.

"Ah, Heather," he whispered, pressing his cock harder between her lips, sinking into the velvet depths of her mouth as her teeth scraped, her tongue rippled and her soft little mouth suckled at him hungrily.

She moaned again, the sound vibrating on his flesh as he halted at the entrance of her slender throat. She wasn't taking enough. His hands clenched in her hair again, hearing her groan, one of greedy need, rather than pain.

"Suck me, Heather, harder," he whispered, poised on the edge of a lust so sharp, so desperate, he wondered if he would survive it. "Suck it, baby. Give me what I need."

He pulled back, moisture glistening on the flesh she had held within her mouth as her teeth and her tongue raked again. A delicate prickling of almost pain that had hard shudders of pleasure racing over his body.

Fucking her mouth was exquisite. Watching, staring down at her as she enveloped his cock in her mouth was paradise. He pushed in again, feeling her tighten on him, suck him in, her tongue a heated brand as she whimpered around the engorged flesh.

"I have to fuck you." He was nearly mindless. Control was nothing more than a memory as he gripped her head with both hands, feeling her hands wrap around his cock, silken cool hands, an erotic contrast to the hell's-hot mouth sucking hungrily at the head.

He held her head still, fucking his flesh into her suckling mouth, groaning at the pleasure, fighting himself, fighting the needs ripping through his body. He didn't want to take her like this. He wanted soft and easy, but God help him, when he got around her, all he could do was take. Take like he was taking now, fucking into her mouth over and over again, feeling his seed boil in his scrotum as it tightened, his cock pulsing, throbbing.

He wanted to hold off. Wanted to wait. Wanted to enjoy every damned minute of it. Wanted to commit the expression on her face, the feel of her lips, to memory so he could have it to hold him when she was gone. Because she would leave eventually. He knew she would. He wanted to thrust inside the hot depths of her mouth forever.

But one of her hands moved, tucked between his thighs, then her nails scraped. Scraped flesh scarred and nearly insensitive. They scraped over his flesh, a pleasure/pain that seared his cock, shot up his spine and destroyed any chance of waiting for the release building inside his balls.

He heard his own cry shatter the stillness of the stables. He thrust hard, burying himself as deep inside her mouth as her tight hand along the stalk allowed. Once. Twice. Fire streaked through his body, traveling to the base of his spine, then back to his bursting cock.

He couldn't hold back his release. "Heather. Take me. Take it all, baby."

His back arched as he shattered. He felt the hard spurting jets of his seed erupting from the tip of his dick. Flooding her mouth, shooting to her throat as she sucked, swallowed, her lips tightening as his cock jerked in time to each hard eruption into her mouth.

He held her head to him, his release rippling through his body as she continued to suckle his still hard flesh. Not enough. God help him, he would never get enough of her.

He pulled back, watching her, the glazed fire in her eyes, her swollen lips, and knew he was a dead man. A dead man because he couldn't let her go. Because he knew how she could be hurt, and how easily she could die, and he knew it would kill him.

"I'll fuck your ass first," he growled, unwilling to let her enter into anything without knowing what was coming. "I'll tie you down, Heather, because I need to see you, hear you, control you, rather than the other way around. And I'll fuck your ass until you're screaming for release, until you're begging. And it won't stop there. I'll fuck you until you can't move, and then I'll fuck you some more. Because I've waited too damned long, and fought too damned hard to stay the hell away from you."

He drew her to her feet, watching her eyes widen as he talked. He leaned in close, staring into her dazed expression, his cock still throbbing for her; still so damned hard he was in pain.

"And then, Heather. Eventually. When I can't take the pressure anymore. When the demons are like snakes twisting in my guts, striking like knives through my nightmares, then I'll share you. I'll watch you. I'll hold you, Heather, as Cade fucks you. As Brock fucks you. As you scream and beg to come, because you're that important to me. So important to me, so much a part of me, that I won't have a choice. No choice, Heather, because that's what we are. That's who we are. And I pray to God we both survive it."

He had fastened his jeans as he talked. Armed himself as her eyes narrowed, fire flashing in the green depths. But before she could curse, before she could accuse him of being the vile, depraved monster he knew he was, he turned and stalked from the stables. She had no idea what she had set in motion. No idea the needs he held back, even from his family. But she would find out. And she would find out tonight.

# Chapter Eleven

The front door slammed. Cade, Sam and Brock turned in unison to meet the fury Heather directed at them all as she stood in the entryway. She was enraged. Her body throbbed in arousal and anger. It pumped through her blood stream, tightened her muscles and eroded her self-control.

"Heather." Sam's eyes were dark as he watched her, filled with grief, with apology. She didn't want to see either. She didn't care if he was hurting, didn't care about the wounds to his soul. She would be damned if she would allow him to wound hers further.

She advanced on the three men, her eyes narrowed, her breathing rushed as her heart raced in her chest. Damn him. She had spent a year fighting his withdrawal from her, a year fighting her own needs in her attempt to better understand him. There was no understanding such sheer male stubbornness.

"It occurs to me." She straightened her shoulders, her jaw clenching as she watched the latent sensuality that filled Sam's expression and began to peak in the other two men's gazes. "That the three of you are just a little spoiled for what I consider fair."

"Heather." Sam's tone was warning, his body taut.

"Going to tie me down are you, big boy?" she spat out. "And tell me, who will help you in this little chore? These two?"

Her tone was more than insulting. The interest that filled their eyes was infuriating.

"I wasn't aware I would need help," he said softly, his gaze flickering over her body. "I'm quite a bit stronger than you are, sweetness."

The very tone of his voice had her womb quivering in lust almost as hard as the rest of her body was trembling with anger.

She snorted. "And quite a bit dumber too, but we won't go there." She looked back to his brothers. "Do the three of you ever get tired of living through your dicks?"

Surprise, shock, filled their expressions.

"That's enough," Sam ordered harshly, his own eyes narrowing as anger began to cloud the lazy sensuality that had filled his gaze.

"Were you informing your brothers of your plans?" Her fists clenched. "Did you tell them how hard you came in my mouth, Sam? How you left me sitting in the fucking hay with only a warning of what was to come?" She threw the accusation in his face. "Whatever possessed you, darling, to believe that I was so weak that I would just put my head down and submit to your plans?"

She was yelling at him and she didn't give a damn who heard. She watched Cade as he stared up at the ceiling as though praying for strength before he cast Sam an accusing glare. Brock shook his head and stared at the floor, though she could have sworn he was hiding a grin. Sam crossed his arms over his broad chest, and though the sight of him was mouth watering, she was so pissed she wanted to kick him rather than fuck him now.

"Could have been that excited little gleam in your eyes when I told you what was coming," he fairly snarled back at her. "What's wrong, Heather? Couldn't wait until tonight?"

"What's wrong, Sam? You have to tie your women down to make sure they can't touch that bleeding heart you possess?"

His arms slowly unfolded from his chest, his fists clenching as he stared at her in angry surprise.

"Sam, what the hell have you done?" Cade growled with a mixture of amused resignation and irritation.

"None of your damned business," he growled.

Heather lifted a brow mockingly.

"None of his business? Well, Sam, you did include him in the coming attractions. Too bad you forgot to ask permission from me." She smiled with a cold, tight turn of her lips. "Tell me, boys, is it August prerogative to get yourselves off and leave your partner sitting in the dust with nothing but empty warnings?"

Cade cursed, his expression flashing with guilt. Brock sighed heavily and shook his head.

"It's that male dominance that they seem to have such a healthy streak of." Sarah came down the curved stairs slowly, her gaze going to Brock and warming with love and with memories before she cast Heather a grin. "I can see Sam has made his usual impression on a woman."

"Dammit, I thought she liked me now," Sam muttered to Brock as the other man shook his head, obviously fighting to contain his laughter.

"I love you, Sam," Sarah soothed with grinning patience. "But I know you too well."

Heather watched as she stopped beside Brock, her dark blonde coloring a pretty contrast to Brock's dark, brooding good looks. His arm went around her, and Heather glimpsed in his eyes the overwhelming love that filled him. It never ceased to amaze her, the relationships that had evolved within this family.

Cade and Sam watched her with fondness as Brock placed a kiss on her forehead. Her head met his shoulder, making her the perfect height, in Heather's opinion, for her tall husband. Marly was several inches shorter and would have only stood as tall as Cade's chest.

"I need a shower. Excuse me." Heather couldn't rage at the brothers over their lust while Sarah was around. It was just too weird. The dynamics within this family was unsettling at the best of times.

"Heather." Sarah's voice stopped her as she made to skirt around the family.

Heather stopped, staring at the other woman suspiciously.

"The next time Sam takes his pleasure without returning it to you would be a good time to show him what teeth can really do," she said gently as she touched the corner of her own lip, and Heather felt her face flame in embarrassed fury.

She sliced an accusing look at the offender as she reached up, touching the corner of her lips and felt the small bit of evidence of his pleasure. She could feel herself shaking, trembling, so angry now she could have shot him with no remorse if she thought she would get away with it.

"You know," she said sarcastically, staring him in the eye, ignoring the dark hint of remorse in his gaze. "It's a good fucking thing I'm paid to protect your ass. Otherwise, I'd save your stalker the trouble and kill you myself."

She pushed by him, moving quickly up the steps as she heard Sam curse with violent heat. A shower, definitely, she thought. A cold one. A very cold one. If she didn't cool down the flames of anger burning in the pit of her stomach, she may very well kill him anyway.

* * * * *

Sarah found Marly stretched out comfortably beside the pool, her slender body clad in the dark blue thong of her swimsuit, though the top was missing. Marly was almost hedonistic in her worship of the sun, the water and her lovers. In the months Sarah had known her, she had learned Marly's enormous depths of love, as well as her maturity for one so young.

Accepting the lifestyle the August brothers shared hadn't been easy for Sarah. If it hadn't been for Marly's acceptance of it, and of her, Sarah knew she would have never made it through the transition. She loved Brock, more than she had ever believed possible, and though he had helped her to understand the needs of her own body, it had been Marly who had helped her understand and sort out the confusion that came with it. Her acceptance and understanding of the brothers never failed to amaze Sarah.

"Aren't you afraid the bodyguards will peek?" Sarah sat down on the end of the lounge chair, watching as Marly grinned.

Heavy-lidded against the bright rays of the sun, her eyes opened as amusement glittered in the dark blue orbs.

"Naw, Cade would kill them." Her voice was lazy, slumberous.

Sarah looked up at the hill behind the pool. Brock had told her that the stalker had once hidden there, taking pictures of Marly and spying on her. The base of that small rise was now heavily guarded with a team of Rick's best men through the day. Specially trained dogs roamed the pine-wooded area there, and kept assurance high that it wouldn't be used again for that purpose.

Sarah sighed, then turned back to Marly.

"Sam took a page out of Cade's book. Instead of the barn, he used the stables though," she said softly.

Marly was quiet, though her brow tightened in a frown as she sat up on the lounge chair. Pulling a silk robe from the back of the chair, she slipped it on slowly.

"What happened?" she finally asked.

Sarah pushed her fingers through her hair and blew out roughly. "When she stomped into the house she was madder than hell and confronted all three of them."

Marly grimaced. "Sam shouldn't have done that," she sighed. "It's going to put everyone on edge."

Everyone was already on edge.

"They want her, Marly."

Marly sighed, propping her elbow on her knee and cupping her chin in the palm of her hand.

"You upset?" she asked softly.

Sarah sighed. "No, not upset..." She stopped, wondering what she did feel and unable to put a name to it. "I don't know, maybe upset. It wasn't so bad last week, but the closer Sam gets to her, the closer Brock wants to get."

"That's an answer." Marly's soft laugh had Sarah grinning in agreement. "I know how you felt now, in a way. But I know how Heather feels, too. And Sam isn't making it easy on her. He keeps her aroused with no satisfaction in sight."

Marly's gaze brightened. Sarah frowned. The other woman had that scheming look on her face. The one that worried the men through sleepless nights when they saw it.

"What are you up to?" Sarah asked her suspiciously.

"Well, I know she has toys." Marly smiled conspiratorially. "But she was only able to bring the one," she pointed out.

"She was?" Sarah lifted her brows, wondering how in the hell Marly came up with the information she often had.

"Well, remember, until her attack, and coming straight here from the hospital, she didn't use the house much?" Marly crossed her legs, the epitome of the graceful lady. If one discounted the conversation she was carrying.

"Okay, I can see why just one toy." Sarah nodded then frowned again as she shook her head. She had to ask. "Which kind of toy?"

Marly grinned playfully. "I thought you would never ask. She only brought her Pocket Rocket. Small, light, easy to hide, but not really practical for the pressure she's under now."

Sarah nodded, though she felt like shaking her head in wonder. "How do you know this?"

"Oh, I heard her and Tara arguing when Tara caught her trying to order something on the company laptop. " Marly shrugged, her lips quirking in a smile. "Now, we have all that stuff those men bought for us a few months ago, still sitting in all their boxes. I say we take her a few gifts. Since Sam is being so stingy with her right now."

That wicked look owed little to Marly's sweet nature. The look spelled trouble for whichever of the brothers she was out to get at the moment.

"I don't know, Marly. Sam's pretty bad off right now." But like Marly, Sarah figured he needed to be shaken up just a little bit more. That darkness in Sam needed to be soothed — or freed — she wasn't certain which.

"So, Heather can make him worse." Marly lifted her brow mockingly. "With a little help from us, of course."

\* \* \* \* \*

"I'm sorry."

Heather turned from the coffee pot to face Brock hours later, irritation and arousal still surging through her body.

"You should be." She glared back at him, furious. "All of you should be sorry. All of you should be on your knees begging for forgiveness and expecting the kick in the teeth that you deserve."

A grin tugged at his lips as he stepped into the room.

"Sam is sure as hell stronger than I was; I have to give it to him." He moved around her as she tried to slide out of his way, but his body still brushed against hers, the heat of him searing her.

God, she was so fucking aroused she could barely stand to breathe. So aroused that the unthinkable was happening. Just the brush of Sam's twin against her had trembling in need.

They were infecting her, she thought fatalistically. And she didn't consider it a good thing.

"Honey, getting on my knees in front of you wouldn't be a hardship," he chuckled then. "But it wouldn't be your foot in my teeth that I'd be considering."

Her pussy creamed. That easily, that quickly. She felt the juices gush from her vagina and had to take a deep, controlling breath before she picked up her coffee cup and headed to the door.

"Heather?"

She stopped, refusing to turn back to him, refusing to see the arousal in his eyes.

"Love is a gift. A rare and precious form of acceptance. If you can't love all of him, then maybe you're right, you're better off without him."

"If I can't love all of you, you mean?" She turned back to him, intending to blast him. To tell him just what she thought of overbearing, blackmailing men.

Instead, the words stilled on her lips. It wasn't arrogance that faced her, but a mixture of acceptance, affection, lingering arousal and pain.

He stood, his fingers pushed into the pockets of his jeans, the cotton shirt he wore stretching across the broad planes of his chest. Sexy as hell. Mouth watering. All male. And honest. This wasn't seduction, it wasn't pretty lies to get into her pants. It was stark, blinding truth.

"Whether you not you come to all of us, is your choice," he said softly. "You don't have to love us, to love Sam. You don't have to fuck us, to fuck Sam. But how much longer are you going to deny the fact that you love Sam for a reason. That kind of love is a gift, rarely given, when you find two people that complete each other, in all ways. That's love, Heather. That's true love. That's 'meant to be love'. He emphasized the last phrase. "And it's the only kind of love that really counts."

She didn't answer him. She couldn't answer him, because she knew if she did, she would have to lie to him. He saw things she didn't want him to see. Knew things she hid, even from herself. And because of that, she couldn't face him any longer.

She turned and left the kitchen.

# Chapter Twelve

Some days, it just didn't pay for a girl to get out of bed, Heather thought after entering her bedroom and finding the letter Sam had left for her.

Be waiting on him!

Heather tossed the answer she had quickly scribbled to him on her pillow and then slipped quickly from the bedroom. Her anger had built through the day. Sam's autocratic order and his brothers' self-assurance that she would willingly fall into his arms irked her pride more than she wanted to admit.

Sam seemed to think that because he wanted it, then things were going to automatically go his way. She didn't think so. She admitted to herself though, that she had really wanted to be waiting on him there. That she would have gladly let him restrain her, let him do whatever his kinky little mind could come up with. The sharing thing… She growled in frustration.

The confusion building inside her where it was concerned was causing her more sleepless nights than she wanted to admit.

The few confrontations with his brothers had filled her with conflicting emotions. They were growing on her, and she hated it. Her dreams were being infected with the misty images of the three brothers, their lips and hands touching her, holding her, as thick cocks pushed into her untried body.

She shivered as she slipped into the dark silence of the night. They looked too much like Sam. They were too alike, and yet too different inside. They were caring of Marly and Sarah. Damned indulgent, in her opinion. At the rate things were going, she would be the one cooking in that damned house out of desperation. She was getting hungry for more than the meager fare she was being offered. A girl got tired of soup and sandwiches eventually.

She moved slowly through the pool area until she reached her assigned post for the night. The lounge chair had been placed beneath several thickly leafed trees; beside it laid a pair of night vision binoculars to use on the high hill behind the house. There had been evidence of movement on the far boundary the night before, though no one was certain if it was human or animal. To be on the safe side, Rick wanted someone in position to watch the area that offered access to the house.

Personally, Heather thought a few tons of dynamite and a couple of bulldozers could have done the job better. Take that baby down, end of problem. She nodded to herself as she sat down on the end of the lounger, sighing wearily as the bodyguard covering until she got there moved from her post along the other end.

"It's quiet tonight." Helena's voice was soft, reflective. "I love nights like this."

The other woman was older, but nice in a quiet sort of way. Heather had watched her mother the other agents for months. She had heard Helena even cooked for the crew in the bunkhouse. Dammit, she was getting desperate.

"Yeah. It's beautiful," she finally agreed. "Gives you plenty of room to think in, too."

A soft chuckle greeted her words. "I heard one of the August boys say the same thing. Sammy, I think it was. He told Rick he needed room to think in one night when he was caught sneaking out."

Heather smirked. Sam wouldn't like knowing the nickname was catching on.

"Hopefully, we can keep him contained a little bit longer," she chuckled, then sobered. "He's getting antsy, though."

"Yeah, he's the wild one of the bunch all right," Helena laughed. "Tara cusses him daily."

"When she's not cursing Raider, you mean?" Heather shook her head. Tara and the other agent seemed at odds more often than not.

"Rick better be getting rid of that one," Helena sighed. "He has his eye on Tara, you watch and see. He's trouble. Always sneakin' around and watching everyone besides the Augusts. That boy's too nosy."

The other woman sounded exasperated with Raider's antics, but the comment caused Heather to pause. This was the first she had heard of any of the other agents not concentrating on their job. Especially Raider. With the information Dillon had given them, it wasn't looking good for the other agent.

"Raider's always been different," Heather murmured, making a mental note to say something to Rick about this.

"Yeah, he's a strange one, all right." Helena shrugged. "Well, I'm headed to the front. Rick wanted me out there for a few hours while he took care of some things in the RV. I'll talk to you later."

"Later, Helena." Heather nodded, her thoughts still on Raider.

She wouldn't have suspected him of not doing his job, but she admitted as she thought about it, that he seemed more secretive than usual, quieter, darker than he had been when she first met him. That wouldn't have seemed possible at the time, but Heather admitted it was true. Raider seemed angrier now, rather than just broodingly quiet.

She sighed deeply. She couldn't imagine one of their agents was actually the person stalking the Augusts. Raider had been on personal time during the trouble with Marly and with Sarah, but he had been with them during the Stewart assignment, a time when Marly had been home, and he could have met up with her.

She nibbled at her fingernail thoughtfully. If it was Raider, then catching him wouldn't be easy. It would be damned hard. He was smart, smarter than most of the other agents with several years of SEAL training behind him. It was one of the reasons Rick had taken him on when he came to the agency. Raider was damned smart, and good at what he did. Covert ops had been his specialty, with particular emphasis on assassinations. She shuddered in dread. If it was him, then their problems had just multiplied. He wouldn't be easy to catch, and she knew Rick and Tara. They trusted him, trusted him too much for the short time they had known him.

Heather was certain Rick didn't share Tara with Raider though. Raider seemed too possessive, too dark and intent on having what was his, all to himself. Heather was certain there would be no sharing if he was involved with Tara.

She breathed out deeply then nibbled at her lower lip as she picked up the night vision binoculars and brought them to her eyes. Directing the lenses to the hill outside the pool area, she searched it carefully. It was the only weak spot on the property. The one place he could hide and watch, wait for the opportunity, for the perfect chance to get off a clear shot.

The doors and windows in the house now held the latest in bullet resistant glass, but there was still artillery that could penetrate it. Nothing was foolproof. And the bastard wanted Sam. Her heart clenched. Could she bear it if anything happened to him? If he was taken from her forever?

She couldn't. She loved him, regardless of the complications it brought and the nights she was spending agonizing over it. She loved him. Now, if she could just help heal him, and somehow, someway, love him enough to help him to let go of the past, and his brothers' lovers.

* * * * *

*"I truly meant to be here as you ordered. Satisfying your every wish is, of course, my fondest desire. Alas, I was called away. I am*

*certain you can find other ways to amuse yourself though. If nothing else, use your hand!"*

The sarcasm in the letter wasn't easy to miss. Sam's eyes narrowed as an involuntary grin tugged at his lips. He raised the scented paper to his nose, inhaled and closed his eyes as nostalgia and hot, searing lust washed over him.

Windsong. It had been many, many years since he had smelled that particular scent. Damn, it had been even longer since he had heard of it. The smell of her perfume sent a shaft of bittersweet longing through his soul. He had been a teenager the last time he had smelled it. And none too impressed with the romance of the scent. Now, it touched him, as few things had in the past years.

He folded the letter carefully, took a last lingering smell of it then tucked it into the back pocket of his jeans. He looked around the room with narrowed eyes. Of course, he wasn't about to let her get away with this.

*Use his hand*, he snorted silently. He had been using his damned hand too often in the past months. The memory of the stables, Heather on her knees, his cock tunneling into her mouth, overtook him. Okay, twice he hadn't used his hand, and he wasn't about to use it now. The first being months ago, beneath the rays of a full moon as she kissed her way down his body. Tara had, of course, walked up on them not seconds after he shot his release down Heather's throat. Her fury, and Heather's chagrin, had been thick in the heavy silence of the night.

He looked around the room, wondering where the hell she could be. He knew she had come up here after dinner. Knew she must have found the brown paper sack he had left, with very complete instructions on what to do and how to be waiting for him. She evidently wasn't taking him seriously.

But she would, he assured himself. As soon as he found her she would learn exactly how serious he was. He turned and strode quickly from the room. Closing the door carefully behind him, he glanced down the hallway. The rest of the family was in the living room, enjoying the rare movie that they took time to watch. He had seen them not ten minutes ago, and Heather hadn't been with them.

He moved down the stairs, determined to check again anyway, just to be on the safe side. She wasn't there. Cade and Brock had their women stretched out on the couches with them, watching the flickering screen silently. Marly looked worn and sleeping. Sarah didn't look much more awake. They were dressed in short silk nighties, their robes pooled on the floor. He had a damned good idea that his brothers had satisfied their own raging hungers earlier. Hell's fire, he cursed silently, where could she be?

He stalked to the front door, careful to turn out the entryway light before he stepped out on the front porch.

"Sam." Rick moved within the shadows on the far end of the porch as Sam stepped behind the concealing pine shrubbery that had been planted in front of the wide cement landing months before.

"Where is she?" He didn't have time to argue or to beat around the bush. His cock was a raging brand beneath his jeans, his blood pounding with his need.

Rick tensed, his muscular body coming to instant alert.

"She's on duty. That means she doesn't have time to play," Rick snapped out.

Sam frowned. "This ranch pays her fucking salary. I say she's off tonight."

His voice was just as harsh as Rick's now. There were few things he had needed in his life like he needed Heather now.

"Don't pull this shit on me, Sam," Rick growled. "She's part of the force. I need her to work sometimes, you know."

Sam pushed his fingers restlessly through his hair. Rick wasn't just an employee, he was a friend. That made the whole situation a hell of a lot harder.

"Dammit, Rick. I need her." He fought the weary vulnerability in his own soul. "She ran from me because she was pissed off. Now tell me where she's at or I'll go looking for her."

Silence thickened between them. Even in the dim light of the moon, Sam could see Rick's impatience, his indecision.

"You're a menace to yourself," he finally snarled back. "She's out back, around the pool. She's providing backup if it's needed."

"Make damned sure it's not needed then," Sam snapped, turning on his heel and stalking along the large porch that wrapped around the house.

At the back corner, a high stone wall protected the pool area and back garden. It rose higher than his head and sheltered the pool area from the eyes of the ranch hands while they worked. Cade had ordered it built when Marly was barely sixteen and he saw how the area filled with men while she used the pool.

He slipped silently through the entrance, moving along the back porch, his gaze wandering around the area as he sought her out. The blood was pounding through his body, hardening his cock past the point that he considered bearable.

He found her moments later. One of the large, padded, wooden lounge chairs had been pulled into the shelter of several low-branched trees. She was stretched out on it, one arm thrown above her head as she watched him approach her.

Blue jeans conformed to her hips, thighs, and slender legs. And in the dim light of the moon that filtered through the trees, he could see the arousal, the longing in her gaze. Her flame-red hair flowed out around her, her emerald gaze stroking the fire raging through his bloodstream to a greater height.

He stopped at the foot of the lounger, staring down at her, dying inside with his need for her. "You weren't waiting for me."

He watched as she shifted her legs then tilted her head to watch him mockingly. "Shame on me." Her tone held such indulgent sarcasm that it had his teeth gritting as he fought for his own patience.

She had been around them long enough to know what a sexual challenge did to them. How it heightened their arousal, made the need so sharp, so imperative it was like a demon raging inside them.

"That's okay, baby." He smiled wickedly. "I found you. You should have known I would."

She rose up on her elbows, the position highlighting her breasts, the slender line of her ribs and stomach.

"Sam, sweetie," she said with exaggerated patience. "I'm on duty. I don't have time to fuck with you tonight."

"You're off duty," he snarled. "You work for me, by God. I decide when you're on duty and when you aren't."

She arched her brow as Sam gritted his teeth at the deliberate mockery in the movement.

"So fire me." She shrugged. "You're so testy lately I'd consider it a vacation to leave this damned ranch."

He clenched his fists. The smell of Windsong and woman drifted in the air, making him weak, making him need.

"Why are you doing this?" he growled, restraining himself, determined to keep the control he was fighting so desperately for.

"Because I'm not your puppet, Sam, nor do I take orders real damned well. Get used to it, baby, because submissive never was an adjective that fit me very well."

"Stubborn and bullheaded maybe," he informed her, anger throbbing in his voice. "You're pushing me too far, Heather. Farther than I would have thought possible. Keep it up, and I'll hurt both of us."

Her laughter was soft and filled with silky amusement as her smile lit the darkness around her.

"Be still, my heart. You do have a way with romance, Sam. It just makes my heart go all aflutter to hear your sweet nothings." Her tone of voice pricked at him. She was pissed—no, he took that back—she was furious. Still.

"I'm not an easy man," he whispered. "The laughter and jokes, Heather, are gone. I can't find them anymore. And there never was much romance, baby."

"Poor Sam." There was a definite lack of sympathy in her voice now. "Why don't I go down on my knees and suck you dry again in recompense. Would that help?"

He narrowed his eyes. The memory of her on her knees, his cock pushing in her hot mouth, had his cock twitching in need.

"Would an apology help?" he asked her curiously.

"Would you mean it?" she asked him archly.

He sighed deeply as he moved closer, stopping at her shoulders then hunching down beside the lounger.

"Likely not." He grinned as her eyes flashed with ire. "That was a damned pretty sight, Heather, and hot as hell. Watching your mouth move on me, driving me crazy."

She snorted. "I'm sure it was, Sam. Too bad you don't like returning the favor."

His lips tightened as a grimace of regret flashed across his face.

"If I get my tongue inside you, my cock won't be far behind it," he warned her. "I want you too badly."

"Really? Strange, I don't feel so wanted, so I don't think I'll put myself out to believe it. Go see if you can convince Marly or Sarah. They might be willing to go along with your line of crap tonight."

Sam winced. Hell, she was past mad.

"What do you want, Heather?" he asked her softly, regretfully. He understood why she was upset, knew he had pushed her when he shouldn't have, knew his own demons were driving her away from him.

Her eyes widened with exaggerated surprise. "What makes you think I want anything? I was out here minding my own business. You're the one intruding."

The garden was dark, but the light of the full moon was enough to see the hard peaks of her breasts beneath her shirt. Her breathing was harder, and she appeared more than a little agitated as he raised his gaze slowly back to hers.

"I want you so bad I'm shaking with it." He shook his head, more than a little amused at his own lack of control. "Surely that counts for something?"

She shrugged, watching him closely. "Not for much on this end, Sam," she told him coolly. "Try me again tomorrow. Maybe I just need to think about it for a while."

His eyes narrowed on her. She was provoking him and she damned well knew it. He looked at the lounger. The special build, like most everything in the August home, was wide and made for comfort. Before Heather could catch his intent, before he could give it much thought himself, he moved from his position quickly. Before she could do more than gasp, he had pinned her body to the thick pad, his elbows holding his weight from her chest, his legs parting hers as he settled quickly between them.

"How about I help you decide?" he bit out then and lowered his head.

Sam meant the kiss to be forceful. To show her, prove to her, his claim that he could only hurt both of them with his desire for her. But the moment his lips met the petal soft curves of hers, he hesitated. He held her still, his tongue stroking over the seam of her closed lips as he stared down at her opened eyes. He nudged at the soft curves with his own, stroked them with his tongue, fighting the compulsion to devour with greed as he savored the taste of her.

A small whimper of longing came from her as her eyelids lowered partially, sensually, a second before she parted her lips just enough to allow his tongue entrance. Sam couldn't halt the groan that vibrated in his own chest. He couldn't stop the need that burned in his loins like an inferno threatening to rage through his senses.

She was heat and soft, silky desire. Her lips opened to him with a hesitant wariness, much as she had with their first kiss. A tentative acceptance that had his body tightening with lust. His cock throbbed with imperative demand even as he fought its insistence.

"Heather." He whispered her name as he sipped at her lips, then stroked inside her mouth once again.

His hands moved from hers as his need to touch her overcame his need to dominate her. Her skin was so soft, so silky and smooth. He wanted to feel it against his fingertips, luxuriate in her response to him. And she was responding.

Her thighs tightened on his. Her hips jerked against his, grinding her cunt against the length of his erection as his tongue stroked over hers, his lips sipping at her as he groaned at the erotic tastes he found there.

Before he ever realized his intention to do so, he had pulled her shirt from the waistband of her jeans, and his palm was sliding up her waist, his fingers trembling with the need to cup the swollen mound of her breast. Her nipples were hard; he knew they would be hot, knew she would cry out when he captured one between his thumb and forefinger.

Her nails bit at his skin through the fabric of his shirt as he rotated his hips firmly against her cunt. He could feel her heat through both pairs of jeans, and the need to sink inside her was nearly driving him insane.

"I could eat you up, right here," he groaned as his lips moved to her throat, his hand cupping her breast as his fingers gripped her nipple, milking it and caressing the hard point as a strangled groan tore from her throat. "You make me lose all common sense when I'm around you, Heather."

"What common sense?" Her voice was torn, ragged, as she arched into him, her neck tilting as his tongue raked over her collarbone.

Sam couldn't help but smile. Her sharp tongue was lethal. But he had his own weapons. He shifted back, exposing her breast further as he moved toward it, his mouth watering at the thought of the pleasure to come.

* * * * *

Heather fought for breath as his lips covered her distended nipple. Heat seared her flesh, stroked her nipple as his mouth suckled at the mound firmly, his hand gripping it, fingers caressing the underside erotically. She arched to him, a broken moan whispering from her throat.

"Someone will see," she whispered brokenly. "Hear me."

"Mmm." Evidently, the thought didn't bother him. Then she remembered who she was talking to. Sam. The same man torturing her body with the needs tearing through it was the man who would want to share her, to watch as his brothers took her.

His teeth rasped at her tender nipple as the thought flared through her. She couldn't halt the desperate clench of her womb, like a soft blow to her stomach as the image of it drifted through her mind.

"I want you." His lips pressed beneath her breast as his hands moved to the clasp of her jeans. "I need you, Heather. I need you more than the air I breathe."

And she didn't have the strength to deny him. Not now, not while the fire of the arousal he called up, poured through her body. As though her blood was lava and her nerve endings receptors of heat that only made it burn brighter.

Her jeans loosened. Heather watched Sam as she gasped for breath, shadowed sensuality in his expression, the intent in his dark eyes. His head lowered again as he kissed his way down her stomach, her smooth abdomen, his hands pulling her jeans and panties down her thighs with teasing strokes of his hand along her skin.

She was shaking as he blew a puff of air across her burning cunt, then shuddered as he finished removing her clothing.

"I want to taste you," he growled. "Lick you like smooth, warm chocolate, Heather."

He dropped her jeans and panties to the ground a second before he moved between her thighs, spreading them slowly as he stared up at her.

"Sam." She could barely speak as she fought for breath. "Someone will see…"

"See me lapping at you, fucking you with my tongue, drawing liquid paradise from your body, Heather. Let 'em watch, baby. Let them see how fucking pretty you are as you come for me."

Her hips jerked, rising from the lounger as his tongue swiped through the narrow slit of her inner lips then licked around her swollen clit. The breath halted in her chest, then released on a rising moan. Smooth flame, his tongue was like snaking fire as it licked and probed at her soaked cunt.

He licked around her clit, pulled it into his mouth for a second less than it would have taken for her to climax, then licked down again before his hard hands lifted her hips and his tongue plunged inside her clenching pussy.

She could hear the wet sound of his suckling at her vagina, drawing the cream from her body as more replaced it. Her hands gripped the rails of the lounger as she twisted against his mouth, fighting for more. She needed him deeper, harder, licking her like that to her very womb.

He slurped at her cunt, his lips smacking as he released her, then his tongue plunging again. His hands moved to her buttocks, holding her open as his fingers spread the delicate mounds, one placing exquisite pressure on the puckered entrance to her anus.

She twisted in his grip, needing more. Her vagina shuddered around his tongue, her clit pulsing, throbbing as her fingers went to her nipples to ease the heated ache there. She pinched lightly, biting her lower lip as she fought back her moan of rising ecstasy.

"So good, Heather." His voice washed over her senses. "Like candy, baby. Like warm, sweet chocolate."

His tongue plunged deep, the tip of his nose burying against her clit, stroking it, caressing it. Heather gasped, caught her breath, but when the resulting explosion hit her she couldn't contain the low, breathless wail that tore from between her lips.

Her body tightened, her cunt spasming as the pleasure streaked over her in drowning waves of sensation. Sam was crooning as he licked her, sucked her, his tongue fucking her through the sharp bursts of exquisite pleasure until he moved back with a groan, his hands going to his own jeans.

"You'll scream for me this time," he promised her. "And everyone will know you're mine, Heather. Mine."

He was within an inch of freeing his cock to take her when the tree behind them cracked, spraying shards of the wood as the first gunshot rang out.

* * * * *

They rolled from the lounger in a tangle of limbs and virulent curses as the bullet struck the tree at the same angle that Sam's head would have been had he not been lowering it to her body. Heather grabbed her jeans, cursing as she pushed Sam behind the shelter of the trees, struggling back into the suddenly uncooperative denim.

"Dammit," Heather cursed as she jerked her gun from beneath the lounger. She struggled against Sam, cursing as he plastered himself to her back, holding her harder to the bark of the tree. Dammit, he was trying to protect her.

She was supposed to be protecting him.

She jerked her comm link from the back pocket of her jeans, bringing it quickly to her ear as the raised voices of the agents rushing for the pool area could be heard.

"Rick, dammit, where the hell are you? Sam's with me and we have incoming gunfire."

Raised voices began to fill the night as bodyguards rushed into the pool area. Several more unknown shots were fired, but none returned as the men rushed to surround Sam as the sound of a helicopter lifting from the front yard cut through the din of raised voices.

"Contain August. Get his ass in the house." Tara's voice was sharp as she barked out the orders to the bodyguards swarming around them. "Dammit to hell. If he gets hit I'll kick all your asses."

"Chopper's in the air," Rick called out. "Stay put until we know where the hell it's coming from. Goddammit, how the hell is he doing this?"

Heather struggled against Sam as he pressed her closer to the tree, his body a heavy weight in front of her, an effective shield between her and any bullet that might cut through the darkness. The other agents surrounded them, guns drawn, watching the darkness with the night vision goggles attached to their faces.

"Stay still," he growled as she struggled against him.

"Dammit, I'm supposed to be protecting you," she hissed. "Let me move!"

"Listen to me." His voice roughened, savagery reflecting so harshly in his tone that she automatically stilled. "You will not take a bullet for me, Heather. Do you understand me? You will not stand in front of me, you will not try to protect me, or so help me God, I'll make sure you regret it."

Then he was gone. "Sam." She cried out his name as he jerked from her and began pushing his way through the small garden. The bodyguards surrounded him as he stalked toward the house, rushing to provide a force of protection around him.

The agents scrambled to move around him, to place themselves where they could protect him as he pushed them roughly aside. Heather propped her hands on her hips and watched his furious face, breathing out thankfully when he made it into the relative protection of the house.

"Son of a bitch is going to get himself killed." Rick stalked toward her. "Did you tell him that, Heather?"

She shrugged, fighting the rapid beat of her heart. She made certain her shirt was in place as she faced her boss, thankful she had managed to pull her jeans back on. Only God knew where her panties were.

"Does it do any good to tell him anything?" she asked furiously as she tucked her gun back in the holster. Glancing over the wall surrounding the pool, she checked the helicopter's progress as its bright lights swept over the hill behind the house. "Where were those damned dogs? I thought they were patrolling the hill back there."

"Not in the dark." Rick shook his head sharply. "It's just too damned dangerous for the animals and the men. It would be a hell of a lot easier if you could keep Sam's ass in the house."

"Me?" Incredulity rocked her system. "What in the hell makes everyone think that man listens to me?"

"He follows you around like a fucking buck during rut," he snapped. "Don't pretend he doesn't. You have house duty from now on, no exceptions."

Heather shook her head desperately. "Forget it. You know what goes on in there at night, Rick. I'd get everyone killed. I'd never keep my mind on the job."

For some reason the August men thought the family room was the place to fuck, rather than their bedrooms. She avoided that room at all costs. She avoided any room but her own until after everyone else had settled down for the night.

"Do what the rest of them do," he snarled then. "Join the others in the kitchen for coffee or park your ass at the front or back door. I don't fucking care which, but keep your ass in the house. That bastard gets his ass killed and Cade will kill us."

"Why don't I just go ahead and fuck him then?" Sarcasm laced her voice. "Hell, Rick, that would solve everything, wouldn't it?"

"Damned right. And it's not like you're not itching to do it." He faced her, anger tensing his body as bodyguards milled around them and the helicopter continued to search the hill behind the house. "I don't give a damn how you keep yourself in the house, just fucking do it."

She would have snapped back. Would have told him where the hell he could shove his orders if he hadn't stalked off as her mouth opened to blast him. A growl of frustration broke past her lips as she barely restrained herself from stomping her foot in fury.

"Damn, Heather, I can't believe you don't want to guard that hard August body." Amusement echoed in the female voice as a chuckle reached her ears.

Heather turned back again as she watched Helena approach her. She was still breathing hard, sweat gleaming on her face as her blue eyes regarded her with a laughing glint.

Heather shook her head as she took a deep, weary breath.

"Men should be outlawed," she decided. "Excuse me, Helena, I'm going to go see if I can find out if anyone, anywhere, has any idea what the hell happened to security tonight."

Not that Heather had much hope for answers at this point. All she had was questions. The least of which, was how the hell the stalker had gotten on that damned hill without being spotted. And had he even been on the hill? That bullet had been too close, the aim too precise. Somehow, it wasn't adding up.

# Chapter Thirteen

Heather couldn't forget her confrontation with Sam in the pool area the night before, or the stalker and how easily a bullet could have taken out the back of his head. Chills raced over her body each time she thought of it, and she knew beyond a shadow of a doubt that if Sam were killed, then the August family would be irreparably damaged. Until they all faced the past, there would be no true healing for any of them.

The three men had formed an exceptional bond together in their sharing, one Sam had denied all but once over the past months. He hadn't gone to his brothers' women, and his brooding anger had only intensified.

The conversation the night before between her and Sam wore at her suspicions regarding them all. She had noticed over the months the lengths the other men went to in protecting Sam, in keeping the memories carefully hidden. She had thought it was a form of mercy. Their own memories were brutally clear, she believed. She had believed they hadn't wanted that for him. But now she knew it had to go much deeper.

She knew Sam didn't possess many memories of the time spent confined in his abuser's basement. He knew what had happened, he knew the pain, and he remembered clearly the first weeks there. But after that, she knew that many of the events were hazy.

Cade had not been very forthcoming with Rick on actual events. The notations in the files Rick made available to her the next day showed an incredible amount of frustration regarding the information he was given. It had taken nearly a year to track down anyone who could have known or seen any of the events that happened that summer. And it was taking even longer to track down the missing Jennings brother.

The old servant of Marcelle's that Rick had tracked down had provided information on the drugs Marcelle had used on the men. Potent drugs that sustained a sexual erection for hours, even days, on end. Keeping their cocks in a state of readiness, no matter the state of their minds. They had been young. Brock and Sam were still in their teens, Cade barely over twenty. At a time when their manhood was most important, it had been stripped from them.

Reginald Robert Jennings, the man suspected now of threatening the family, had attempted to follow his brother's footsteps in a medical career, but had been unable to succeed. Marcelle himself had been a well-respected member of the medical community for decades before an early retirement beneath a cloud of suspicion that arose in his final years. Suspicion of drugging several of his male patients and abusing them. Rick had found the men who first made the complaints and learned they had been generously paid to retract their statements. But it didn't change the stories they had to tell, or the hazy, drug-clouded memories of abuse.

The suspicions of sexual perversions hadn't abated then. The winter before the brothers had been sent to his ranch, Marcelle had visited a doctor in Madison for a broken nose, cracked cheekbone, and severe bruising. A result of Sam's rage after the bastard had snuck into his bedroom during a visit to the August ranch.

Cade had known what had happened, but when his father ordered them to the Marcelle ranch to learn a new technique in ranching, his father had assured the boys they could leave the moment any impropriety was suggested. Old Joe August had sworn the ranch's livelihood depended on those new techniques. The only techniques available for them to learn, though, had been those in pain and torture, Heather thought as she finally closed the last of Rick's files.

The servant's accounts of those days were frightening. The screams that filtered from the basement, the horrendous amounts of blood sometimes shed, was reported as sickening. As a doctor, Marcelle had known how far he could abuse their bodies and yet keep them alive, and he had pushed them to their limits. Especially Sam. It had always been worse for Sam.

The files she had managed to dig up on Raider gave her no evidence, period, to suspect the other man of having a reason to want to hurt the Augusts. Russell "Raider" Kincaid was known for his loyalty, his abilities, and his determination to get the job done. Considering his credentials she couldn't help but believe if he wanted Sam dead then Sam would be dead.

Heather tapped her fingernails against the table she was sitting at as she stared outside the RV the Agency was using on the August Ranch. Heat rose in waves outside the air-conditioned comfort of the motor home. Horses dozed beneath the shade of several large trees, as cattle lay in small gatherings along the shaded stream that ran through the pasture.

It was late afternoon, and the ranch had settled down as the heat built outside. Late summer was a scorcher in Texas, and this wasn't turning out to be any different.

She drew in a hard, weary breath as she shook her head. Where did she go from here, she wondered. Obeying his every sexual command didn't sit well with her. Especially those in the written note he had left on her pillow when he had slipped into her room around daylight. She snorted. The directions were explicit, the reasons clearly explained.

An inflatable butt plug had accompanied the note. How to prepare her body for him and keep it ready to accept his pleasures. She shook her head mockingly. Did Marly and Sarah actually put up with that nonsense? A mild anal douche, a tube of lubrication, directions on how to use the butt plug, how often, for how long, when to prepare... The sheer arrogance of it amazed her. But the depth of strength it had taken to survive, even at these extremes, made her heart clench.

"Sam's heading back, Heather." Rick's voice was soft in the comm link at her ear. "You have twenty more minutes."

Heather had been hesitant to go through the files at a time that Sam could come looking for her, possibly even surprise her in it. She still remembered the shame that flared in his eyes after Rick had returned from Utah and began giving his report.

The three men's expressions had been cold, emotionless, but their eyes had swirled with shame, guilt and remembered pain. It had been more than she could bear. And sometimes she wondered how Marly and Sarah held up under the pressure.

"I'm heading back in, Rick," she told him as she restacked the files and stored them back in the security box Rick used.

She locked the box and shoved it back beneath the bench before leaving the motorhome and locking the door behind her. Rick met her at the front of the RV, his brown eyes dark, questioning. "Did you find what you were looking for?"

She tucked the mic up, cutting off sound from the other members of the group. "No," she sighed. "Just more questions."

"See if you can get any of them answered, Heather," he told her softly. "This is dragging on too long. At this rate, Jennings could attack and easily catch us off guard due to sheer boredom, just like he did last night. The men are getting tired of playing cowboys, and the Augusts are damned tired of being confined to the house. We need more information if we're ever going to make headway here."

"Unless Jennings messes up," she pointed out.

"Unless he does," Rick nodded. "Which could be anytime, or a year down the road."

"Or whenever he figures out Sam has taken me," she said softly. "That he's happy."

Tension thickened between them as her implication widened Rick's eyes.

"No." He gripped her arm firmly, staring down at her with a hint of anger. "Marly and Sarah barely escaped the bastard,

Heather, and you know yourself just how serious he is. Don't put yourself in harm's way."

"I'm already there, Rick," she reminded him bleakly. "Jennings just thinks he has time. He thinks Sam is suffering and he's reveling in it. As long as that comforts him, he won't mess up. He'll plan carefully and meticulously until he takes Sam out. We can't allow that."

Heather could feel that knowledge gathering inside her. He wouldn't come after anyone, not seriously, as long as Sam suffered. He had to be convinced Sam was no longer paying for whatever crime he imagined Sam had committed.

"What do you have in mind?" Rick asked her carefully.

"I'm not sure yet. Give me a little more time, and I'll let you know." She pulled away from him as the Augusts rode into the ranch yard.

Her eyes met Sam's across the distance and her body tingled in awareness.

"Whatever it is, be damned sure you let me know," Rick ordered her wearily. "Don't go off half cocked, Heather. Tara and Sam both would kill me if anything happened to you now."

"I promise, I'll be careful." She moved away from him, aware of Sam's eyes following her, but not just Sam's. The combined heat of three men, watching her, wanting her, followed her into the house.

\* \* \* \* \*

Sam's gaze sliced to Rick as Heather disappeared into the house. He could sense the tension in the other man, the suspicion in his gaze. Dismounting, he led the horse into the stables, ignoring Cade and Brock as they watched him curiously. They were tense, had been for days, and it was only building. He knew the cause and would have welcomed the relief. He needed the relief, the escape from the burning awareness inside his own body. The escape from the brutal memories, the twisting shadows, the knowledge that his escape from the hell of the past was about to backfire.

"I hate checking fences," Brock muttered, as he threw his saddle over its rack and handed the horse into the capable hands of one of the ranch hands.

"Someone has to do it," Cade growled as he did the same and began unbuckling the leather chaps he wore over his jeans.

"We have ranch hands, Cade," Brock reminded him tersely as he removed his own chaps.

Sam could feel the tension building between the two men, and it tightened his own body. He sensed the needs swirling between them all. The effects of ignoring the past, and the need to understand the future. Weariness lay on all their shoulders, but it only served to strengthen the needs rather than to weaken them. It strengthened his own sexual aggression, his need to hear the trembling, erotic cries that poured from Sarah or Marly as they shook in passion.

"You're getting lazy, Brock," Cade snapped. "All this laying around the house is making you soft. You'll survive."

Sam unbuckled his own chaps and threw them on a convenient hook. He was silent, but he had welcomed the physical labor for a change. A chance to get away from the house, to ease the battle waging between himself and Heather. He grimaced. No, the fight wasn't with Heather; it was between his arousal and his conscience, which was even worse.

"Goddammit, Cade, it's dangerous to leave like this," Brock finally snarled. "We left the women alone. What if the bastard strikes while we're gone?"

"It's not the women he'll go after." Sam raised his head, watching them both as he spoke softly. "They're safe for now."

He watched his brothers' expressions tighten.

"And you aren't making things any easier, Sam," Cade said darkly. "Stop stomping around the house like a bear with a sore paw. Do something about it before you drive us all crazy."

Sam faced them, aware of the building tension growing between them. It had been there before, he knew, but he hadn't noticed it, hadn't really been aware of it before now. It was an anger, a steady remorseless anger that was growing. But not at each other. Sam sensed no anger toward him from the other two men, and he knew he wasn't angry with them.

It crept through them though, steadily building in strength until they relieved it with the cries and sexual release that spilled from the bodies of the women they shared. Then it would still. Quieting for a while before it began to build again.

"I can't," he finally answered Cade's demand. "You know I can't, Cade."

He turned from them, leading his horse to its stall and a supply of oats and water. He could feel his body tightening, needing. In the back of his mind he could almost hear Heather screaming out her release for the three of them. It was a tempting thought, but one he knew would never come to pass. He couldn't, he wouldn't, place her in danger again.

Behind him, Cade and Brock were silent. It wasn't the first time he had refused to participate, but he knew the time was coming that he wouldn't be able to deny it any longer.

"She knows, Sam," Cade said, his voice immeasurably tired.

Sam shook his head. She knew, but there was no way she could understand. Hell, sometimes he didn't understand it himself and for months now he had been fighting to make sense of it.

"I know that, Cade." He shrugged as he turned from them and headed back to the house, and hopefully a cold shower. "I'm more than aware of what Heather knows."

As he walked away from his brothers, his memories kept returning to the first time, the very first time he and his brothers had shared a woman. It wasn't after the abuse, but before. Several months before Joe had sent them to Utah. Cade had been more than a little drunk that night, and his partner was more than a little easy. They had all been skinny-dipping at one of the ponds several miles from the ranch house. An evening away from the callus, bitter old fool they called their father.

A little too much beer and raging hormones had triggered the sharing. But Sam remembered afterward more than anything. Something had changed within them. They had always been close, but after that, the bond had felt deeper, stronger. Then after the hell of that summer was over, it had been there to draw them together again.

Sam remembered the bleak isolation of those days, before Cade brought the first woman home. They made certain to never touch each other, so terrified that even the smallest touch would bring back the pain that they had been forced to inflict on each other. Not that it was ever forgotten. It was always there.

He jerked his hat off as he stepped into the house, breathing in a sigh of relief as the cool air slid around his overheated body. Sleep came hard most nights now, and he felt tired to the bone. Tired and horny and aggravated—a hell of a combination. As he closed the door, Sarah stepped from the stairway, looking toward the door curiously.

"Brock coming in?" She was dressed in one of those short, gauzy skirts that looked so damned good with her long tanned legs. A matching peach tank top brought out the honey color of her tan on her shoulders and neck.

"Yeah, he'll be in soon." His hand tightened on the brim of his hat. For all her sweet gentleness, Sarah was a wildcat, and he could use the aggressiveness right now. Her nails biting into him, her teeth nipping at him.

"You okay, Sam?" She walked to him easily, comfortably. There was no hesitation, no reluctance as she came into his arms. There was no fear. And it never ceased to amaze him.

"Whoa, I'm hot and sweaty, hon." He dropped a kiss to her smiling lips. "I need a shower before I dirty you up."

"You look so sad, Sam." Her gaze was compassionate and a little aroused as she stepped back from him. "Is everything okay?"

"Everything's fine, darlin'." He attempted a smile, but her expression never changed. "If you want the truth, I want to fuck you silly, but the middle of the hallway might be the wrong place for that."

"Liar," she whispered. "You're after that hot little redhead who escaped into her room to apply her Pocket Rocket before you got here."

Sam blinked in surprise.

"How do you know?" He glanced to the stairs, wondering if he could catch her in the act. Damn, he would give anything to see that.

"Sam, hon, I'm a woman," she laughed as she patted his chest in comfort. "Besides, somehow Marly found out that was the only toy the poor little thing possessed. We're thinking of giving her some of the new stuff you boys ordered."

The thought of Heather, her body stretched out on the bed, legs spread, the honey-slick folds of her pussy glistening as she fucked herself was making him crazy now.

His body tightened. "The Rabbit," he whispered. "Give her the Rabbit." He spoke of the exceptionally powerful dildo that vibrated, rotated and stroked deep inside the vagina as the soft ears pulsated against the clit. The twin sensations drove Sarah and Marly crazy. "Do that for me, Sarah, and I'll owe you."

Her eyes widened in surprise. "I don't know, Sam, that might be a little advanced for her..." Her voice sounded hesitant.

He could see her, moaning, the Rabbit driving her crazy before allowing herself to come. That's what he wanted for her. Wanted her so primed for him that the first thrust inside her tight pussy would send her careening over the edge of sanity.

"Sarah, give her the Rabbit," he told her desperately, fighting to keep his excitement, his need under control. "Do this for me."

"Sam." She shook her head in confusion. "Why don't you satisfy her? The woman needs a man, not a chest of toys."

He needed to. God help him, he wanted to, more than anything, and it terrified the hell out of him. The thought of hurting her, of being the reason she was hurt, was more than he could bear. His brothers had damned near been destroyed because of him. What if that fucking stalker hurt Heather in a similar way...more than she had already been hurt? And yet, he couldn't restrain his needs. Couldn't restrain at least a small part of the pleasure that zipped through him at the thought of Heather and those toys.

"Sarah." He gripped her arm imperatively as his cock thickened and throbbed beneath his jeans. "Do this for me. Promise me."

She watched him, tilting her head as her gaze held his.

"You can't fight it forever, Sam," she finally said softly. "You can give her all the toys in the world, but you won't be satisfied until you take her yourself. You know that."

"I need this, Sarah." His voice was just as low. "More than you know. She won't take them from me, but she would from you. Do this for me. Please."

She sighed deeply as she shook her head. "I'll do it, Sam."

He closed his eyes and when he opened them he could have sworn he caught a flash of amusement in her eyes before it was quickly hidden.

"I owe you big time," he growled, unable to still the thought of maybe, just maybe, catching Heather in the act of using the intimate devices.

His hand ran up the outside of her thigh as he leaned forward, giving her a lingering kiss before he pulled back. "Brock's a bear today. Fuck him out so he'll quit bitching at me." He grinned. "Now I'm gonna shower. I'll see you later."

He hurried away from her before his urges could get the better of him. He strode quickly up the stairs and to his own room and a cold shower that he prayed would still the heat in his body.

* * * * *

"He's such a goner." Marly stepped from the doorway of the study, a huge grin splitting her face as she peeked around the wall to the stairway.

"Shh, Brock and Cade will be here in a minute." Sarah was having trouble stilling her own laughter. "We'll take them to her this evening. Just make sure Cade knows we're doing it, too. The three of them are driving me nuts."

Marly shook her head, her blue eyes filled with such mischievous laughter that she resembled a teenager more than she did an adult.

"Marly, have you considered the fact that we are deliberately setting her up to be fucked by Cade and Brock?" Sarah suddenly shook her head at the thought. "I would have never believed anyone if they had told me I could have accepted this."

Being with the three brothers herself, and seeing their interaction, the knowledge that it wasn't sexual so much as it was truly loving, had eased any jealousy she would have felt. Brock often had sex with Marly, either with the other two present or alone, whenever the need was there. Just as Cade and Sam would come to Sarah as they needed. The unique relationship that was evolving among them all often surprised her. She had three lovers, and she loved them all, but Brock held her soul, just as she knew she held his.

Marly shook her head, her rioting black curls rippling to her hips. "We love them." She finally shrugged. "Just as they love us. I couldn't imagine anything else now, Sarah."

Sarah admitted that she couldn't either. Knowing Brock was with Marly no longer caused her jealousy or hurt. It was no more than a hug, a kiss on the cheek. It was a sharing of the bond he had with his brothers, and with her.

"Well, let's take her the gifts then." She grinned, more than a little curious as to the reactions the men of the house would have. She felt a little naughty, a little nervous, but she would be damned if she wasn't looking forward to it.

# Chapter Fourteen

"The Snake?" Heather blinked down at the carefully wrapped adult toy. The deep purple color was bad enough. It was nearly seven inches, slender and extremely supple. Nearly an inch and a half beneath the flared head, in the middle of the supple device, there appeared to be a small, metal motor.

"What does it do?" she whispered as she stared at Marly and Sarah, afraid to speak too loudly in case someone would hear her.

Marly laughed gently. "It vibrates," she whispered back, her eyes widening with amused naughtiness.

Heather swallowed nervously. "Vibrates?"

"Uh huh." Both women nodded.

"Why?" She asked then, frowning at them as they watched her expectantly.

"Why does it vibrate?" Sarah looked at her in surprise.

"No," Heather said slowly. "Why are you giving it to me?"

Sarah and Marly glanced at each other before Marly sighed deeply.

"Because sometimes, Sam needs a little push to realize what an ass he can be." She smiled. "Besides, it will hold you over until he gets his commonsense back."

"Oh, he gets his commonsense back?" she asked curiously, not really believing it. "Strange, I haven't seen any proof of it." She laid the wrapped dildo carefully on the bed.

"Oh, we have more." Sarah reached into the tote bag she had carried into the room.

"More?" Heather stepped back, wondering what in the hell they were going to come out with next.

"The Rabbit," Marly explained as they handed her the box.

Heather stared down at it in shock. "You guys have a thing for critters, right?"

Marly sighed as she rolled her eyes. "Heather, if you don't want the toys, we won't be offended."

And she wouldn't be. Heather saw the understanding, the compassion in the younger woman's eyes as she stood before her. She blew out a hard breath and sat down on the end of the bed, careful to keep some distance between her and the erotic "snake."

"I wasn't expecting this, ladies." She tried to smile as, unselfconsciously, they pulled the chairs at the side of the room closer to the bed.

"It's not exactly something we were expecting either." Sarah relaxed into the high backed chair, her hands lying loosely at the end of the chair arms. "The situation here is unique, Heather, as you know. Sam is important to us, too."

Suspicion washed over her then. "Are you afraid I'm going to try to take Sam away from the two of you?" she asked them. The impropriety of the discussion was nearly laughable.

Marly grinned. A smile of such confidence, such loving assurance, that Heather felt vaguely ashamed of herself.

"Heather, Sam will always be a part of us, even if he never touches us again. Whatever makes him happy, makes the shadows ease from his eyes, makes us happy. This isn't about the sex. Not in any way."

Heather shook her head. "Excuse me, Marly, if I pause to consider how ridiculous this whole situation is becoming. You are aware that Cade intends to fuck me. Right?" A thread of anger moved through her voice, despite her attempts to keep it covered.

"Heather…" Marly stopped and glanced at Sarah as though for support.

Sarah shook her head in denial as a light laugh escaped her throat. "Not me. You see if you can explain it."

"I am very well aware, Heather, that Cade intends to fuck you," Marly answered softly. Heather was amazed that there was no jealousy, no anger in her words.

Heather watched both women, confusion building within her until she couldn't stand it any longer.

"Marly, he's your lover," Heather whispered. "I know you love him. Why do you allow it?"

Marly's head tilted as she stared back at Heather curiously. "You know I fuck Sam. You saw us get out of the limo, and you knew I had, Heather. Yet, you weren't filled with fury. Why was that?"

"There's no commitment between us." She shook her head, coming to her feet, refusing to admit to the point Marly was making.

"But you love him, and you can't deny it," Marly pointed out. "I saw your face, Heather. You knew. You knew, and for one brief moment jealousy flared, then something dimmed it. Why?"

Heather shook her head. She couldn't answer that. She wouldn't answer it.

"We're not here to convince you either way, Heather," Sarah spoke up. "We have no intention of trying to convince you. We brought you the toys for two reasons. One because we know you have to be horny as hell. Two, because the thought of you having them will make Sam insane with need. There are few things that turn him on more than the toys do."

Heather turned back to them, tucking her hands into her jeans pockets nervously as she watched them. They were relaxed, friendly. They watched her with understanding, with sympathy.

"I love him," she admitted, shaking her head. "But I won't beg him."

"You won't have to, Heather," Marly said gently. "Sam is just as much in love as you are. But he hurts so deeply. When the stalker attacked you, he placed scars on you that remind Sam, when he thinks of them, of his belief that it's his fault you were attacked. Until he deals with the past, until they all do, that pain will always be there."

"As will the sharing?" Heather hunched her shoulders, fighting the shiver that fought to race up her back at the thought of it.

"The sharing." Marly frowned thoughtfully. "I don't think it will ever change, Heather. If you ever see them together, sharing, you'll understand what I mean. They are an extension of each other, as I told you. Their every thought centered on whichever of us they are with. Every touch, every kiss, made for our pleasure, our satisfaction. I don't think it's because of the pain. I think it eases the pain though."

It was no more than Heather believed herself. "They're too much alike," she muttered.

"In some ways," Sarah agreed. "In others, they're completely different. I love Brock with all my heart and soul, Heather. I don't know if I could stand it if I lost him. But I love Sam and Cade as well. It grows when you don't realize it, and they become a part of you even when you try to separate yourself from them. You can't help it. You can't fight men who want nothing more than your safety, your happiness and your pleasure."

"You could want fidelity," she said softly.

"But we have that, Heather." Marly's voice was low, yet filled with conviction. "We have their complete fidelity. Cade and Brock would have no desire for you at all if Sam didn't love you. You're a part of Sam, so you're a part of them as well. That's not cheating, that's loving."

"It's an excuse," she sighed wearily.

The two women looked at each other, then rose to their feet.

"The toys are a gift. With no ulterior motive, Heather," Marly said, as they placed their chairs back in their proper places by the window. "Use them or throw them away. Teasing Sam with them would be pretty damned effective, though." She grinned. "If you need to talk to us, anytime, you know where we are."

"Heather." Sarah turned to her. "Think about something. Is it our excuse? Or are you attempting to judge something that convention and morality has taught you is wrong? Think about it long and hard, then come and tell me where the excuse lies."

Heather stared at the toys after the two women left. She paced her room, she fretted and she worried until she felt as though she would go insane from it. She opened the toys and inserted the required batteries that had been left as well. She washed them, she looked at them, but she didn't use them. She wanted to. Her pussy clenched at the thought of it, because she knew damned good and well Sam would hear the distinctive buzz through the thin panel of the door.

Unlike the walls and the outer doors of the bedroom, the connecting door was damned near as thin as paper. You could hear everything through it. He would hear, and he would know.

Would he come to her? Would she want him to? Her need kept rapid pace with her pride, until she could barely stand the pressure from it. It was a relief to finally go to dinner. Until she got there. Sam watched her heatedly. Of course, he would have heard the toys as she held them, feeling the vibration beneath the flexible latex that covered their motor packs.

Conversation flowed around the dinner table as Rick, Cade and Brock discussed the lack of clues on the stalker, and the close call in the pool area the night before. Sarah and Marly discussed the next day's appointments, and teased the men whenever the chance presented itself. Sam was quiet. Heather was silent.

After the meal was over, the family retired to the family room, and Heather escaped to the dark kitchen. A pot of coffee waited for her there, and a dark lonely night stretched out ahead of her.

She sent up a silent prayer that if family fun occurred in the other room, they would at least have mercy and muffle the noise a bit. She was riding on her last nerve, and her arousal level was reaching meltdown. If she didn't do something soon to relieve the pressure building in her pussy, then she was going to explode. The only problem was, she was uncertain how to do so. Her Pocket Rocket seemed to only make the situation more desperate, and from her previous experience with vibrators, she doubted the dildos, no matter how much they wiggled and squirmed, would help.

Quietly she checked the locks on the back door, the ones on the kitchen window, then made certain the dark, rubber-backed curtains were completely closed. The incident more than a month ago, where the bullet proof glass had been shattered, had terrified them all, Heather knew. No chances were being taken now.

Reasonably certain that the room was safe, she flipped on the small light over the sink after securing the curtains there and fixed a cup of the strong coffee. A recliner sat in the far corner of the kitchen now, a comfortable resting place for whoever guarded the back door. Rather than sitting in it, she leaned against the counter and sipped at her coffee as she leafed through one of the ranching magazines that had been left lying on it.

She glanced over her shoulder as she heard the door swish open. As she began to turn around, a large male hand patted her ass affectionately as the broad form passed her.

"Excuse me." She turned as Cade reached over her head for a coffee cup in the top cabinet.

His large, muscular body had her pinned against the counter as his hips pressed intimately into her lower abdomen. There, the distinct feel of a thick, fully erect cock could be easily felt.

"Coffee still fresh?" His deep voice was a rough rumble as he flicked her a heated glance while moving away from her.

She didn't know whether to kick his ass or scream bloody murder.

"Don't try my patience, Cade," she warned him instead. "It's extremely low at the moment."

He poured his coffee, then leaned against the counter as he watched her. His eyes were gray, not blue-gray like the twins'. His face was harder, more chiseled and set into lines of stubbornness. He didn't smile as much as the others did, but as the months had passed, Heather had watched as the shadows in his eyes seemed to lighten.

"Yours isn't the only one," he grunted. "Sam's pacing like a caged cat."

She narrowed her eyes warningly. "Do not suggest that I fuck him again."

She had the distinct impression from the look he was giving her that it was all he could do not to roll his eyes in exasperation.

"I wasn't going to suggest anything of the kind. When he can't handle the pressure anymore, he'll take care of it." He shrugged.

"Which means?" she asked as she fought not to grit her teeth.

His lips kicked up into a smile. "Which means, Heather, I hope you've been practicing with that plug I know he's left you by now, because you can bet you'll be wishing you had."

Shock washed through her body. "What is with you men and anal sex?" she asked furiously. "Maybe I believe that's an exit only. It's not exactly natural. And why the hell am I even discussing this with you?" she hissed, wondering if she were finally losing her senses as well. "You guys are driving me crazy." She wasn't about to admit that she had indeed, and even now, was using the little device.

He chuckled. The sound was rich and warm, and laced with arousal. He watched her with those hot eyes of his, his face drawn into lines of sensuality, and it nearly sent her running.

Did he know, she wondered, could he tell somehow, that she was using the plug his brother had left for her?

"You'll get used to us in time," he assured her, and she wondered if he had any idea how close she was to just shooting them all.

"Why are you even in here?" she asked with exaggerated patience. "Shouldn't you be in there doing the family thing or something?"

The heat of arousal seemed to flare brighter in his eyes. "Marly wanted to relax tonight. She headed on to bed."

Which didn't answer her question. "And Sarah?" she asked, wondering if even now the other woman was enjoying Sam's heated touch.

"Sarah too," he grinned. "She and Brock just went up."

"Where's Sam?" She couldn't stop the question from rolling past her lips.

He leaned closer as he set his cup in the sink behind her, but he didn't draw back when he was finished. He was close, so close she could smell the clean male scent of his body, so like Sam's. She could close her eyes, and almost convince herself…

"Sam's in the family room, watching TV," he whispered, his lips too close to hers, his heavy body too warm, too tempting.

"Stop." She drew in a ragged breath as she moved back from him. "You're trying to seduce me."

His eyes widened as he straightened. "Actually, I was just flirting a little." His lips kicked into a slight grin. "I must be getting old, or out of practice."

"You're plenty practiced," she promised him warily as she edged away from him.

"You act frightened." He frowned then. "Do you think I'd hurt you, Heather? Or take anything from you that you don't want to give?"

She shook her head, fighting the impossible, traitorous desires that coiled in her womb. Her cunt gushed with need, spasming with arousal as he watched her broodingly.

"No." Her breathing was rough, and she knew he could see the desires pulling at her.

"I won't even try to touch you without your permission, Heather," he promised her, and he meant it. She could see it in his eyes. "It doesn't work that way, you know that."

"Did Sam send you?" She wanted to sound angry, but she knew she only sounded needy. Damn them. All of them. What they were doing to her body, to her heart, should be outlawed. She could see the need in his eyes, his arousal, his emotional response, and it was tearing her apart. He wasn't Sam. She loved Sam. Not his brothers.

But her breasts were swelling, her nipples peaking, and between her thighs, her clit was throbbing from the excess arousal pouring through her body.

"Did Marly and Sarah bring you the toys today?" he finally asked her curiously, throwing her body further into its rioting confusion.

Heather's face flushed. She knew her whole body must be a perfect shade of red by now.

"That's none of your business," she strangled. "Geez, Cade. Isn't there any privacy in this damned house?"

She crossed her arms over her breasts, praying to hide the desperate hardness of her nipples.

"If you need help figuring out how to use them, I could help you out," he offered.

Heather choked on her strangled curse as he moved close again. She wondered if he could see the steam that should be pouring from her pussy.

"I'm sure I can figure it out," she finally gasped. "Go watch television or something." She turned from him, and would have put the distance of the room between them if his arm hadn't come gently around her waist.

He exerted no pressure, but she was so damned weak he didn't have to. She fought for breath as she felt his erection against her lower back, his lips at her neck.

"Push it inside you first, Heather. Then line up those little ears to grip your clit between them. When you turn it on, the dildo will move and flex inside you as it turns in little circles. The little pearls in the base will flip and beat around, stimulating your tender opening, and the ears?" His teeth raked her neck. "Those little ears will pulsate and massage your clit as your hips twist and thrash, driving you closer to orgasm."

His hand pulled her shirt free of her jeans as the door opened again and Sam stepped slowly into the kitchen. Heather whispered his name, terrified now, caught by his brother and the erotic words pouring from his mouth as he pulled her T-shirt up her abdomen, and Sam, who watched it all, his eyes darkening, his sweat pants tenting with his own erection as he watched his brother's hands.

Hands that pulled her shirt along her body until the full mounds of her breasts met the cool air of the dimly lit kitchen. She was fighting for breath, her eyes locked with Sam's, a plea on her lips, but she was unable to force the words out.

Cade's hands cupped her breasts as Sam came closer.

"The dildo will fuck you slow and easy, stretching your tight pussy, Heather," Cade continued. "It's not as large as we are, or as long, but it will get you ready. When you climax, your body will tighten, the sensation ripping through your womb…"

"Oh my God." She arched as Sam's head lowered to one of the ripe breasts Cade was cupping and directing to his mouth.

She was helpless, caught, trapped by the sensuality of the act as Sam's mouth covered the hot, aching peak, his tongue raking her nipple as his mouth began to draw on her with a firm, suckling motion. Her hands rose to Sam's head, whether to push him away or pull him closer she wasn't certain. But she wasn't able to do either. He caught her hands, trapping them in one of his larger ones as the fingers of the other went to her jeans.

Her moans filled the room as his fingers jerked the buttons open.

"Think about it, Heather," Cade whispered sensually, his voice thick and rough. "And later, after Sam gets over his stubbornness, he'll lay you on your stomach." Sam's hands breeched the opening of her jeans. "And you'll have that Rabbit trapped inside you." Sam's fingers raked her swollen clit. "And while it's fucking you nice and easy, he'll push his cock up your tight ass, making the sensations multiply…" She screamed out in desperation as Sam plunged two long fingers deep inside her weeping cunt.

She shattered. The orgasm that tore through her body had her rising to her toes as his fingers twisted inside her, his mouth drawing on her breast, his tongue flaying her tight nipple. The room darkened as her eyes dazed, her body jerking, shuddering as the explosion rocked every cell within it.

Caught between the two men as their hands touched her, lips on her skin, fire streaking through her veins, she could only cry out Sam's name. She trembled, her body shuddering spasmodically. She felt her release pour over his fingers as her legs tightened, her pussy milking the fingers fucking her, stealing her sanity.

When it was over, it was Sam's arms that drew her close, his lips that whispered soothing phrases in her ear, his hands that ran gently over her back.

"Come to me, Heather, when you're ready," he growled, his voice hard, tight with his own unsatisfied arousal. "But don't wait too fucking long, or I might come to you. And when I do, I might be flat out of control."

He moved her to the recliner, sat her gently upon it as he kissed her lips. A soft, gentling caress, before he turned and stalked from the room. Heather blinked, then stared at Cade where he stood by the swinging door.

"It's your gift to give, Heather. He won't take it from you. But you might find you get in return a hell of a lot more than you ever believed possible."

# Chapter Fifteen

Three in the morning was a hell of a time, Heather thought as she trudged wearily up the stairs. After Sam and Cade had left the kitchen, the night had been quiet, leaving her to reflect on the events that had destroyed many of her beliefs and left her fighting the inner knowledge that she was a goner as far as Sam and his brothers were concerned.

She knew the history of the men, knew the abuses they had suffered, and she suffered for Sam now. But there was something so dark and lonely inside him. She shook her head; she couldn't put her finger on it. Something was raging inside him that almost frightened her. As though he were fighting himself as much as the past.

She pushed her fingers wearily through her hair and walked into her room, closing the door behind her. She glanced at the door on the other side of the room. It led to Sam's room. Interconnecting rooms.

She stood and stared at the door. It wasn't closed as she had left it earlier. It had been opened just enough that she would know the offer was there. She stared at it somberly, wondering if she dared.

She licked her lips and shook her head wearily. Damn him, he wasn't making this easy for her. Do this, do that. As though she had no idea, and wasn't in the least prepared for him. She snorted silently. She had known for months what was coming, and had fought to prepare herself for it. Marly and Sarah had helped to an extent. Those two women amazed her.

She undressed, her eyes closing as she stepped out of her jeans, feeling the butt plug she had inserted earlier as her muscles tightened around it. The erotic, naughty feeling of wearing the device had nearly driven her crazy in the kitchen with the two men.

Heather wondered what he would have thought, what he would have done if he had known that what he had threatened to do to her, she had already done to herself. Shaking her head at the thought, she moved to the bathroom and removed it. The sensual feeling of the plug sliding free of her stretched anus had her pussy throbbing. She closed her eyes, wondering how Sam would feel, his cock pulsing, burrowing in and out of her as he had threatened her countless times.

She washed the device, smiling a bit regretfully as she left the bathroom and moved to her dresser. She stored the item away, and moved toward the bed. Then she stopped, frowning, uncertain.

"No..." The sound came again, a moan of pain, of rage.

Heather trembled. Sam's voice was broken, enraged, filled with disbelief as he fought his nightmares once again. Her body tightened as she turned to his door. She knew what would happen. He would rage and cry out, bringing himself from the dream then stalking from the house. Rick would have to track him, watch him, otherwise he would ride out and head into the darkness of the open land.

She pulled on her robe, moving quickly for the door.

"So much blood..." His voice was strained, agonized, as she stepped through the doorway. "Oh God, Cade, what did I do? What did I do, Cade... No... No, Cade... NO!"

He twisted on the bed; the blankets kicked away from his nude body as he fought whatever demons haunted his nightmares.

"Too much blood..." he cried out again. "Oh God, Cade it hurts..."

He twisted, his voice ragged, fighting the memories, the horror of the past.

"Cade...too much blood..." He cried out the words again.

Heather moved closer to the bed, the light from the bedside lamp was dim, but she gasped in horror at what she saw. Scars, unimaginable scars, scored his body from his abdomen to his thighs. Razor thin, crisscrossing. She swallowed tightly, wondering what could have possibly cut him so deep, and yet with such thin precision to leave such scars. She had seen him naked before, but never like this, while he was helpless. And she realized that though he had never tried to hide his erection from her, he had always made certain the scars weren't so visible.

"No." He thrashed on the bed. "No, goddamn you. I did it. I did it..."

Heather cried out, jerking back as he came up in the bed, his hand gripping her wrist and jerking her to him.

"Sam?" she cried out as his eyes, nearly black with pain and shock stared into hers.

His hand tightened on her wrist as he blinked at her, perspiration covering his body as the air around them grew thick with tension. Heather shuddered as she watched him, wondering how in the hell he had remained sane with the strength of these nightmares haunting him.

"Sam." She reached out with her free hand to touch his face.

"No." He gripped her wrist, holding it away from him, staring back at her as though he wasn't certain why she was there, or what she wanted.

"You were having a nightmare." She swallowed tightly, licking her lips in nervous awareness of the sexual heat beginning to build in his expression.

She felt her breasts growing heavy, swelling as his gaze dropped to them. Her face flushed as her nipples hardened beneath his stare, feeling his interest even through the cool silk of her robe. Her body was flushed, her cunt heating, dampening further.

"Heather." His hands tightened on her wrists. "I'm sorry."

"Sam?" She watched the intent fill his expression, bleak and hot, desperate.

Sexual tension wrapped around them, and as her gaze flickered to his lap she watched his cock swelling, thickening before her eyes. She tried to pull her wrists from his grasp, suddenly nervous, uncertain. Sam was at his most dangerous after the nightmares, and though he had never been known to hurt Marly or Sarah when the nightmares raged within, she knew that his sexuality was at its peak then.

"I need you." His voice was hoarse, hungry, yet still shaded with horror.

"Sam," she gasped his name as he pulled her to the bed, releasing one of her wrists only long enough to transfer it to the other hand as he released the loose knot in her robe.

He jerked her across his lap and she fought for balance. The robe was nearly torn from her as he reached to the nightstand, fumbling with a drawer as she fought to move away from him.

"No." His hand pressed against her lower back. "Stay still. For God's sake, stay still, Heather. Please."

She struggled against him, not frightened, yet unwilling to just submit to whatever he needed. Everyone submitted to what Sam needed. They pampered and coddled him, and tried to ease memories and nightmares that only grew as the years went by.

Heather refused to pamper, or to submit. She knew that taking him wouldn't be easy. She knew what he wanted, what he needed, and knew the rough ride she would receive in the bargain. But she was determined to break the rage growing in his soul. If she had to fight him to do it, then by God, she would fight.

She pushed against the bed, struggling to come to her knees, when his hand landed on the cheek of her rear. She stilled in shock. Not in shock that he had done it, in shock at the flash of pleasure that struck her sharper than his hand.

"Stay still." He moved, flipping her to her stomach on the bed.

Before she could struggle away, do more than bring her knees up, he was there. His hands gripped her wrists, stretching them out until he could restrain first one, then the other to the heavy posts of his bed with the leather restraints he had obviously brought back to his room.

The long straps with their wrist cuffs were secured quickly, her strangled screams of outrage doing little to deter him as he moved to her feet. Excitement raced through her body, though she fought him, kicking out at him, fighting to keep him from restraining her legs as well. She wouldn't submit. She wouldn't give in. Despite her halfhearted struggles, he managed to clip the leather restraints on her ankles and attach them to the footboard posts.

Then his hand went between her thighs. She cried out as his fingers slid through the folds of her pussy, gathering the thick cream that flowed from her vagina. Proof that she was aroused; that what he was doing was more exciting than anything she had known in her life.

There was only enough slack in the straps that restrained her ankles to allow her to lift her hips. She pressed closer to the mattress though, struggling to evade his fingers as she heard his breathing, harsh and heavy behind her.

"I told you, stay away after the nightmares, Heather." His voice was broken, gasping as he bent over her. "I warned you, and you came anyway."

"Let me go, Sam." She jerked as she felt his cock nudge between her thighs. "You won't get what you want this way."

"Won't I?" His lips were at her ear, his breathing heavy, hot as they moved to her neck.

She fought the insidious pleasure as he kissed the sensitive flesh between her shoulder and her neck.

"I need you." He licked her skin, his hand smoothing up her side, caressing the curves of her breasts. "I need you, Heather. More than you know."

Her eyes followed his arm as he reached to the side of her, widening as he grabbed the tube of lubrication from the bed table.

"Sam." She fought the restraints then, knowing what was coming, suddenly nervous, wary of her ability to accept the invasion.

As he moved back, his free hand slid over her back, the curve of her ass, then inward, closer, moving inexorably toward the entrance to her anus.

\* \* \* \* \*

Sam was riding the edge of sanity and he knew it. As always, the nightmares, foggy and uncertain, left him grasping, fighting for something to hold onto, something to fight back the demons haunting him. And suddenly, in the midst of the nightmare, there was Heather. Smelling of romance and desire, soft and satin, warm, tempting him further than his fragile control could bear.

He stared down at her, watching her ass flex as she fought the restraints, hearing her whispered cries, knowing arousal filled them. He could smell her heat like a midnight rain, feel it flowing from her tight little pussy below. But he needed more right now. He needed something darker, more erotic, an acceptance, a submission that came from only one act.

He flipped open the cap of the lubrication and smeared a large amount across his fingers. Then with his other hand separated the cheeks of her ass as he widened his knees, forcing them under her thighs, forcing her to lift the soft curves of her rear closer to him.

He stared at the little entrance in surprise. It was reddened, loosened marginally, showing evidence of having recently been stretched for more than a few slight seconds. She had been wearing a plug. He swallowed tightly. Dear God, had she worn it earlier and he hadn't noticed?

He watched, entranced, as his own fingers moved for the flexing entrance.

"Sam…" Her wail was one of reluctant arousal as the cooling gel touched the heated area.

"So pretty." His own voice was guttural, his lust barely leashed as he fought to prepare her with gentleness.

Had she moved away from him, had she done anything other than moan his name and press back against his invading fingers, then he could have stopped, could have halted the spiraling loss of control surging through him.

But he could only watch, tortured, as he pressed two fingers against the little rosebud. It opened, spreading reluctantly as she bucked against him as though to draw away, gasping, crying out his name.

His cock was thick, hard, throbbing in increased demand as she writhed beneath his touch.

"No, don't fight me." He followed her movements, watching, his mouth watering as his fingers sank into the tight—so fucking tight—depths of her anus.

She clenched on him, her muscles struggling to accept the intrusion as he pulled back then pressed deeper. She thrashed, tightening on him, but taking him as he worked his fingers inside the searing heat of her ass.

With his other hand, he clumsily smeared more of the lubricant from the tube over the thick length of his cock. When a long line of the thick, cool gel had been applied, he tossed the tube aside. He stroked the gel over his cock as he watched, never taking his eyes from the sight of her tender back entrance opening around his fingers as he slowly fucked her with them.

"Sam, you're killing me."

She was panting for breath, her voice weak with arousal and stunning desire. She wanted him, wanted his possession. Just him. This wasn't Marly or Sarah, who took him because of his brothers' needs; this was Heather, who took him because of her own.

"Feel how good it is, Heather," he whispered desperately. "Forbidden and hot, with just a touch of pain, just enough bite to let you know you're alive, that you need." He pushed his fingers deeper, watching as she accepted him, her body jerking as the pleasure rippled over it.

As he pulled back, he added a third finger. She cried out as he worked them inside her. Her ass tightened and he groaned, imagining the bite of the muscles around his cock as he took her. She jerked as though to move away from him, her hips thrashing, her thighs quivering as she fought him. But she took him. He fucked her slow and easy with his fingers, imagining, knowing the exquisite pleasure to come.

Assured that she was ready, knowing if he had to wait a moment longer he would lose all sense of control, he pulled his fingers back, easing from her as his hands gripped her hips, holding her still as he knelt behind her.

"I need this," he growled. "First this, Heather." He cock nudged at her prepared opening.

"Why?" she cried out. "Tell me why, Sam."

He shook his head, fighting the answer. He couldn't answer her, couldn't put the need to words. He watched instead. Watched as his erection pressed against the little hole, forcing it to flower open, to stretch to take the bulging head.

"Sam." The fear in her voice suddenly stopped him. "Sam, please don't hurt me."

Oh God, no. No, don't hurt me... Sam shook his head, fighting the twisting nightmares that fought to release.

He stared at her, saw her tight hole easing open, stretching around him.

"I won't hurt you," he gasped. He couldn't hurt her. If he hurt her, what was the point? He had to replace the horrific memories with pleasure, only then did they ease. Only then did he regain the control he needed so desperately.

"Sam, why?" She opened further, and Sam grimaced as half the head buried inside her. She was hot, so damned hot and tight already that all he wanted to do was plow as deep and hard inside her as he could. The scars on the head and shaft of his cock did little to dim the pleasure to be found in a hot, tight anus. The bite of the tight muscles on his flesh was exquisite, the sensations too shockingly arousing to be denied.

"Stop, baby." He gripped her hip as she tried to jerk from him again. "Please, please, Heather. Stay still."

"Why?" She managed to jerk to the side, escaping the invasion he had started.

"No." He jerked her back, held her still as he pressed forward again. "God dammit, Heather, you want it. I know you do."

"I want to know why." Her back bowed as he pushed the flared head of his cock inside her ass with a desperate move of his hips.

He gritted his teeth, feeling his control slipping.

"Stop." He smacked her ass as she jerked again, nearly tearing him free. He watched her muscles flex from the small stinging caress, heard her gasp of pleasure. "Please God, Heather. Please. Take the pleasure, baby. Take it, so I can forget the pain."

The words that left his mouth penetrated his brain. The shock of it destroyed any semblance of control he might have possessed. A ragged cry, fraught with pain and rage, billowed from his chest as he thrust inside her anus. Hard and deep. The instant heat, like fire on his cock, tightening around him, stroking him as she screamed out beneath him, fighting to accept the full, thick length of the cock buried in her tender depths.

Her back bowed, her head thrashing as the long tendrils of her hair rippled over her back.

"Sam…" He knew that husky sound, vibrant with the shocking pleasure/pain of his entrance.

Dark, primitive lust shot through his veins as she took him. Her scream was one of intense arousal. The point where everything is heightened, mingling and searing in its heat. He couldn't stop, couldn't contain himself or his need. He drew back, watching as his cock eased from her tightly stretched hole then thrust back hard and deep. Over and over. He watched her flesh stretch for him, heard her cries echoing around him and felt heaven and hell in her acceptance.

He bent over her then; reason lost, only pleasure, only the white-hot heat of her ass gripping his cock meant anything. His hips moved as he powered his erection inside her, pushing through sensitive tissue, feeling it stretch, tighten to bite at the invader taking it so ruthlessly.

He was groaning as his thrusts became harder, quicker. He could hear Heather screaming beneath him, calling his name, begging, pushing back to him as he fucked her with hard, furious strokes. He throbbed, pulsed. Hurriedly he tucked his hand beneath her hips, his trembling fingers finding the hard, swollen knot of her clit as he began to deepen his strokes.

Her hips were jerking, fucking back at him as the soft syrup that flowed from her pussy coated his fingers and her clit. She was taking him, loving it, accepting it. Lust clawed at his loins then, his scrotum tightening with the excitement, and as he stroked Heather's clit, he felt the climax that tore unexpectedly through her body.

A howl ripped from his throat as he gripped her hips, laid over her and began to fuck her with hard driving strokes. He couldn't stop, couldn't control the driving lust as it boiled through his cock. When his climax came, it was like white-hot death. Streaks of lightning tore through his cock, his body, as he buried himself one last time in the tight depths of her anus and felt his seed explode from the tip of his erection.

Explosive pulse after pulse tore through his body as her anus tightened around him with each jetting release. Her muscles bit at his cock, milked it, sucked the seed from him until he could only lay against her, jerking at each whip of fiery pleasure, gasping for breath, and realizing each gasp came out as her name.

Long moments later he found the strength to draw back, to watch in dazed pleasure as his still hard cock pulled out of her tender, well-fucked ass. The little hole was coated with his cream now. Her body holding it inside her, accepting him, a part of him held within her, at least for now.

She lay still against the mattress, her breathing labored, her small body quivering as he removed the wrist and ankle cuffs that had held her to the bed. His hands caressed the fragile wrists, stroking the skin that the padded cuffs had held prisoner. They were reddened slightly, proof that she had fought the restraints, fought to be free. Free of him? Or free to touch him? Bitterness seared his soul as he realized he was afraid to know the answer.

As she lay there, he moved to the bathroom, wetting a washrag and cleaning himself before wetting another and moving back into the bedroom.

She still lay there, perspiration coating her body as he sat beside her. His hands were gentle as he cleaned her, his heart aching in regret as he glimpsed the slight bruises that now marred the cheeks of her rear, and her slender hips.

He shook his head, fighting the rage that seemed to only build now. He rose from the bed, jerked his sweat pants on and rushed from the room. God help him, he'd hurt her. He had to have hurt her.

"Sam." Her surprised, slightly angry voice followed him from the room. The husky confusion that filled his name called to him, drawing him to turn back, to return to her. But he couldn't. He couldn't face her, couldn't face the possibility of hatred, the possibility that he had finally stepped over a line that had terrified him for years.

Voices pounded in his head, the remembered scent of blood washing over him as his fists clenched and remnants of terror bit at the edges of his mind. He raced down the stairs, threw open the door and ignored the surprised voice of the bodyguard as he made his way into the night.

# Chapter Sixteen

"Son of a bitch." Heather came to her feet, jerking her robe from the floor and pushing her arms through it quickly as she heard the front door slam close. "I'll kill him. I swear to God, this time I'll just kill him myself."

Anger surged through her, mixing with an arousal so desperate, so hot, that she could feel the juices from her cunt trickling to her thighs. He had left her again. Left her body raging, on fire, so damned hot she felt as though her pussy was blistered from the need.

She rushed for her bedroom, grabbed the gun from her dresser and then rushed out the door. She gritted her teeth as she met Cade and Brock in the hallway, barely dressed, their expressions concerned as they headed for the stairs.

"Heather." Cade caught her arm as she rushed past him. "What the hell happened?"

His face was lined with grief, with pain. In his eyes she saw the same shadows, bleak and dark, that filled Sam's.

"He doesn't need you," she snapped, knowing what usually came after the nightmares, the lust and brittle pain of the three men forming, coming together, fighting to find ease in the body of their women. Together. Always together, as though in the sharing of the lust, they could ease the memories of the pain.

"You know better than that, Heather." Marly stood in the bedroom doorway, watching as Heather faced off with the two brothers. "You've seen enough to realize what he does need."

"No." Her hand sliced through the air as she tore away from Cade. "He doesn't need your protection. He's not a child."

"Dammit to fucking hell, you don't know what you're doing." Cade's voice was desperate, his expression taut, fierce as he watched her.

"Stop trying to protect him, Cade." Heather faced off with the older man, seeing so much of Sam in him that her arousal only grew. She knew very damned well what they believed would ease the horror that gripped Sam. Knew what they wanted and how it would happen. But she would be damned if it would happen tonight. "Your protection of him is killing him, can't you see that?" Her voice rose as she fought to make him understand. To make all of them understand. "You're babying him, giving him what he needs to hide from whatever is ripping him apart. He has to face it, and he needs to face it now, before that fucking stalker gets any closer to him than he already has."

Cade paled. She watched, surprised, suddenly terrified as he lost the color in his face and denial filled his expression.

"Listen to me." He grabbed her arm again, hauling her close as he stared down at her, his gaze fierce, searing in its demand. "You don't want this, Heather. You don't want him to remember, do you understand me? Sam doesn't fucking remember the details. He dreams of it, he knows it happened, but he doesn't remember it, and by God I won't let you force him to."

Heather's eyes widened as her own fury flamed. "What in the hell makes you think he can survive like this, Cade?" she yelled up at him, jerking back, tearing her arm from his grip. "How much longer do you think he can stand the poison that's only growing in his mind? For God's sake, surely you know better than to try to suppress those memories?"

But they hadn't known better. She saw it on Cade and Brock's faces, just as she saw the confusion on Marly and Sarah's.

"My God," she whispered. "You've encouraged it. All these years, you've helped him hide. Helped that monster to fester in his mind like a fucking cancer."

Disbelief washed over her. She shook her head, backing away from them, terrified now that Sam faced something he would never survive. He had hidden from the pain for over a decade. Fought the memories, and the healing he needed to make sense of the life he lived now. That was why he always seemed so bitter, so unable to accept that Marly or Sarah could find pleasure in the embrace of the three men.

"What have you done?" She raised a hand to her forehead, shaking her head as she stared from Cade to Brock, then to Marly. "What have they done to him, Marly?"

Compassion and concern marked the other woman's sleepy features.

"Whatever it was, Heather, it was done to protect him when he needed protection. I don't doubt that."

"Marly," she whispered. "He had to tie me down. He had to restrain me to assure himself that he wouldn't hurt me." She was trembling with her anger, with her own pain. "He couldn't even take me normally. He had to fuck my ass to assure himself that he controlled me, that he controlled himself. Is that fucking protection?"

She was trembling with the implications of what Sam faced now. Pain surged through her body, overwhelming her desire, overwhelming her senses. How had he born the pain she knew he had faced? How had he had ever stayed sane all these years, fighting the memories, fighting whatever truth lay within his memories? A truth slowly destroying him now.

"Sam won't hurt you…" Brock shook his head. "We'll find him…"

"The hell you will." She gripped the gun in her hand tighter. "You go after him and I'll shoot you myself." Her throat felt raw from the emotion that seared it, roughened her voice and shook her body.

"Like hell." Cade threw her a bitter look before his muscles tightened and he began to stalk to the stairs.

"I don't think so." Before he could stop her, before Heather was aware of her own intentions, she had stepped in front of him, bringing her body flush against his, the muzzle of her gun pressing hard and commanding beneath his jaw.

Heather didn't know who was more surprised by the action, herself or the men. Cade stared down at her with arrogant fury, his eyes narrowed, his body tight and furious as Marly cried out behind him.

"You're playing a very dangerous game," he warned her darkly, his cock tightening against the flat plane of her stomach. "A very dangerous game, Heather."

She snarled in his face. "He's mine, Cade. All mine, and I'll be goddamned if I'll let you help him hide any longer. He's of no fucking use to me handicapped emotionally. And he's no use to you, either."

His eyes narrowed. "Go after him then," he challenged her roughly. "Go on, Heather. See if you can stand his pain. See if your heart can take what we've fought so hard to ease for him. And I promise you, the day will come when you'll pay for holding a gun on me."

The threat may have carried more weight if his cock wasn't so thick and so hard against her abdomen. She tilted her lips in what she felt was a smile of savage mockery.

"You know, Marly," Heather sneered contemptuously. "Only an August could have a hard-on with a gun pressed under his jaw. Take your lover and fuck him, before I have to kill him."

She jumped back from him then, turning on her heel and rushing the short distance to the stairs. She was fed up with August men, August pride and August demons. To her back teeth, she had had enough. Sam had done nothing but tease her past any woman's limits of control for nearly two years now. Taking her to the edge, only to deny her the release she knew was waiting just moments away from wherever he stopped.

If she had to hold the fucking gun to his throat, he was going to fuck her and do it right. She was damned tired of his self-pity and his dark demons, and she was determined to force him past them. The brothers might see their protection as a form of easing the pain for Sam, but she saw differently. She saw the man fighting to survive, to make sense of his needs, his desires. A man who loved those around him, yet had no idea how to show it.

A man who loved her, and refused to admit it. She'd be damned if she would let him deny it any longer.

* * * * *

The front door slammed behind her. "Where is he?" Rick was on the porch, agitation tightening every line in his body as he swung around to her.

"You two are driving me fucking crazy," he bit out. "What the hell is going on?"

She speared him a furious look. "I'm going to save the stalker the trouble and kill the bastard myself. Right after I fuck his brains out. Now tell me where he went."

Rick eased back as the hand that carried her gun twitched.

"Heather." He cleared his throat, but she still caught the edge of humor in his voice. "Maybe you should give me the gun first."

"Where. Is. He." Her teeth were gritted, fury and lust surging in equal parts through her body.

Rick blew out a hard breath. "Dammit, Heather, just don't kill the dumb bastard. We don't get paid if he dies."

"Where?" She was tired of arguing with stubborn men.

"He headed for the barn. He's barefoot though, so I don't expect him to take a horse out. He dared anyone to follow him, Heather. And he looked mean enough to make it stick."

"He's trouble looking to happen," she snorted furiously. "Expect anything."

She stepped from the porch.

"Uh, Heather, you're a bit underdressed," Rick pointed out.

"Overdressed," she snarled. "But I'll take care of that when I find him."

Thankfully, she had thought to slip her feet into the thin ballet-style house slippers that matched her robe. The thin rubber soles protected her feet from the concrete of the walkway and the rough dirt area in front of the barn and stables. She stalked across the distance, determined to finish this once and for all. She was ready to pack up and leave the ranch for good. Sick to death of the conspiracy and veil of secrecy that bound the brothers together.

They could deal with their pasts however they pleased. She wasn't a fainting miss. Hell, she had been intrigued by Sam and his brothers from the beginning. But it was Sam that set her body on fire. Sam that kept her in such a state of lustful preparation that she couldn't keep her mind on her job, or her own protection, let alone his. It was a dangerous line she was treading.

She entered the interior of the barn, stopping as she saw the dim light behind a stack of hay toward the back. She followed him, listening carefully to the shuffle of hay, a muffled curse. She moved purposely around the high bales then stared at him coldly as he stared up at her from the rough bed he had made in the thick loose hay behind it.

A battery-powered lantern lit the area. A thick blanket was spread over the rough dried grasses, perfectly formed to make a comfortable bed.

"Pouting?" she sneered as she watched him angrily.

She could feel every cell in her body burning, demanding. She would be damned if she would pamper to his stubbornness or continue to let him drive her any crazier than he already had.

"Go back to the house, Heather." He frowned at her fiercely, and yeah, he looked mean enough to make it stick, but by God if she didn't feel a whole lot meaner right now.

"Take those sweat pants off." She pushed the words through gritted teeth, her body so hot, so desperate for release she could barely think coherently.

His dark brows arched in surprise, his gaze flickering to the gun in her hand. Heather didn't give him time to comment further, or to refuse her. Training could be handy though, she thought, as she moved in quickly. Before he could do more than gasp, she was straddling his tight abdomen, her wet pussy flush against his clenching muscles, the gun muzzle beneath his chin, much as it had been Cade's. She was damned near mad enough to pull the trigger, and the amusement that suddenly lit his eyes did nothing to cool her down.

"Take the sweat pants off," she gritted out.

"Do you have the safety on?" he asked her, arching his brow as his hips lifted, his hands moved.

"What safety?" she questioned him harshly, hissing out a hard breath as his abdomen tightened further, rippled beneath her swollen clit.

"You're playing with fire," he warned her as he slid the sweat pants away from his hips then worked his legs until she knew the pants were separate from his hard body.

"I'm so damned hot I am the freaking fire," she groaned, swallowing tightly as she edged back until she felt the naked tip of his engorged cock nudge between the cleft of her ass.

"Heather." His hands caught the rounded curves of her butt as she wiggled against the engorged head of his erection. "Baby, please." His voice stopped her.

She could feel the juices of her pussy leaking onto his tight abdomen, his cock nudging at her. She stilled, staring down at him, dying to shift, to bring his thick flesh in line with her hungry cunt.

As her gaze cleared, she saw the gun tucked into his jaw, the ragged emotion on his face. Dear God, what was she doing? She whimpered, lowering the weapon then tossing it to the side.

"You've driven me to rape," she told him angrily, her hands bracing on his chest. "I swear to God, Sam, if you don't put out this fire…"

"Heather." One hand lifted from her rear, his fingers gently tucking back the strands of her hair as he cupped her cheek.

His expression was somber, though his eyes were lit with a lust that flamed in the blue-gray depths.

"Not like this," he whispered, his hand trembling. "I'll hurt you…God damn!"

She moved, not wanting to hear any more protestations, no more apologies. She pressed down on the thick shaft, taking the bulging head, feeling it split through the entrance of her vagina, stretching her, sinking into her as her muscles trembled in protest.

She stilled to adjust then watched in amazement as his eyes darkened, his expression transforming. His eyelids lowered as an expression of pleasure, sensual, lustful and all consuming, washed over his face.

"Damn," he growled, his fingers tangling in her hair, the other hand gripping her hip. "You're tight, Heather. So fucking tight…"

Only the thick tip was buried inside her, but Heather could feel her muscles gloving it, milking at it, fighting to draw him in. She needed him hard and deep, needed to feel the little bite of pleasure/pain that would send her soaring into ecstasy.

She cried as he moved then. A smooth display of power as he shifted, rolling her to her back, and never once losing the penetration of her body. She was beneath him, staring up at him as he rose between her thighs, his knees spreading her, opening her to him as he stared down at where his flesh split her cunt open.

"I warned you," he whispered. "I tried to, Heather. Tried to protect you." He shook his head, grimacing as his cock pulsed inside her.

"I don't need you to protect me, I need you to fuck me. Now, Sam."

Her breath rushed from her throat as his cock slammed inside her pussy. Every hard, hot, thick—oh God, so thick—inch, tore through the small channel that had never known an invasion other than the slender vibrators she used irregularly.

Every muscle in her body screamed in protest. Her head thrashed, her hips bucking against him as he ground his pelvis into the swollen knot of her clit.

"You're tight, Heather." His voice rumbled from his throat as he stilled inside her. "So tight I can feel your pussy sucking at every inch of my cock."

His hand smoothed up her stomach, her ribs, his hands finally cupping her breasts as his fingers gripped the hard nipples that peaked them. Heather was dazed, fighting the knowledge that only a slender thread separated pleasure and pain, and at the moment Sam's cock had her held precariously upon it.

She could feel her vagina clenching on him. To force him out, or force him to stay? Each ripple around his thick flesh was a sensuous bite of sensation that became nearly orgasmic as he ground himself deeper inside her.

"Sam." Her head thrashed against the blanket as he pushed his knees closer together beneath her thighs, angling her harder onto the thick spear piercing her tender flesh.

"Do you like it, Heather?" he whispered sensually. "Your cunt's so tight it's almost painful on my cock. Burning me, Heather. Your hot, wet pussy is burning me alive."

She whimpered in protest as she felt him moving back then. Her hands gripped his arms; his fingers tightened on her nipples. Her eyes flew open, staring into his face again as he massaged the little peaks firmly. Fire bit at her nipples, agony resounded through her vagina as he drew back until once again only the head of his cock penetrated her.

His face was taut, his eyes blazing as he stared down at where his flesh met hers. "You're so wet for me, Heather." He sounded amazed, as though he had never expected her to need him as desperately as he needed her.

"Sam, please." She arched to him, trying to press his cock deeper into the heated depths of her vagina. She was on fire, so achy, so desperate for an end to the incredible arousal that she felt like howling out her demand.

"Easy." His hand pressed against her abdomen. "Easy, Heather, just lay there, baby. Just lay there and let me show you how much I've wanted this sweet little body of yours."

He pressed in, grimacing as she stretched around him. Heather's thighs trembled, ached as she fought to take him deeper, harder.

"Harder," she whispered. "Harder now, Sam."

"Shh, baby." His hand moved from her breasts, cupping her hips as he controlled the desperate thrusts against him. "Slow and easy, baby."

He began to move inside her, long slow thrusts that pushed her apart, stretched her with exquisite patience. Her muscles protested the thick intrusion as much as they greeted it. Nerve endings she had never known she possessed screamed out in sensation.

She felt perspiration soak her flesh, felt her cunt spasm around his erection, spilling more of the slick juices that lubricated the tight channel for his invasion. Over and over. Not even giving her the full length, but torturing her with the half thrusts that pierced her vaginal tissue, pressing it apart, teasing her with the pleasure/pain, the threat of the hard brutal thrust that she knew she needed to send her over the edge.

And Heather wasn't willing to be tortured. Months, agonizing arousing months of waiting were going to come to an end. Her heels locked around his lower back, giving her the purchase she needed to thrust herself onto the slow impalement.

She cried out as he sank to the hilt, a curse blistering from his lips as his hands tightened on her hips.

"Don't," he growled. "Dammit, Heather."

She ground herself against him, sensation flaying her body, piercing her womb as she felt her release building inside her.

"Stop." He came over her then, holding her still, his hands gripping hers, holding them to the blanket as his hips pressed deep and hard against her, immobilizing hers.

"Listen to me, Heather. My control is hanging by a thread, dammit. Don't make me hurt you."

"If you don't fuck me I'm going to shoot you," she cried out desperately, clamping her vaginal muscles on him, milking him, sucking him in deeper.

Heather felt his muscles bunch, his hands tighten on her hips as a ragged cry was torn from his throat. Her eyes widened as he began to move, a throttled scream ripping from her as he drew back and began to pummel her body with hard, driving strokes.

He was thick. So fucking thick and hard that he tore through her untried cunt with each hard, brutal thrust. But it wasn't pain, it was a pleasure mixed with a hard bite, the forceful dominance, the hard uncontrolled thrusts that drove her into her first orgasm.

Her body tightened, her cunt spasmed and she was thrown through the release with such violence, such shattering sensation that she could only whimper, her nails biting into his shoulders, her body jerking, shuddering as the whiplash of sensation ripped through her womb, her breasts, her cunt, drenching them both with the excess fluid that rushed through her tight channel.

Tara had assured her that the first time didn't last long for men. That even an hour later, the second time, that stamina wasn't always their strong suit. She collapsed beneath Sam, expecting an end. Expecting him to tighten, to spill his seed inside her. But he didn't.

He gripped her hips harder, groaning against her ear as her cunt tightened further on his pistoning erection. Hard thrusts into the swollen flesh. Muscles tightened from her orgasm were being stroked steadily, harshly, no quarter given to the sensitivity that flared within them.

"Sam...Sam..." She chanted his name, desperate now as she felt the sensation building again, harder, deeper, nearly painful in its intensity.

She thrashed beneath him, fighting to escape, to pull away from the intensity of feeling, the pleasure that was too close to pain, the explosion she knew would destroy her, remake her, bind her to him in a way she would never escape.

"No!" She screamed out the word, pushing at his shoulders, desperate to escape him, to escape the binding that terrified her. She loved him, but God help her, this she couldn't handle.

"Don't you fight me!" His voice was a growl, a primitive, feral sound as she fought beneath him. "No, damn you. No, don't you fight me."

She fought, bucking against his body, clawing at his hands, desperate to escape the ethereal, unknown emotion as well as the violent pleasure building inside her.

"Damn you!" He threw himself back, and for a moment, just a moment, she was free.

Until he flipped her over on her stomach, gripping her legs between his as his hands gripped her hips, lifting her. He mounted her, thrusting into her hard and fast as her juices gushed between them.

"Sam," she screamed his name as she fought, but there was no release. Her cunt shuddered, tightened on him further, burned and pulsed, and before she could control the sensation, it tore through her with a force that pierced her soul.

"Yes," he cried out as she tightened on him further, the blast of her release renewing, ripping over her over and over again as her pussy exploded around him.

The sound of wet, sucking flesh filled the silence of the barn as his balls slapped at her swollen clit, firing it, exploding it in time to the contractions ripping apart her vagina. The sensitivity built, but the thrusts never diminished. His cock seemed to swell thicker, harder inside her, his brutal strokes driving her higher. Then his hand slid along her rear, spread her cheeks desperately and two fingers, slick from her vaginal juices pierced her ass.

Heather lost her sanity. There was no other way to describe the explosion that ripped her apart. It hurt, the impalement of her tender anus. Not in a tearing brutal way, but in a way that drove the pleasure higher, tightened her cunt, speared through her mind, and destroyed her sense of self. She couldn't stop the ragged cry that wailed from her throat, or the tearing explosions in her womb.

Behind her, Sam pushed his fingers deeper, thrust into her cunt, hard, fast. Once. Twice. His cry joined hers as she felt his semen jet hard and hot inside her gripping, milking pussy. It threw her higher, triggered the explosion again until her body was racked by the brutal shudder, her thighs soaked from the hard spray of her own cream deep inside her quaking flesh.

She collapsed. His cock was still throbbing inside her, his spurting release filling her, spilling from her body as his fingers jerked inside her anus. She shuddered again, the pleasure never ending, echoing through her body until she felt herself drift. Drift. Exhaustion closed over her. Desperate emotion, brutal satisfaction taking the last edge of consciousness and freeing her from the confusion as well as the knowledge. The knowledge that she would never be free now. That forever, Sam would hold her soul.

# Chapter Seventeen

"She fights it, like Marly does." Cade's voice didn't surprise Sam as he pulled from Heather's exhausted body, his hand running over the perfect curve of her ass as he did so.

He flipped her robe over her nude body, knowing she would be hurt, angry, if he allowed Cade to see her, knowing he was looking. He had suspected that one of his brothers was behind him. He always knew. He always had known. Just as they knew when he was watching, taking in the sensuality of whatever act they were engaged in, soaking in the knowledge that there was no jealousy, no greed where the other was concerned.

"I knew she would." He kept his voice quiet as he rose to his feet, snagging his sweats and pushing his legs into them. "I always knew she would."

She was independent, fiery. There was nothing like Heather in full rage. When she had come over his body, the muzzle of that damned gun almost cutting off his oxygen, he had swelled thicker, harder than he could ever remember being. She was tired of waiting, tired of wanting, and her aggression had set his own aflame.

He pushed his fingers through his hair before he collapsed on the hay beside her. He propped his back against a bale of hay and regarded her silently as Cade lowered himself at the bottom of the makeshift bed and stared back at Sam.

"Feeling better?" His voice was carefully calm.

"I'm fine, Cade." He shrugged; he wasn't about to tell Cade about the nightmares, the blood and the death.

*I did it, Sam! I killed him!* Sam looked at Cade's hands. He didn't remember seeing blood on them. But he remembered seeing the blood, thick and brilliant, staining his own.

He stilled the tremor that wanted to wash over his body. He was exhausted, drained emotionally and physically, the aggression that had raged through his body relayed through his lust and his need for Heather.

He met Cade's penetrating look and gave his brother the crooked smile he knew Cade needed. He was good at that, he thought bitterly. Allaying the fears of his brothers, easing their consciences, their own demons.

Cade flicked a look at Heather. "She's a hard one to figure." He nodded at her. "She put a gun under my chin tonight, Sam. I wouldn't want to piss her off too often."

Sam grunted and looked around. He found the gun beside her shoulder and lifted it gingerly.

"Son of a bitch," he breathed out softly as he thumbed the safety over. "She had it cocked and ready, too. She had the damned thing under my chin about the same time she was working her cunt on me." He shook his head and laid the gun carefully out of the way.

Cade's face reflected his own surprise then he shook his head, his lips tilting in a grin. "She said only an August would have a hard-on with a gun under his chin. Maybe she was right."

"Yeah." Sam tried to laugh, he wanted to, but the laughter wouldn't come.

He watched Cade closely, seeing the strain on his brother's face, the worry in his eyes.

"Sam?" Cade questioned him softly.

Sam bit back an oath. His brothers had spent twelve years trying to protect him, to ease the pain, the horror of what had happened to them all in that dirty basement. His own memories of it were distant, as though it had been a dream, but lately,

lately they had been clearer, returning with a vengeance and magnified by the scent of death.

"What happened that night? The night he died." He hadn't meant to say the words but they rumbled from his chest as his body tightened at the injustice of reminding Cade of those horrific days.

He watched Cade draw within himself. His eyes iced, growing cold, his expression emotionless.

"It's better forgotten, Sam," he bit out. "I told you that."

Sam laid his head back against the hay, watching Cade, his heart breaking for them all.

"But it's not forgotten," he said softly. "We still wake up shaking from the nightmares, and we never talk about them. We punish the women who love us enough to tolerate our perversions, and still, we never talk about it. Neither of you have even asked me why the bastard hated me so much. Or why he punished you along with me."

"There's no sense in discussing it," Cade growled, moving restlessly to his feet. "Let it go, Sam."

"No, Cade." He stood as well, facing his brother over the helpless, naked form of the lover he had just taken. The lover he would eventually share. The need was there, rising within him, to see Heather between the three of them, screaming in pleasure, begging for them. For all of them. "We have to discuss it. I'm remembering things..."

"Forget it." Cade shook his head desperately. "Whatever you're trying to remember Sam, forget it. It's over."

The tone of voice was well remembered. It brooked no refusal, no argument. But Sam wasn't a kid anymore, and Cade was no longer the final word in any of their lives. In a flash he realized how he and Brock had given Cade what he needed at that time. Control. They followed his lead, did as he said, and let him guide them through the horrific days after the death of the monster. He had killed for them, hadn't he? He had, with his bare fists, defended himself against the knife-wielding psychopath who had held them helpless. But Cade's hands weren't scarred. Cade's weren't, but Sam's were.

"It's not over, Cade." He stared his brother in the eye, seeing the pain, the shame that seared the other man's soul. "It's not over, because we still haven't accepted it."

"Wrong." Cade's voice was harsh, tempered with steel, hot with fury. "You're wrong, Sam. The bastard is dead and we're still alive, so it's over."

"And some fucking maniac is trying to destroy it all again." Sam's voice rose with his own anger, his own pain. "Every fucking bit of it, Cade. He'll take it all away from us if he can, and if he's caught, he'll tell the world. He'll tell them how we were held, how we were raped and how we were forced to fuck each other, goddammit. We can't hide from it anymore."

He watched Cade's face pale as fury blackened his gaze. Cade's fists clenched at his as sides and he snarled with a violence Sam hadn't seen in him in years.

"Then I'll fucking kill him when he's caught," he snapped furiously. "Because I'll be damned if I'll see us destroyed any further."

Shock held Sam speechless for long moments as he stared into Cade's eyes and saw the violence, the commitment to protecting all they had fought so hard to build within their lives.

"Why?" Sam asked him softly, unable to shake the feeling that there was more, so much more to what Cade was protecting. "It was in self-defense. It's been twelve years, and it would be a crazy man's word against ours. Why kill him? Why not face it ourselves, Cade, and deal with it?"

"Because it's fucking over. Forget it, Sam. I killed him. I killed the dirty bastard, and he'll never take another breath again. Forget it."

*Forget it, Sam,* as he wiped his hands over Sam's, smearing the blood from them to his own and showing it to Sam. *I killed him, Sam. I did it. Forget it. Just forget it, Sam.*

Sam shook his head as the image snapped in front of his eyes. There, then gone, but not forgotten. He blinked. He thought he had remembered. Cade with his hands wrapped around the bastard's throat as he sliced at them with the scalpel, but it wasn't Cade, suddenly it was Sam. Then Cade. Then Sam.

"Fuck!" he snapped out, shaking his head to clear it of the dreamlike memories. "Just tell me what the fuck happened. Tell me, Cade, so I can remember."

"I killed him. And I'll do it again if I have to, Sam. I'll do whatever it takes to protect us this time. This time, I won't fail any of you." Cade's voice was a broken, ragged sound of pain as he turned and stalked from the barn.

"God damn." Sam turned, his fist plowing into the bale of hay behind him, the force so extreme that the bales trembled, shuddered as his hand bounced back.

His chest heaved with his breaths as he fought for control, fought to make sense of the foggy memories that assaulted him at will.

"The bastard will destroy us again," he whispered to himself, hearing his hoarse whisper as it settled in the air around him. "And once again, it's my fault. All my fault."

\* \* \* \* \*

Feigning sleep had never been one of Heather's strong suits. But she had done just that as she lay and listened to Cade and Sam's argument. After the older brother left, Sam's torn, ragged cry had her heart clenching in pain. The shadows in his eyes, the dark nightmares, it all made sense now. And as she lay there, drifting in exhaustion and worry, a horrifying suspicion began to bloom within her mind. She could feel the seeds of knowledge ripening, and she hated it. Hated the truth she knew was being hidden from the man she loved. A truth she didn't want to face herself.

Finally, after long moments, she heard him sigh and move. She almost jerked in surprise as he wrapped the robe around her then turned her over and picked her up in his arms. Strength and heat surrounded her. Safety. She was safe. She had never quite known this feeling in anyone's arms before, especially a man's. Men were generally intent on release from what she had seen from other relationships. Tenderness was merely a bribe to get them there, quickly forgotten when the end had been achieved.

But he was tender. Careful to hide her nakedness, to hold her in arms that lacked the rough dominance of his sexual embrace. Not that she would dare protest that embrace. Despite the exhaustion and the lingering aches in her body, the pleasure had been more than worth it. He had taken her higher than she had ever dreamed she could go. Pushed her to limits she would have sworn she didn't possess. And now, he was tender.

If she had the strength she would have blushed when she felt Sam step up to the porch and heard Rick's muttered curse as the front door opened. Sam ignored him and strode quickly through the house and up the stairs. Within seconds he was opening a door and closing it quietly behind him.

Surprise rushed through her as she opened her eyes lazily and recognized her own room. She stared up at Sam as he tucked the blankets over her and stood looking down at her. His eyes were still shadowed, his face drawn into lines of somber regret.

"Sam?" She whispered his name, confused now.

"I'm sorry." He sat beside her slowly, a sigh shuddering from his body as he stared down at the floor.

"For what?" She kept her voice quiet, fought to keep him with her.

He raised his head and breathed in deeply, though he still didn't look at her. He stared at the wall, seeing the past, or his own fears, she wondered. His profile was shadowed, his broad shoulders straight and tense, though she suspected the weight that dragged at them.

"For hurting you. For restraining you." He wiped his hands over his face and shook his head as his jaw clenched violently. "I'm as bad as the fucking monster that destroyed us, Heather."

She could feel the violence vibrating in the air around them. The restrained hunger, like a dark, powerful beat in her blood, still throbbed in his voice. She knew what the nightmares of the past did to these strong men. Had watched it for over a year. Sam would fight within himself until he restrained it as tightly as possible. He would put up the barriers at all costs, and he would try to smooth the worry or the fear that he felt he was causing.

"Sam." She sat up, desperate to touch him, to take away the bleak pain that resonated from him. To help him face the demons that were rising from within the lost memories.

"Don't touch me, Heather." He caught her hand, staring at her then, and the hard, slate gray gaze had her gasping in concern. She had never seen Sam's eyes so dark, so ridden with shadows.

He released her wrist carefully as he laid her hand on her thigh. Each move was carefully coordinated, the muscles in his hand and arm tense from the hold he had on whatever urges were driving him.

"Sam, tell me what to do," she said softly, fighting her tears, her need to comfort where she knew there was no hope of it.

He watched her silently, almost calculatingly. It was as though he were gauging her sincerity, her needs.

"Why did you stay here?" he finally asked, his voice rough. Angry. "Your life is in danger and you live with the knowledge that in accepting a relationship with me could mean accepting one with my brothers as well. Is that what you want, Heather?"

Fury pulsed in the air around him, a carefully contrived insult, Heather thought, delivered to her heart. She nearly flinched in response.

"Why are you hiding again?" she asked him instead, fighting to keep the hurt from her tone. "Every time I get close to you, Sam, you throw up the same barriers. You know, this was my first time with a man, rather than a vibrator. The least you could do is lay down beside me, maybe hold me for a while. Or have I just been relegated to a line in a little black book? Maybe under the header: August Plaything Wannabe?"

His eyes narrowed in surprise before he shook his head, a sarcastic snort of laughter coming from his throat.

"You want to be in there?" he asked her coolly. "I could put you in there, baby, if that's the position you're looking for. But you have a hell of a lot to learn before you're up to taking on all of us."

"Learn?" The inelegant snort was deliberately pulsing with sarcasm. "Really, Sam. What's there to learn? Say 'yes, sir' and 'no, sir' and 'up the ass please, sir?'"

His eyes narrowed further, his body shuddering once, hard as she watched him fight for control.

"You're dangerous to yourself," he sighed bitterly. "And I'll be damned if I'll sit here and listen to you bait me."

"Then leave." She lifted her hand, waving her fingers to the connecting door. "Marly and Sarah brought me some new toys today, so I don't even need you. That bunny promises to make men obsolete anyway."

His face flushed with sexual promise, though his eyes flared with anger.

"A Rabbit," he growled. "It's a fucking Rabbit."

"Bunny, rabbit, whatever." She shrugged. "I'm certain it will do everything but give me someone to cuddle up with, and I know where the electric blankets are kept if I get cold enough. So just run along to bed, hon. I'm sure me and Bugs will get along fine."

"Bugs?" His voice sounded strangled as she pushed her tangled hair back from her shoulders then leaned on her elbows as she watched him. She was aware that his eyes latched instantly on her upthrust breasts and hardened nipples. Arguing with him made her tingle. Her cunt, her nipples...hell, her toes. Every cell in her body seemed primed and ready and more than willing to take the rough, dominant touch he could give her.

"Oh really, Sam, who cares what I call it?" She shifted her legs beneath the corner of the blanket, causing it to fall away until it covered only her lower hips and mound.

She felt more than a little naughty as his jaw tensed, his body became tenser, harder, as his sweat pants tented with the heated length of his erection.

"Stop pushing me, Heather," he growled.

She allowed her fingers to play lightly over her abdomen.

"Pushing you?" His eyes followed her fingers as his fist clenched by her hip. "I told you to go ahead and run away, Sam. I have Bugs and something called a Snake. Plenty of company. Why would I need you?"

"You know, Heather, if I weren't very well aware of the fact that your ass couldn't take another pounding, I'd show you exactly what you're pushing me into," he growled as he came over her, dark, hungry, his eyes no longer bleak and barren, but filled with a sexual intensity that had her body heating in instant response.

"Excuses, excu—" The sound broke off as his lips covered hers.

Hard, greedy, his tongue pushed between them as he forced her back on the bed, his body coming over her, holding her still beneath him as his hand clasped her head.

Heather moaned in surprise, in pleasure, shocked at the hoarse, desperate quality of the sound. Her arms went around his shoulders, her fingers gripping the hard muscles as his tongue plunged into her mouth, his lips moving over hers with a lustful intensity that sent her blood pounding through her body.

No sooner than she was beginning to luxuriate in the feel of his muscles rippling over his broad back, his lips moving on hers with such naked need it tore through her soul, than he jerked her arms down, holding them flat to the bed as he tore his lips from hers.

His hips were between her thighs, his own spreading her wide as he stared down at her with dark, hungry eyes.

"Keep your smart mouth shut," he ordered harshly as she started to speak. "No toys. No Rabbit, no Snake, no fucking Pocket Rocket, no sex. Go to fucking sleep so I can."

He rolled off her, then in a smooth, powerful display of rippling muscle, pushed his sweat pants from his hips and threw them onto the floor. He jerked the blankets over her, pulled her roughly in his arms then leaned over and shut the light out.

Heather lay silently for long moments, listening to his heart thunder, feeling his muscles bunch, tense as he fought to keep from taking her. She gave him just enough time to almost, almost reach that comfort level where it would take another confrontation to fire his blood. Just enough time to think she would really sleep.

"Sam," she whispered. "What are the nightmares about?"

# Chapter Eighteen

Sometimes, some nights, a man's only friend was his whisky bottle. Unfortunately, night had long passed. The morning was edging bright and hot as Sam sat in the shade of the vine-covered lattice patio as he stared at the still pool. He was dressed in sweats and sneakers, his chest still bare, his fingers rubbing at a particular rough section of scars on his abdomen as he took another healthy drink of the liquor.

*Sam, what are the nightmares about?*

His eyes narrowed as he stared into the crystalline blue of the water. What were the nightmares about? He remembered the screams, the horror and the blood, but like his memories, the details seemed to be lost in a mist that his brain couldn't penetrate.

"Well, I can see you're back to your old habits." He turned quickly as Marly stepped onto the patio and took the chair in front of him.

He pushed his fingers roughly through his hair and sighed wearily. "Don't start, Munchkin. It's been a hell of a night."

"For all of us," she raged. "Cade had nightmares all night, Sam. What the hell happened in that barn?"

"He didn't fuck her." Pain resonated through his body. God, how much more could they hurt the women they loved before it all came apart around them.

Her eyes widened in surprise. "You think I'm upset because I think he fucked her?" She rolled her eyes then, shaking her head. "Hell, I would have gotten some sleep, Sam, if that had been the case. Instead I sat up and cried the better part of the night while the man I love tossed and turned in the grip of the horrible dreams the three of you share. What the hell is going on?"

He shook his head. "You don't want him to fuck her, Marly. You let him fuck Sarah, and I know it has to kill you."

"It does?" She leaned back in her chair, crossing her legs casually as she watched him. "Sarah isn't a threat to me, Sam. And neither is Heather. Do you think I don't know what happened in the kitchen? That Cade didn't tell me what happened after the fact?"

Sam shook his head. No, he knew she would have known.

"How do you share him?" he whispered. "You love him, Marly."

"And you love Heather, Sam, but you would fuck me in a New York minute if Cade were here right now."

He sighed. "I would fuck you without Cade, Marly, and you know it."

"And when Cade saw me later, he would know." She smiled with an edge of excitement. "He would know, and he would touch me, and he would love me, and he would show me all the ways that it brings him pleasure to know that I love you enough to give myself to you, Sam."

It made no sense to him. None of it did. And now the stakes were so much higher. He loved Heather, loved her like nothing he had ever loved in his life, and he wanted to share her. He wanted to see her screaming in pleasure as his brothers took her. See the arousal, the joy, and know she had everything he had to give. His love, his brothers' love, their protection and their caring. To know that no matter where he was, or what happened, Heather would be safe and loved.

But there was more to it, and he was only now realizing it. The bond that had started by that damned pond so long ago, was something too deep to deny, and yet too ethereal to explain.

He hunched forward, lowering his head as he stared at the whisky bottle between his feet.

"I love you all, Marly," he whispered. "Heather holds my soul, but I love you and Sarah, too." He frowned, fighting to understand, to make sense of it himself. "We did all we could to protect you. You weren't raised like we were." He raised his eyes slowly to meet her dark gaze. "And then the abuse... It makes us so different, Marly, and I'm terrified that one of you will be hurt, that we're scarring your souls as much as ours were."

Silence fell between them as he dropped his gaze before bringing the whisky to his mouth once again.

"Sam." She stopped him, her small hand on his wrist as the other lifted the bottle from his grip. "I look at you, and I see parts of Cade and of Brock. And it's the same for Sarah. But we see you as well. We see a man we've grown to love and to respect, one who places our safety and our pleasure above his own. There's no jealousy and no anger, Sam. We're family. A different kind of family, but a family."

"So the family that fucks together, stays together?" he laughed mockingly, jerking to his feet as he paced to the arched opening that led out to the pool area. "God dammit, Marly..."

"No, Sam, a family that loves stays together. However they love, whether it's a love acceptable to the world or not, it's love that holds a family together. Love and respect and the commitment to it, Sam. You know that even better than I do. If you didn't love and respect your brothers, then the three of you would have drifted apart years ago. You wouldn't still be fighting to survive, nor would you be trying to make sense of whatever demons haunt you all. Love, Sam."

She came up behind him, her arms going around his waist as she leaned against his back. Sam turned to her, enfolding her in his arms as he rested his cheek against the black silk of her hair.

"He saved us all," Sam whispered. "Cade, Marly. He saved us, even though he doesn't believe he did."

"You saved each other, Sam," she said gently, and he wondered how much of her statement was true.

"Sam?" Heather's soft voice had him pulling back from Marly, looking over his shoulder as Heather watched them from the sliding glass door that led into the family room.

She didn't look angry or jealous, she looked frightened. Terribly frightened.

"Heather." He turned to her, knowing he had hurt her, knowing this day would come...

"Sam, the sheriff is here. We have trouble."

* * * * *

"You like fucking your brothers, August?" Mark Tate's voice echoed through the room, courtesy of the small recorder Sheriff Martinez held in his hand. He sounded breathless, frightened. In the background you could vaguely hear another voice directing him. "You have two hours to show up at my place, or I send these pictures I have to every newspaper and law enforcement office in the country. Interesting pictures of a dead man."

"You're a dead man." Sam heard his own voice, cold, hard, a promise of violence that he only vaguely remembered.

The sound of the phone disconnecting was loud in the room; those who stood listening were silent, held in shock.

"Oh God." Marly's whispered cry was echoed by Sarah's as they stood in his brothers' arms.

Heather stood beside him, but he couldn't reach out to her, couldn't look at her. He stared down at his hands and saw the blood. Rick and Tara stood somewhere behind the sheriff, witnesses to their shame.

He raised his head slowly, his body tensing in rage as he stared into the cold, hard gaze of a sheriff he had once counted as a friend.

"You should have kept the family out of it, Josh." His voice resonated with a fury he couldn't contain. "They didn't have to hear that."

"Goddammit, Sam." Cade's voice sounded shattered, echoing eerily within his head. *I did it, Sam!* He wanted to shake his head, to rip the shattered words from his head, along with the memories so shadowy and twisted that he couldn't make sense of them. "Why the hell did you leave the fucking house? Why didn't you tell me?"

"It was me he called." He kept his voice low as he continued to watch Martinez. "I would have taken care of it."

"We're a family, Sam," Brock reminded him, his voice tortured.

Sam glanced at him, seeing how Sarah hid her face against his chest. In shame? Did she regret now, allowing him to touch her, to dirty her? Hatred blazed through his mind as he leveled his stare back at the sheriff.

"The only thing that saved your ass from an arrest warrant was the fact that forensics proved Tate was bludgeoned to death with a baseball bat. So hard, in fact, that wood splinters were found in the remains of the body. The coroners had also found traces of a strong narcotic in the battered internal organs." His eyes narrowed then. "If that wasn't bad enough, someone tried to mess with the results at the coroner's office. Luckily, it was discovered. Computer records can be a chancy thing, and old Doc Harper doesn't like them much. His notes were handwritten rather than recorded and transcribed. It appears to me that this is a family problem, Sam. You're being framed, and it looks like there's more than one murder here to solve."

"There's about to be three." He stared at Martinez, his teeth drawn back in a snarl he couldn't contain.

"Sam." Heather's hand covered the fist at his side as she moved closer, blocking him, should he try to move.

He stared down at her, his body tensing, expecting disgust, hatred. What he saw tore into his soul with the force of a knife through unprotected flesh. Tears welled in her eyes, soft understanding shining beneath them.

"Sam, Martinez might think you're serious rather than angry," she said with a smile, yet a warning look. "Sheriffs get serious about death threats, darling."

She moved against his chest, staring up at him, beseeching. An anchor in the storm brewing in him. His arms went around her, terrified if he didn't hold on to something or someone, then he would be sucked into the growing shadows of his own mind.

"Cade. Did Tate have pictures?" Joshua moved further into the room then, and Sam watched as the other man stared at the oldest August brother. "There's rumors he was getting them. That he had proof against the three of you."

"Of what, Josh?" Cade was cold, his voice soft, menacing. "You have unexplained deaths?"

Joshua's gaze was cynical, knowing, as he glanced at Cade before allowing the look to encompass the rest of the occupants in the room.

"No." Josh shook his head. "All I have is an unrecorded phone call to the sheriff's department by someone who went to great pains to disguise their voice. I heard quite a detailed account of a murder in Utah twelve years ago."

A muscle jumped in Cade's jaw, and Sam saw the fury that flared in his brother's eyes.

"Marly..." Cade whispered her name on a sigh.

"No, damn you." She thumped his chest where she rested against it, and Sam could hear her the desperate battle against the tears inside her. "I won't leave. Not again, Cade August. I won't let you face this alone. I won't."

Sam's arms tightened on Heather then. He couldn't let her go. He couldn't let her leave. God help him, if she didn't hold onto him, he didn't know what he would do to the bastard destroying them.

"I'm staying, too." Sarah turned in Brock's arms. Her expression was tormented, filled with knowledge and pain. "We're a part of this, Cade. All of us. It's not just you and your brothers anymore. No more hiding."

"Damn you, Martinez, why didn't you just shoot us and be done with it?" Sam demanded furiously as he released Heather and raked his fingers through his hair. "It would have been more humane than this. I'll be damned if I'll stand here and listen to you destroy my family."

He moved for the door.

"Sam, you walk out that door and I'll arrest you for obstruction of justice and suspicion of murder. I'll lock you up so fast it will make your head spin."

Sam stopped. The memory of the jail cell was fresh in his mind. The memories of another cell were far clearer. He turned back slowly.

"You'll have to kill me first, Josh. Can you do that?" Sam clenched his fists at his sides, fighting the betraying memories welling inside him. They had fought so many years to forget, and now it was being ground in their faces in a way they could never ignore, nor escape.

"Goddamn, Martinez," Brock cursed. "Let him go. We can handle this."

Something inside Sam stilled. He looked at his brothers, seeing desperation and a foreboding fear. He couldn't fight the suspicions any longer, no matter how desperately he needed to. "Protecting me again, Brock?" he asked his brother carefully.

Cade shook his head at the other brother, a clear warning in his eyes as Brock started to speak. Sam advanced back into the room. He looked at Heather; saw her worry, her concern. Rick was observant as always, while Tara watched them all with an edge of sympathy.

"What makes you think we know anything about Utah?" Sam asked him softly. "This is Texas, Josh."

"And Marly's uncle was Jedediah Marcelle. He was killed in Utah twelve years ago by an apparent house fire. Coroner's report suspected he was dead before the blaze. Her natural father, Reginald Jennings barely escaped..."

"No! No!" Marly's shattered voice echoed through the room. "It's not true! Oh God, Cade. Cade, no! You didn't hide this from me." She was screaming at him, fighting the hold he had on her as Cade's face twisted in tortured, agonizing pain as her tears began to fall. "Oh God! Damn you. Damn you, it's not true. Tell me it's not true..."

Rick and Tara moved then, placing themselves between the sheriff and Cade as Sam rushed to his brother, to Marly.

"Oh God. Oh God. Cade."

"Get her the fuck out of here," Sam screamed as Cade fought her, fought to keep her in his arms, to accept the pain radiating through her cries as his face twisted into lines of grief. "Go, goddammit."

Sam felt his heart breaking. He had feared Cade wouldn't share the knowledge with her, the fact that her uncle had raped them, that her father had known. Oh yeah, he remembered Reginald Robert.

Getting Marly out of the room wasn't easy. She fought Cade, broken, despairing. She knew. Sam could feel her knowledge pulsing in every cell of his body. She knew the truth, and it would kill her. Kill Cade. It would destroy them all.

And Martinez had to have known it. He swung around, raw intense rage boiling in his blood, ripping through his body as he jumped for the sheriff.

"Sam, no."

"Did the three of you really think you could keep something like this quiet forever?" Martinez's voice was cold, hard, as he paced the room, flicking a glance at Brock and Sam as he turned at the other end of the room. "Dammit to hell, Sam. You should have known better."

Marly's reaction had shaken them all. Joshua wasn't left unaffected, or unharmed. His eye was nearly swollen shut from the one punch Sam had managed to land before Brock and Rick had taken him to the floor. All he could hear were Marly's cries; all he could feel was Cade's shame. All their shame. It was like an inferno in his gut, searing into his soul.

They had heard Marly's screams for too long, broken, ravaged. Sam was desperate to go up, to help Cade comfort her, as he knew Brock was. But was stuck here instead, dealing with this bastard. Stuck in the memories of a past that never seemed to clearly emerge within his mind. But the screams were there, as was the blood.

"You did it deliberately." Heather accused the sheriff as she sat beside Sam, her hand on his knee, her shoulder pressed against his arm. "You're a cold-hearted bastard, Sheriff Martinez."

Unfortunately, Sam agreed with her. Joshua had always been too damned blunt. Too damned straightforward. He went for the jugular when he needed information, and didn't care whose blood was shed.

"Dammit, Heather, you're out of line," Tara snapped as she faced her from the opposite couch. "You have no opinion in this."

"There's where you're wrong," she argued, obviously fighting to keep her voice quiet. "He was out of line. He had no right to drop that little bombshell the way he did."

Sam could only sit in silence, watching Martinez as he felt the rage ice in the pit of his stomach, and hear the screams that seemed closer than ever before. His eyes were narrowed, watching the man who had once been a friend, a confidant. A long time ago. In what seemed to have been another life.

Martinez grunted sarcastically.

"Of course I was, otherwise, Sam's ass would be in jail for assault and the rest of you for suspicion of obstruction. Unfortunately, I'm about as in the fucking dark as one sheriff could be. Now how the hell am I supposed to keep the lot of you out of prison if you don't fucking help me?" His voice rose as his anger broke the cool demeanor he usually kept. "Dammit, don't you think I knew something happened back then? We were friends, Brock, Sam. Best friends until you returned from Utah. How fucking stupid did you think I was?"

As far as Sam was concerned, it was the wrong question to ask.

"Stupid enough to destroy an innocent woman," Sam yelled back, his fists clenched, his body so tense Heather nearly sat on him to make sure he stayed in his seat.

She stared back defiantly as he flicked her a hard glance. She didn't look ready to move anytime soon. Amazingly enough, there were no recriminations in her look, no sense of disgust, no anger. Understanding marked her dark green eyes, though her face was pale from stress. Her touch was gentle, and though she looked ready to go to battle, it was the sheriff she seemed more than willing to fight.

He loved her. Needed her with a desperation he couldn't explain, but he was damned tired of everyone thinking he needed to be protected. Needed to be cuddled and cared for. He shook his head at that thought. He had spent too many years trying to comfort Cade by playing the prankster, by joking his way through the bleak darkness. Now that he couldn't fight it any longer, his whole family was falling apart around him.

"Who killed Jedediah Marcelle?" Joshua's gaze sliced to Sam. "Don't pull any shit on me, either. If I'm going to pull your ass out of this, Sam, you have to be honest with me."

"Don't answer that, Sam." Rick stepped forward, his voice quiet, steady. He seemed to be the only one in the room not intent on murder. "Sheriff." He turned to Joshua. "You are aware that the phrasing of your questions could be construed as an officer of the law attempting to either entrap, or conspire with my clients. Both of which are illegal." His voice was razor sharp with sarcasm, though his expression remained perfectly bland. Cold and controlled.

Joshua frowned. "Don't you pull any shit with me either, Glaston. I know who the hell you are and just what you're capable of hiding. So we can both go up on conspiracy charges."

"Enough." Sam came to his feet, then jerked his head to stare down at Heather as she placed herself in front of him. "What happened to that bastard doesn't matter. He's dead and gone..."

"And someone knows one of you did the killing," Joshua reminded him coldly. "I'm willing to help, Sam, but not if you can't cooperate with me."

"What do you want, Josh?" he sneered. "Do you want to hear how the bastard drugged us, made our dicks so hard that his crazy half brother could slice into it with a scalpel and it still wouldn't wither? Or how about how he would take a whip and lay it to my back until he forced Brock or Cade to rape the other, or even me? Do you want to hear how many times we had to suck each other off while he cackled..."

"Goddammit, Sam." Brock came to his feet then, his face pale, his eyes tormented. "Shut the fuck up."

Sarah sat on the couch, her arms wrapped around her waist as she rocked silently, her head lowered as tears fell to her lap.

"Sarah, baby. Sarah please..." Brock went to his knees, his hand touching her cheek. "Please, let me take care of this."

"No. I'm okay. I'm ok—" Her voice broke as she seemed to heave sickeningly.

Sam cursed silently as he turned away from the sight. He was no better than Martinez. He shook in the grip of his rage, the twisting images, the sudden sight of bloody hands pushing him to his limits until he had no care for who his words sliced into.

"God. Sam." Martinez drew in a ragged breath as he nearly collapsed in the chair that sat to his side. "God damn."

The blood had drained from his face as he stared at Brock and Sarah, seeing their pain, the ravages the past was causing. He shook his head again.

"Coroner has filed his report," he said bleakly. "You're cleared of Tate's murder, but whoever was with him..." He shook his head. "If they have pictures, Sam..."

"Then the bastard would have used them," Sam bit out. "I appreciate your help, Joshua. But I have to say, you've caused a hell of a lot more harm than you did anything else. Why don't you get the hell out of here until we can figure out what to do."

Joshua frowned, his eyes narrowing. "You think these women are too weak for this, Sam?"

"No." Sam shook his head, pain rioting through his body. "I think they're too damned strong for all of us. Just go, Josh. Just get the fuck out of here so we can deal with it now."

"It's not over, Sam." The other man stood slowly to his feet. "Whoever the bastard is, he's gotten a taste for blood. None of you are safe. He's losing control."

"So am I, Josh. Let me assure you of that. So am I."

# Chapter Nineteen

Heather knocked timidly on Marly's bedroom door. She had heard her and Sarah both caustically ordering their lovers from their rooms. She had seen the bleak pain in all three men when they returned to the family room and headed for the whisky.

Cade was a man tormented. Tortured. For hours they had listened to Marly cry, to her rage that she should be related to someone who had aided in the brother's pain. It was be a piece of knowledge she would be years coming to grips with.

She couldn't believe she was doing this. Couldn't believe their pain and their need was affecting her to this point.

"Cade, go away." The door jerked opened.

Heather stood before the other woman warily, nervously, as she smoothed her hands over her jeans-clad hips.

"Oh. Heather." Marly's tear-drenched eyes widened in surprise. "Come in. You can help me plot Cade's murder."

Marly was as furious as she was hurt by this new knowledge. Realizing that Cade had hidden it from her, Heather knew, would strike the deepest.

Heather eased into the room, glanced at Sarah then cleared her throat.

"I'd rather you two help me plot something a bit more pleasurable." She felt her face flush.

Heather blinked in surprise as Sarah rose slowly to her feet.

"You're going to them?" Marly asked her in amazement.

Heather could feel her heart pounding out of control, fear, arousal and need clamoring through her body. "Sam, he's…"

She swallowed tightly. "He's hurting. Bad, Marly. And the others…"

"They hurt just as badly," Marly said softly, sighing. "None of them deserve it, you know." She frowned sternly.

Heather took a deep breath. She could feel small tingles of electricity moving along the nape of her neck, her scalp. Her body felt warm, yet chilled, and her pussy was drenched at the thought of what was coming. If she could keep her nerve up.

"Damn, this could get embarrassing," she sighed, pushing her fingers restlessly through her hair.

"Why are you doing it, Heather?" Sarah stepped forward then. "If it's just for Sam, you'll never accept it. You'll never enjoy it."

She swallowed tightly. "Brock is pacing, and I can see the tension, the pain in his eyes. He's hurting for them, and doesn't know how to help. Cade is tortured. Sam's starting to remember and he knows it, and he can't stand it. Sam…" She licked her lips as she fought the conflicting emotions inside her heart. "Sam is almost broken, Sarah."

"Not good enough, Heather," Marly whispered gently. "I won't give you my permission, or my help in fucking the man I love with such a flimsy excuse."

Heather frowned. "You knew it was coming," she accused her.

Marly shook her head. "You're not pissing me off, either. Why do you want to do it, Heather?"

She twisted her hands together. Dammit, it shouldn't be this hard.

"It's time." She struggled to push the words out.

"Heather, you're not ready." Sarah's voice was regretful, firm.

"They're breaking my heart, goddammit. I have to do something." Tears welled in her eyes. She knew what they needed, knew what broke the desperate distance that occurred between the men when the demons rose so bleak and cold inside them. "All of them, Sarah. I can't bear it. I can't bear how much I need them, anymore than I can stand their need any longer."

Marly smiled. A slow, gentle smile that eased the desperate fear filling her.

"Let's get started then. And don't balk because of the preparations it takes, it makes it easier for you, and for them."

Balk? She was horrified. An anal douche? Lubricant? She stood inside the bathroom an hour later, the inflatable butt plug once again inserted, inflated to its fullest width. She had showered, shaved, paid special attention to making her cunt as soft, as smooth as possible, and berated herself for her shaking hands as she pulled her robe on quickly.

Stepping back into her own room, she faced the two women who sat cross-legged on her bed, waiting on her.

"Do you realize how depraved this is?" she asked, her voice breaking as she fought for control.

"You'll love it." Marly waved her hand dismissively. "I promise, there is nothing more seductive, more pleasurable than those three men concentrating on you, and on your pleasure. You'll be begging for it again tomorrow."

Heather looked at her in horror. "God, this is so unreal." She trembled, unable to believe she was taking the final step, actually preparing to…

A tingle shot up her spine, the base of her neck, and covered her scalp as she shivered in anticipation.

"Be sure, Heather," Sarah advised her. "If you even think it's not what you want, they'll know, and they'll pull back. It will hurt them more if you're forcing this."

"Forcing it?" she questioned roughly. "Sarah, I'm so hot I might come before I get down the stairs, and that terrifies me."

"Don't do that." Marly laughed. "Save your energy. I promise, you'll need it tonight…"

"Not to mention in the morning, tomorrow night, the night after...takes them a while to get their fill." Sarah was laughing with Marly as they glanced at each other in amusement.

"That's not possible," Heather whispered, horrified. "No man can go like that..."

"Oh Heather, you don't know the August brothers well enough." Sarah shook her head with amused regret. "Trust me, each of them can go three times a day at the least and never blink. Stamina hardly comes close."

She swallowed tightly. "Will it hurt?" She could barely still the tremor in her voice. Damn, she was too nervous.

"Any pain you feel will be so damned good, you'll beg for more." Marly sighed. "I still say Cade doesn't deserve it, though. He should suffer, for days."

"He was protecting you, Marly," Sarah murmured. "You know that."

"I don't need his protection." She propped her elbow on her knee and regarded Heather solemnly as her chin sat atop her fist. "They try too hard to protect us. It's their greatest flaw. Sometimes, you have to kick them, hard, to make them stop."

Heather stood uncomfortably in the middle of the room, waiting for the plug in her rear to ease her muscles. They had told her before she went to the bathroom that it was essential to give her body time to adjust. They loved anal sex as dearly as they did vaginal, and Marly had warned it that it was possible, entirely possible that each of them would need her there before the night was out.

"I think I'm scared," she finally said as she fought to control her breathing, the hard beat of her heart.

"No you're not," Marly assured her softly. "Not really. It's like being a virgin all over again. The unknown is the scariest part. The actual act is more beautiful than you can imagine. This isn't fucking, Heather. It's loving, and I promise, you'll understand that when it's over."

"If I survive it?" she joked nervously.

"You'll survive it," Sarah promised with a smile. "Now, it's been an hour. If the worst of the pinching is gone, then you're ready to go downstairs."

And it was. The fiery tightness in her rear had all but eased, just leaving her feeling stretched, full.

"Here, take this." Marly rushed to the closet and jerked a small satin comforter from the shelf there. "Take off the robe and go to them wrapped in this. Trust me, they'll love it."

Heather removed the robe slowly and wrapped the blanket around her shoulders. She took a deep breath for courage, a smile trembling at her lips.

"You're sure?" she asked the other two women.

"If you are, Heather." Sarah nodded. "But you have to be certain yourself."

She breathed out heavily. She was sure. Turning, she left the room and without looking back, headed downstairs to the men awaiting her.

# Chapter Twenty

Bleak silence filled the house after the sheriff left. Marly and Sarah were quiet, though they had thrown the men out of their rooms and holed up together in Heather's several hours ago. Now Sam sat with Brock and Cade in the family room, watching, listening to the silence.

"I killed Jedidiah Marcelle, didn't I?" It wasn't a blinding stroke of knowledge. He had suspected for years. The blood on his hands, the nightmares, the demons that haunted him, had assured him of it.

He saw the truth in the sudden fear in Cade's face, in Brock's.

"I did it," Cade gritted out roughly.

Sam shook his head, staring at Cade as he let the knowledge sink into him. "I remember the blood, Cade. I remember you wiping it from my hands to your own. And I know why you did it. But I don't need your protection any longer."

Cade came to his feet in a surge of anger as he paced to the French doors. "The son of a bitch deserved to die. It doesn't matter who did it, Sam."

Sam lowered his head, shaking it wearily.

"He did it because of me, Cade. Because I rejected him. Because I humiliated him. It was my fault."

"No, Sam." Brock's expression was sadly quiet, accepting. "It wasn't your fault. Marcelle was a sick man, and he focused on you because you were stronger than he was. Someone he wanted to break. We wouldn't have allowed that, no matter what happened."

Sam shook his head, unable, unwilling to accept such simplicity in the reasoning. "You should hate me, Brock. Look what happened to all of us."

"Exactly, to all of us, goddammit." Cade swung away, fury vibrating in his voice. "We weren't alone, just as we always swore we wouldn't be, Sam. We protected each other as best we could and we came out of it fucking alive, what more do you need?"

"I need to fucking close it," Sam screamed back, surging to his feet. "I want to end the goddamn nightmares, Cade, and the smell of blood and semen that nearly fucking chokes me at times. I want to stop hurting the women I love, and fucking to be normal."

Cade stilled. "You think we're hurting Marly and Sarah?" Amusement struck his voice then, surprise glittering in his eyes.

"We share them, Cade…"

"And you don't want to share Heather?" Cade asked without anger, with no recriminations.

"Son of a bitch, I want it so bad I can nearly taste her fucking cries." His fists clenched at his side.

"Why?" Cade crossed his arms over his chest. "If you think it's going to hurt her, Sam, then why do you want it?"

He stopped. He felt every muscle in his body tighten in knowledge.

"She would love it," he whispered. "She would be loved with everything I have."

"Why would she love it?" Cade shook his head in irritation. "What the hell makes you think we're hurting Marly or Sarah with this? Why the hell do you think they accept it, Sam? It's not just for us. Don't fool yourself. Marly and Sarah have more than any other woman you will ever know, or so Marly assures me…"

"Marly has three men, devoted to her, loving her, always protecting her. She has the love of not just one man, but three.

Three men who will love her until death. She has a love I need, Sam."

They swung around to Heather. She stood there, and Sam felt his heart explode with pride and arousal. Naked, aroused, as she closed the door then dropped the brilliant blue quilted blanket she had wrapped around her body.

"Heather." Sam heard the strangled quality of his own voice and fought to clear it as she advanced on him.

"Do you need this, Sam, for you or for the demons?" she asked him softly as she stopped before him, her hands going to the buttons on his shirt, slipping them free with calm deliberation.

"For me." He fought to control his breathing, his excitement. Like nothing he had known before. Lust and love flared through his soul.

"Why? How is it just for you, Sam?" She pulled the shirt from his jeans, her nails raking his abdomen with piercing pleasure.

"They're part of me." Sam struggled to put the feeling into words, to explain the needs. "If you're with them, Heather, you're with all of me."

"How, Sam?" She pulled at the snap of his jeans. "How is being with your brothers being with you?"

He struggled through the morass of sensations and emotions. Her voice was hot, aroused, searing him as deeply as the touch of her hands seared through his flesh.

"Because, Heather." He ran his hands through her hair, gripping the back of her head as he lifted her face until she was staring deeply into his eyes. "Because they love you too, baby. Just as deep and just as true as I love you."

\* \* \* \* \*

218

Heather's heart exploded in her chest as he whispered the words. His eyes, more gray than blue now, stared down at her, his expression creased into lines of arousal and pleasure as Brock and Cade came around her. Hands moved over her back, her waist, lips smoothed across her shoulder.

"Sam." She trembled, aroused past bearing yet so nervous she could feel her body trembling. "I'm nervous. Real nervous." Talking was more difficult than she could have imagined as she saw Brock move from her side and jerk the large Futon mattress from its place on the couch. "You guys really need a bedroom for this," she gasped as she felt Cade move her hair aside and brush her nape with his lips.

The room dipped and swayed as Sam lifted her into his arms and carried her to where Brock had laid out the overly thick pad in the middle of the floor. Sam lowered her gently to the mattress, then rose only long enough to tear his clothes and shoes from his body.

Heather stared up at him, trembling from the inside out as anticipation and a small measure of fear rushed through her body. She looked at Brock, at Cade. They were naked, their cocks thick and hard, their expressions, adoring. It wasn't lust, it was love. Affection, sexual excitement and a sense of bonding, just as Marly had sworn it was. They moved as one, their concentration on her, their expressions tender, loving, darkly sensual.

"You're so pretty, Heather." Sam came down beside her, his arms enfolding her as he pushed her hair back from her face, his hands trailing lingeringly down her cheek. "So damned beautiful that I can barely believe you're here, in my arms, as I need you."

She stared up at him, fighting to breathe, fighting to concentrate on Sam alone as Brock stretched out beside her on his side and Cade knelt at her feet. She licked her lips nervously, her hand gripping Sam's arm as he stroked her abdomen.

"Only as far as you can go, Heather." A smile tipped his lips, but his eyes were filled with confidence.

"I'm not scared," she tried to snap, but her voice was weak with arousal and nerves.

"No, you're not scared," he whispered. "You're a miracle. A miracle to all of us, baby."

His head lowered then, his lips catching hers in a kiss that had her moaning with rising need as she rose up to meet it. His tongue pushed past the barrier of her lips, tangling with her tongue as the extreme eroticism of the three men around her began to pulse through her bloodstream.

She turned in his arms, reaching for him, needing the soul clenching warmth that his kiss instilled in her. As she did, she felt hands behind her, below her, heard whispered phrases a second before male lips brushed her shoulder, then the calf of her leg.

She cried out into the kiss, arching closer to Sam as he moaned hungrily against her lips, and a broad palm, Sam's or Brock's, enclosed the curve of her swollen breast as her leg was lifted, settled over Brock's thigh and warm lips caressed to her knee.

"Sam!" She broke away from his kiss, fighting for breath as the sexual intensity rose inside her.

"Just feel, Heather," he whispered, desperation ringing in his voice as his lips moved down the front of her arched neck. Her head was resting on Brock's shoulder as his lips and tongue stroked the side of her neck, his hand lifting her breast to Sam's eager mouth.

Further below, Cade's mouth was moving closer, closer to the soaked center of her body.

"Dear God!" she screamed as Sam's lips closed over her hard nipple at the same second Cade's tongue swiped through the creamy slit of her cunt.

She climaxed. Just that easily, that quickly, her body pulsed then shattered, the intensity of sensation exploding through her system as Cade thrust his tongue deep and hard inside her spasming pussy, stroking, licking the rush of liquid release that poured from her.

She was twisting in their grip then, hunching against Cade's mouth as he held her leg up to fit himself deeper between her thighs. Sam's mouth was suckling hungrily at her breast, then moving to the next as Brock moved behind her, and she was stretched out, her hips arching to Cade as Brock covered her other nipple.

Heather was desperate. Racked by such pleasure, such sexual extremes she felt as though insanity was only moments away.

"Sam?" Cade's voice was rough, a question, a heated demand as he rose between her thighs.

Looking over the two heads lowered to her nipples, Heather gasped. Cade's cock was thick and erect, pulling down from his body, heavy and demanding. She watched Sam's then Brock's hands as they went to her thighs, lifting them, opening her for the older brother.

"Heather." Sam's head lifted, staring into her eyes as dazed pleasure and excitement ricocheted through her body.

They were too much alike. Looked too much alike, responded sexually too much alike. Dear God, it was like fucking three Sams. Her pussy was flooding, clenching in greedy need as her anus clenched on the thick butt plug she had inserted an hour before.

"Sam, she's using a plug." Heather cried out as she felt Cade's fingers at the base of the device.

Sam's eyes darkened, his expression growing more intent, more sensual.

"Which one?" he whispered, still watching as Heather cried out at the satisfaction, the adoration in his expression.

"Fuck. Inflatable." Heather shivered as Sam's eyes went nearly black in pleasure. The inflatable had gone in easily enough, but it seemed to take forever to get it inflated to its maximum thickness.

Sam's head turned, his gaze going to her cunt as Cade moved closer, his cock kissing the entrance to her spasming vagina. His expression was entranced, and Brock's was damned near as mesmerized as they spread her legs further, watching the older brother.

"Can you take it, Heather?" Sam sounded strangled.

"Damn you, if one of you doesn't fuck me, I'll shoot all of you." She arched, driving the head of Cade's thick erection into her pussy.

She gasped and stilled, her head tossing as moisture glazed her body and creamy liquid flowed from her cunt. She clenched on the intrusion, feeling the desperate tightness of her vagina as he eased slowly forward.

"Sam. Sam." She chanted his name, nearly screaming as she felt the muscles spreading, protesting, yet making room for the wide stalk moving inside her.

One hand clenched Sam's arm, the other Brock's. She knew her nails were piercing skin and didn't care. She shook, shuddered, crying out yet pleading desperately for more. He was thick and hot, moving in inch by inch as she tightened on his cock, tightened on the plug stretching her ass and felt impaled by a shaft of sizzling steel.

"Sam, damn, I can't hold back," she heard Cade groan desperately as he began to pull free of her. "She's too fucking tight."

"NO!" She arched closer, knowing if he didn't continue, if he didn't force the thick erection inside her then she would die of need. "Sam, please. Please don't let him stop."

They stilled. The air was thick with heat, the smell of sex and clawing arousal. She looked between her thighs, seeing that less than half of the throbbing cock was buried inside her. She felt full, stretched beyond bearing and she was dying for more. She raised her eyes beseechingly to Sam.

"I can't stand it," she cried out, her hips working her cunt on the wide shaft. "Please, Sam. Please fuck me."

Cade jerked as she whispered the words, his cock sliding marginally deeper as her back arched and a growl tore from her throat. Brock and Sam still held her thighs, keeping her open, watching as her cunt flared around Cade's erection.

"Sam…"

He glanced down at her, and Heather saw his excitement, his complete pleasure as she begged for his brother's cock.

"Take her, Cade," he whispered deeply. "Let me watch her. Let me see her pleasure." And in his voice she heard his need for just that. To see her enraptured, pleasured, loved.

Heather couldn't stop the scream that escaped her throat as Cade pushed inside her. Her eyes widened, her vision blurred as pleasure and pain collided, streaking through her system, driving her so high, so hard, she wondered if she would survive it. It wasn't a hard, fast lunge inside her protesting pussy. It was a gentle, remorseless burrowing inside the slick grip of her narrow vagina until he seated himself in to the hilt.

"Damn. Sam. Fuck. She's too tight." Cade held himself deep inside her, unmoving, his hands holding her hips still as she fought to grind herself on his impaling cock.

He pulled back slowly as Brock and Sam seemed to snap from their dazed concentration at the sight of their brother buried inside her pussy. Heather watched, unable to look away as the sight of his shaft, coated with her thick cream, slid back from her.

"No," she whimpered, fighting the hands holding her as she rocked on the hard flesh. "Please. Please. No."

He slammed inside her then. Heather writhed on the mattress, her breath lodging in her throat at the desperate stretching and fiery pleasure attacking her overstretched cunt.

"Sam, I'll come in her," Cade warned tightly. "Son of a bitch, if I don't get my cock out of her, I'm gonna lose it. She's too fucking tight like this."

Heather's eyes rose to Sam. He was on his knees beside her, one hand holding her thigh close to his body as the other stroked his own erection. He stared down at her, his face twisting with lust and anticipation.

She felt Cade's fingers between her thighs, his thumbs at each side of her swollen clit, massaging the flesh around it, making her fight to churn her hips, to work her pussy on the thickly lubricated shaft throbbing inside her. She allowed her hands to reach out to each side of her, covering the male hands that stroked their own cocks. Brock growled out his approval as he moved his hand, allowing her smaller one to stroke the bulging erection tormenting him.

Sam's hand covered hers as she gripped his cock as well, holding her hands still though, rather than allowing her to stroke him.

"I want to watch you," he whispered. "If I fuck you now, Heather, I won't have the control to watch your climax as you explode the first time with us."

"If someone doesn't make me come, I'm going to kill you all," she panted desperately. "For God's sake, Sam, why are you teasing me like this?"

"No, baby," he whispered, his voice pulsing with need. "You don't understand."

"Sam, son of a bitch, this isn't going to last." Cade pulled back and then groaned in defeat before sliding forward again.

"Sam. Sam. Oh God. Sam." Her hands forgot the cocks they were holding and clawed at his arms as pleasure tore through her body. "Please. Please, Sam."

She fought to free her legs, to impale herself on the erection tearing her pussy apart. She was desperate to climax, to be free of the building pleasure, the overwhelming sensations rocking her body.

Cade cursed again, then heaved back, pulling his cock from the gripping desperate flesh of her vagina as she cried out in shock, in pulsing need. At the same time Sam and Brock released her legs, and Heather surged forward. She turned on

Sam, her lips moving to his, her hands gripping his hair as she pushed him to the mattress.

She heard his chuckle, the happiness, the joy in it a second before she mounted the hard cock rising between his thighs. She gave her body no time to adjust to it, no warning before she impaled herself on the bulging erection rising eagerly to her hungry cunt.

Her wail was one of pleasure, pain, sensation tearing through her body as her muscles parted for the desperate thrust. Sam groaned out beneath her, his hands gripping her hips as Brock moved before her, his cock nudging at her lips.

Control was stripped away in the desperation of the moment. Behind her, she felt the relaxing of the anal plug as Cade released the air that had inflated it. Then she moaned in rising pleasure as he pulled it free of her gripping depths.

"Now, Heather," Sam growled, holding her thighs tight, stilling her as Brock's cock pushed into her mouth. "Now, you see…"

Her eyes widened as she felt Cade move behind her as Sam's hands moved to the cheeks of her rear, parting them, revealing the stretched hole of her anus. A second later, the broad head of Cade's cock tucked against it.

"Easy, baby," Sam whispered beneath her. "Slow and easy, Heather."

She moaned around the flesh filling her mouth, suckling at it desperately, whimpering as she felt Cade slide slowly, so damned slow past the tight ring of muscles that spasmed around his flesh. Her cunt clenched around Sam's cock, growing tighter, ever tighter as Cade forged into the heated depths of her anus.

Desperate male groans and whispered accolades shimmered on the moist air around them. Heather trembled, shuddered, weak with arousal and more than thankful as she felt Sam's hands brace her upper body, holding her arm, aiding her in maintaining the position needed to nurse at the thick cock thrusting in and out of her mouth. The clean male taste of the burgeoning flesh, the heated length rasping over her tongue made her hungry, greedy for more. Behind her, Cade was splitting her muscles apart, the hot tight pinch of pain a heady contrast to the exquisite pleasure of Sam's cock stretching her cunt.

She was filled, overfilled, and couldn't help the intense cry that escaped her throat as Cade surged those last inches inside her ass. She was impaled, taken, possessed. She was the center of three hearts, and the holder of one desperate man's soul, and she gloried in it all.

As though the last impalement behind her was all that was needed, the three men began to move. Perfectly synchronized, their bodies rising and falling, pushing in, pulling out, in perfect accord. A natural, heady dance of such sensuality, such erotic excess that Heather lost all sense of reality. A pulsing tempo of desire, passion, lust and love filled the air. Heated male groans, whispered entreaties, and thick hard flesh stroking her most sensitive, tightest regions was more than her system could process at one time.

Her mouth tightened on Brock's cock, her hands tightened in Sam's hair as his mouth latched on an engorged nipple, sucking it deep and hard into his mouth. And further below, as thick, throbbing cocks began to power hard and deep inside her, she tightened sensitive muscles, growling as the hot flesh stroked delicate tissue in ever increasing thrusts.

She was fighting for breath, fighting for sanity as electricity began to travel through her body, lightning arcing, sensation ripping through her spasming womb as Cade and Sam began to fuck her harder, groaning, cocks throbbing as Brock gripped the halfway point of his cock and began to stroke harder inside her suckling mouth. She was going to come. She was going to explode. Disintegrate.

Her body stiffened, tightened, her gaze darkening as she lifted her eyes to Brock in supplication. She couldn't stand it. Couldn't bear it. The pleasure, the sensations, the very depth of emotions were rocking through her like a tidal wave of ever increasing pleasure.

As though that connection, that pleading glance lit a fuse, she felt Brock stiffen.

"Sam, I can't wait." His body bucked, his cock drove into her mouth again, then again as behind her, below her, Cade and Sam increased their thrusts, the pleasure, and she died.

She was only vaguely aware that the sound of suckling lips was overly loud to her dazed senses. The sound of wet thrusts, male groans and heated adoration was too much. She exploded as Brock pulled free of her mouth, a cry tearing from her throat.

She felt her body jerking, convulsing, her juices spraying from her cunt as her body shuddered in hard, involuntary spasms. Her womb rippled, clenched, her anus tightening as Cade groaned behind her a second before he blasted the hot depths of her ass with his desperate release.

Sam cried out below her, words of love, of need, emotional, intense, as another climax tore through her, pouring over his cock as he thrust harder, deeper inside her. And still her pussy milked him, clenching on his flesh.

She could hear Cade behind her, a last groan tearing from his chest as her muscles continued to tighten on him, on Sam, before he slowly pulled free of her. Then amazingly, shockingly, Brock gripped her hips, his still hard cock thrusting into her ass as Sam stilled for only the time it took for his brother to begin a series of hard, quick thrusts inside her.

"Sam, Sam..." she chanted his name. "God help me, I love you, Sam."

Pivotal, intense, the words shattered his control. He heaved beneath her, burying his cock deep and hard inside her as Brock blasted her with his own release. Sam filled her. His seed jetted to her womb, triggering another harder, deeper climax that had her body tightening to a point that she felt she would shatter. And then she did. Like a veil of night, the pulsing emotion and deepening, agonizing pleasure overwhelmed her senses as she slumped against the man that she knew would hold her, heart and soul, for eternity.

Sam held her close, still a part of her body, unable to pull himself free, to move her fragile weight from his chest. The scent of sex and semen, and raw, unbridled emotion still filled the air. But there was no scent of blood. For the first time in his life, he could smell the raw, earthy scent of sex, and smell no blood.

Her body was soaked with her own release, as well as theirs. Her hair was thoroughly damp, falling over her shoulder and his to trail to the mattress beneath them. He pretended that the moisture on his face was his own sweat, but he knew it for the tears it was. He held her close, rocking her, and let them fall.

It wasn't the sexuality or the lust that fulfilled him in sharing her. It went deeper, further than that. She knew a pleasure now that he alone could never give her. It was an unselfish giving from his soul. In sharing her with the men who were as much a part of him as any other human could be, he gave her more than he could ever give her alone. Sensations, emotions, a protection and an acceptance that would never dim.

In his soul he realized now why one of his brothers could walk into a room, smell the scent of the other on his woman, and know pride rather than jealousy, regret or guilt. They would be there when he couldn't be. She would have three measures of support, rather than just one. She would have three of him.

"Sam?" Cade's voice was soft, relaxed. Sam hadn't heard that quality in his voice in years.

He shook his head, the weakness of his tears hidden. He wasn't a kid anymore, but a grown man, and still his greatest joy, his greatest sense of security was in knowing that all he was, all he cared for, was being watched over by the brothers who had been his salvation throughout his life.

"When you're holding Marly, touching her, loving her, I know in my soul it's the same as if it were myself," he said softly. "I know what you're feeling, and it's okay. I'll be damned if I didn't cry in her arms when I bathed her after that first time."

He smoothed his cheeks over Heather's shoulder, feeling her even breathing, knowing the exhaustion that gripped her.

"She needs to be bathed, Sam," Brock advised him gently. "So she won't be too sore, or wake up uncomfortable."

He moved her gently, aware of the hands that helped him. His brothers. They laid her back on the mattress, and Sam could only smile gently as she cuddled closer to his warmth, a slight chill rippling over her skin from the air-conditioning for a moment before Cade jerked the blanket over her.

Ready hands to see to her comfort if he couldn't. To see to her pleasure, her happiness. He sighed deeply as he rose to his feet and dragged his jeans wearily over his legs. It was a ritual, a necessity. She had given them the greatest gift a woman could give, and now it was time that he saw to her comfort and her wellbeing.

He wrapped the blanket carefully around her as Cade and Brock dressed. They would return to their own rooms now, shower, and then love their women, either separately or together. There was no censure, no sense of doubt or possessiveness among the women, or the brothers. Sarah loved Brock, but she understood that sometimes Cade needed her as well, and there were times, Sam knew, that Sarah had sought out that connection as well. Just as Marly did. As Heather would soon learn to.

It wasn't pushed on them, it wasn't taken for granted, the gift they gave. Each woman set her own limits, and without argument, without disapproval, each of the brothers accepted those limits.

As he left the family room, he drew up warily, stopping outside the door as he glimpsed Tara standing militantly by the stairs. He expected rage, expected a screaming fit. But it was sadness that marked her features instead.

"If she gets hurt, I'll kill you," she whispered, and Sam knew she meant it. "Some way, Sam, somehow, I'll kill you."

He held Heather closer, glancing down at her slumbering features as joy pulsed in his heart. When he looked up at Tara, there were no doubts, not in his heart, not in his voice.

"If she gets hurt, Tara, you won't have to. I'll take care of that myself."

Her lips firmed as she drew in a ragged breath. She said nothing more though, merely stepped aside and allowed him to carry his woman to his room. The pain that marked her features worried him, for Heather's sake. He knew that pain would concern her, would weigh on her. Despite their differences, the two women were close, almost as close as he and his brothers were. Almost, but not quite.

He stepped into the darkened bedroom, flipping the light on as he kicked the bedroom door closed then came to an abrupt stop. Nightmare and reality collided. Hopelessness, horror scarred his soul.

"Hello, Sammy-boy." The voice whispered demonically. "Been a long time ain't it, son?"

# Chapter Twenty-One

Sam prayed that Heather continued to sleep. He laid her on the bed as directed, tucking the blanket carefully around her, tucking her hair back from her face as he stared down at her with a sense of agony. If he could just get the threat out of the room, out of the house, then the rest of them would be safe.

"You dirtied her," the voice sneered. "You and those bastards touched her and soiled a good, decent woman, just like you did Marly. You were supposed to protect them, Sam. Protect them, not turn them into camp whores."

"Yes, I know." He stilled the rage and the denials that rose in his soul. He would do whatever it took to keep Heather safe, no matter what he had to say, what he had to do.

He rose slowly and turned back to face the past.

She wasn't the beauty she used to be. Her long, black hair was cut almost manly short. Her eyes, once a deep blue, now seemed faded. The once pure, creamy skin was mottled, with small scars along her cheeks. She was pitifully thin, almost emaciated.

"You killed Tate." He shook his head, knowing it was true.

"Of course I did," she sneered. "He was a blight on society, no better than Reginald was."

"Was?" Sam asked her carefully.

"Was." Cruelty reflected in her gaze. "He's dead, Sammy. Poor bastard, thought he could help Jack take me, punish me for running away. I showed him. I killed him just like I killed Tate."

Sam swallowed tightly.

"This will kill Marly, Anna," he whispered painfully. "Did you think about that?"

She grimaced, her lips twisting with an ugly sneer as she aimed the gun at his heart.

"Marly will never know," she sneered. "I'll kill you, Sam, and remove your influence forever. It's your fault. All your fault. If you hadn't killed Jedediah, then he would have kept Reggie under control. Would have kept him from hurting me. He controlled Reggie and Jack, and you killed him. Then, when I would have forgiven that, you turned my baby into a whore. Made her as diseased and dirty as you are."

"Do you know what he did to us, Anna?" he whispered bleakly. "For God's sake, he would have destroyed us."

"Of course I knew," she growled. "I lived there, Sam. I heard every scream, every plea out of your pathetic mouths. Whining bastards that you were."

Shock shattered his system, weakening his knees, sending his stomach dipping with horror. He could only stare at her, his body tightening with ragged, enraged fury.

He remembered how he had once looked up to this woman. When he was younger, before his father's abuses, his mother's death. Remembered how she would come to Cade when Joe's screaming rages first started, huddling in a bed with the three boys, trembling in fear.

"You're insane," he whispered. "You'll never get out of here. Never get away with this."

"Of course I will," she cooed almost gently. "We're going to walk out of here, Sam, and go to the back door. The guard there is sleeping his final sleep. And we'll walk out into the night. You'll never return, and neither will I, until Rick's crew pulls out, and Heather will go with them. No one will know me then. No one will suspect when I return." She waved the gun to the door. "Let's go before your little whore wakes up and I have to kill her, too."

He moved to the door, praying for a chance to catch her off guard. He couldn't do it in the house. Couldn't take the chance that Cade or Brock, or one of the women would be hurt. His best chance would be outside, in the dark.

"Don't try to screw me over, Sammy," she snarled as he reached the door. "Make sure no one's out there. If they are, they'll get hurt."

He paused, opening the door slowly.

"You first," she hissed, waving toward the hallway.

He stepped from the room, his body tense, tight, desperate to get Anna from the house before anyone else, especially Marly, saw her. He stayed where she could see him, knowing he had to get her away from Heather, then away from the house. After that, he would make damned sure she paid for the hell she had put them all through.

She stepped carefully from the bedroom, tucking the gun in the pocket of her light jacket as she motioned him forward. He headed for the stairs.

"Sam, is Heather awake yet?" Cade's bedroom door opened and Marly stepped from the room. Between him and her mother.

Sam swung around, moving in front of her, placing his own body between her and the crazy woman intent on death.

"Momma?" Her voice was dazed, confused as she fought Sam. "Move, Sam. Move. It's my mother." Joy lit her voice as it rose in volume, until she glimpsed the gun Anna had jerked from her jacket and aimed at Sam's heart. "Momma?"

"Stay back, Marly. Get the fuck back in your room." He fought to crowd her to the open doorway, as Brock moved from his own bedroom behind Anna.

Sam glanced at his brother, seeing instant understanding as Anna started to dart back to Sam's room, and Heather. Brock moved quickly, placing his body between her and the room, ignoring the gun wavering between him and Sam, and the desperate-eyed woman watching them with hatred.

"If you fire that gun, you'll wake her up," Sam warned her. "You can't get to her, Anna."

"Momma, what are you doing?" Marly fought Sam as he held her back, terror thickening her voice. "Damn you, Sam, get out of my way."

"No, Marly." He pressed her against the wall, turning to her, holding her in place. "Baby, she's fucking crazy. Please. Please God, Marly. Stay behind me."

"Let her go!" Anna screamed, the barrel of the gun homing in on him.

"Pull the fucking trigger, bitch," he yelled, turning back to her, fury marking his face. "Do you think I'll let you have her? Let you close enough to hurt her? You're crazier than Marcelle was if that's what you think."

Anna blinked. "She's not your woman, Sam. I could take Heather instead. She'll be out here in a minute," she sneered. "Would she trade herself for you, I wonder?"

Sam snarled and glanced at Brock. His brother moved closer to the bedroom door just in case. "Brock will protect her, Anna. The same as I'll protect Marly."

"And if you die?" she screeched. "I'll kill you, Sam."

"You won't get Marly before Brock gets you, Anna," he warned her. "Either way you go, one of us will get you."

"And one of you will die," she spat out. "What then, Sammy?"

"Then the other will protect what's his, Anna," Brock spoke for him. "The same as we protected what was yours when you brought her to us. Family, Anna. We protect each other."

"Protect!" She growled the word. "You dirtied my baby. You made her your whore, the same as Jack and Reggie tried to make me. You raped my baby and you made her accept you. Monsters, just like they were."

"Momma, no!" Marly cried out, tears thickening her voice, pain echoing in it. "What are you doing? Why would you do this?"

Anna paused. She stared at Sam, then at Marly as she fought to see around Sam's wider body. "Because they destroyed it all, baby," she whispered gently. "Don't you understand? I gave Marcelle Sam. It was my idea, honey, so he would make Reggie and Jack leave you alone. Don't you remember your daddy, baby? Always wanting to touch you, to cuddle you." Anna shuddered. "And Sam ruined it. He ruined it all in a way that made me lose you. I had to let you go until I could find a way to destroy them. To keep them from you."

Marly cried out in pain behind him as he held her close, feeling her body sag against the wall.

"No," she cried out. "Please, no. Oh God Momma..."

"Marly, you don't understand." Anna shook her head, her eyes glittering with demonic fervor. "He protected us, baby. All he needed was Sammy. But Sam had to go and hit him and piss him off, and then Cade and Brock hit him. They had to pay, baby. Jedediah was a great man, Marly. Hell, they deserved it; even then the bastards shared their stupid girlfriends. Perverts. They all were."

"He nearly killed Cade," Marly screamed out in pain, fighting Sam harder now. "Damn you. Damn you. You're not my mother. Never. Never, by God, will I know you as my mother." She kicked at Sam's legs, clawed at his arms, fighting to be free as voices began to raise the alarm downstairs and Cade came barreling up the stairs.

"Fuck. Anna." He slid to a stop beside Sam, confusion marking his features as he stared at the gun and the wild-eyed woman waving it.

"Well, there he is," Anna snarled viciously. "Big brother. Ever tell your lover how often you fucked your brothers, Cade? Or how many times they fucked you? Since we're all here, maybe we oughta just reminisce for a while." Gleeful laughter echoed in the air for a brutal, agonizing second before the shot was fired.

"I hate stupid people." Sam watched in shock as Heather stepped from his room, fully dressed, her revolver held carefully in front of her as she stared at the fallen woman.

Silence reigned for long seconds, then rushing feet as Tara and Rick and nearly two dozen body guards ran upstairs.

"Call an ambulance, Tara," Heather barked out the order roughly. "She's not dead, but she's not in good shape.

"Momma." It was Marly's broken, tear-filled voice that drew their eyes from the scene of the bleeding, unconscious woman slumped along the wall.

She moved slowly from behind Sam. Her eyes were wide, dazed, as Cade caught her slight body in his arms.

"Keep her back, Cade," Rick ordered abruptly as he knelt in front of Anna. "Damn, it was Helena," he whispered again.

"Her name's Anna. She's Marly's mother," Cade said wearily, pain vibrating in his voice.

"Explains why she refused house duty. She couldn't take the chance that any of you would see her." Tara knelt beside the fallen woman. "I allowed it because she seemed so quiet, so sad."

Rick shook his head. "She signed on with the agency a few years back, when we worked on the Stewart case. She worked with us off and on after that until we came here. She had perfect papers under the name Helena Doraga."

"That was Grandmother's maiden name," Marly whispered, her voice hoarse. "She was going to kill Sam. She tried to kill Sarah." She looked across the room to where Sarah watched the scene in amazement.

"Munchkin." Sam touched her cheek as Cade held her upright. "This wasn't your mother, baby. Not this woman."

Sam saw the tears that rolled down her cheeks, saw Cade's bitter helplessness in his eyes. The rage was gone from his brother's face though. The dark, grief-stricken anger that had lingered there for years was missing. Sam realized since finding Marly, his brother had slowly come to terms with the past.

He turned back to Heather, arching a brow sardonically as she tucked the pistol in its holster behind her hip. "Hey, Hot Stuff," he growled. "I was supposed to be protecting you."

He moved to her, jerking her into his arms, his lips covering hers in a kiss of thanksgiving, of joy. Her lips opened to him, her arms tightening around his shoulders as her breath hitched in her chest.

Pulling back, he stared into her damp eyes. "What?" He frowned down at her. "Don't even think about leaving me, Heather. I won't let you go."

"Leaving you?" she questioned him roughly, her green eyes sparkling with her tears. "Sam, I was terrified. Completely terrified. You would have let that evil woman kill you. I know you would have. You walked right out of our room like a fucking sacrifice." Her fist bounced on his upper arm as she struck him harshly. "Damn you. You know better than that."

Sam laughed. He couldn't help it, couldn't stem the happiness overflowing inside his soul. "Oh no, baby. The minute I had her outside she was done for. I would have come back, Heather. I wouldn't, couldn't let you go, baby."

He held her close again, her slight weight enfolded in his arms as Sam looked over her head to Brock. He had stood before the door, knowing what would happen if Heather walked out unwarily. He had covered the slight crack she had made when opening it, had eased aside for the gunshot. But he had stood there, protecting her, ensuring her life. The same as he had protected Marly.

Rick's men applied first aid to Anna, prepped her for the ambulance and moved her quickly downstairs as Cade and Marly followed. It would be hard on Marly, he knew. Her gentle heart, her dreams of her mother returning, were shattered forever. But she wasn't alone. And she never would be.

"I owe you a bath," Sam whispered into Heather's still damp hair. "A bath and a lovin'. Think you can handle me?"

She snorted tearfully. "You and two more just like you…" She paused. "Well, maybe we'll wait to try that one again."

Sam chuckled, held her closer and drew her slowly into their room. The past was over. There were still questions that needed to be answered, and he knew his returning memories wouldn't be easy on any of them. But the demons were gone. The fears were laid to rest and his life stretched out before him now, devoid of the loneliness, of the bleak, desperate pain. And Heather's gift of love had healed those raw, aching wounds in his soul. Her acceptance, her love. The gift of her heart to them all.

# Chapter Twenty-Two

Several weeks later, Sam sat alone in the dark shadows of the family room, staring out at the night through the glass doors. The bodyguards were gone. The house was silent, safe again. It had been so long since they had all felt safe. Twelve years to be exact. In the past weeks, Sam had realized how oppressive the memories of the abuse had been, how the repression of them had affected his own life.

Slowly, the memories had returned. Bleak, filled with pain, shame, and finally a resigned acceptance.

*It happened, we survived it. Doesn't matter how we survived it, Sam, we did. And we're healing, that's all that matters.* Brock's quiet words not too long ago had slowly made sense to him. With Heather's help, with her smart mouth, her take-charge tone and her sweet loving, he had finally found a measure of acceptance and peace.

"Sam?" He turned as Heather's soft voice questioned him from the doorway.

She walked into the room, her slender body covered by an almost sheer silk nightie that fell only as far as her thighs.

"You should be sleeping." He wrapped his arms around her as she came to him. The sweet scent of her perfume went to his head; the feel of her slender body sent a surge of lust through his cock. He would never get enough of her. No matter how many times he had her.

"You weren't in bed with me." She snuggled into his arms, a little drowsy as he sat down in the chair at his side and pulled her onto his lap.

"I was just thinking." He kept his voice quiet as he spoke, relishing the soft intimacy of holding her like this.

The past weeks had been rife with confusion, with Marly's shattered dreams of her mother and Anna's eventual burial. Heather's bullet hadn't killed her, but her own twisted hatred had. She had died in her attempt to escape the hospital and come after the Augusts once again. After tricking her guard and stealing his gun, she had been stopped as she slipped down the hallway. A police officer's bullet had stopped her after she had fired on him.

"Remembering?" she asked gently.

Sam smoothed his hand over her silky hair, enjoying the feel of it against his palm.

"Questioning maybe," he sighed. "Accepting."

She was quiet for long moments. Finally she sighed deeply, her lips pressing against his bare chest.

"And have you accepted?" she asked him, moving, turning her body until she faced him, her legs spread across his, the heat of her cunt settling against the strength of the erection straining beneath his sweat pants.

Sam laid his forehead against hers, staring into her eyes, a grin edging his mouth. She wasn't going to baby him, nor would she pamper to the memories. She was tough as nails, and refused to let him blame himself, or wallow in the pain of the past. Not that he had any intentions of doing it. Remembering was easier than forgetting, and acceptance had slowly settled over him.

"Would you let me do otherwise?" he asked her as he kissed her pert nose gently.

She snorted. "Like I can control you. You do what you want, Sam. I've always known that."

He shook his head, leaning his head back on the high rest of the chair as he stared at her. Yeah, he did what he wanted. And all he wanted in life was to love this woman. To give her more pleasure than she could bear, to make her life as smooth as possible. Which reminded him...

"What were you doing cooking tonight? I swear, next time I have to wait on the three of you to clean the mess up before I can take you to bed, I'm going to paddle your butt."

"Hmm." She arched a brow suggestively. "Sounds like fun. Wanna go for it now?"

He frowned fiercely. "We could have gone out to eat, Heather. You didn't have to cook."

"I'm tired of eating out." She smoothed her hands over his chest, her nails biting lightly at his skin. "Make Cade hire a housekeeper if you want to help."

He snorted. "She would run off the first time she heard us all fucking in here. Damned prudes."

"We have bedrooms," she chuckled, the sound soft, husky with desire.

"Uh uh." Sam shook his head firmly. "In here. It's good in here, Heather. All of us together, loving, laughing. The bedroom wouldn't be the same."

The openness of the family room, the feeling of freedom, of acceptance, wouldn't be the same in any other room, he thought, not for those occasions. Not that he wasn't prone to take any of the three women in whatever room he caught them in. He was. But those nights when all their desires converged, and the sharing became heated, intense, drawing screams of pleasure, pleas for release, the family room couldn't be replaced.

"Pervert." She rocked against his cock, her wet pussy moistening his pants.

"Nympho," he whispered back. "You've been fucked senseless today, and you still want more."

The women were damned picky. Cycling weeks they were off limits, and this was Sarah's and Marly's week. Damned women seemed to be slowly moving to a matching schedule. It was worrisome. But Heather had been left the lone woman out for the past few days. Cade and Brock had kept her busy.

He shivered as he remembered walking into the kitchen from the barn that morning, seeing her sitting on Cade's lap, her back to his chest, her pretty cunt dripping as his fingers tunneled into it. Cade's cock had been buried hard and deep up her ass as he pushed her into orgasm. The sight of it had been so damned erotic he had nearly come in his jeans at the time. With her big green eyes watching him, helpless, overwhelming pleasure filling her face, he had thought his cock would explode.

Then later that afternoon as she lay by the pool, Brock had oiled every inch of her skin with a thick layer of tanning oil before turning her to her stomach and fucking her through more than one orgasm. She had slept the rest of the evening; he grinned at the thought.

"I always want you, Sam," she said as her lips moved to his neck, her teeth rasping against his skin. "I could keep you buried inside me forever."

Her hands moved between them to pull at his pants. Sam lifted his hips, helping her to pull the sweat pants down his thighs, releasing the thick length of his cock. She whimpered as he positioned himself and began to ease into the ultra tight depths of her body.

"Damn." His fingers clasped the full globes of her rear, separating them until he could feel the base of the plug she had inserted.

"I need it all." She gasped for breath, her nails biting into his shoulders as she impaled herself slowly on his erection. "I need all of you, Sam."

He groaned her name, he couldn't help it. He pushed in hard and deep, giving her the bite of pain she craved as his lips covered hers. She was a wildcat, in bed and out. His tongue plunged past her lips as he gripped the base of the plug, moving it in time to her thrusts on his cock, letting her feel the fullness, the flaring heat of the double penetration.

Her moans rose, her pussy growing wetter by the second, her tempestuous passions burning him alive. She stroked around him, so hot and snug around his erection that he had to grit his teeth to hold on to his control. His hips thrust in time to hers, plunging his cock harder, deeper inside her as he felt the convulsive ripples of nearing climax that echoed through her snug channel.

"You're so tight, Heather," he whispered against her ear as he powered deep and hard inside her. "So hot, so perfect..." His breath caught as he heard the sound of her whimpers change. Breathy, hitching with excitement. "Yeah, baby," he groaned, his cock throbbing, flexing as he neared his own release. "Tighten on me, Heather. Grip me, baby, until it hurts to move."

And she was doing just that. Shuddering, she could only hold herself still then as he gripped her hips, holding her to him as he thrust his cock inside her despite the tight, slick drag of her muscles clasping him. When she came, she screamed his name. Her body jerked in his arms as he pushed his cock inside her hard, deep, before allowing his seed to jet in thick, hot streams into the depths of her cunt.

Her wet flesh rippled around him as she shivered in his arms, fighting for breath. Little cries from her echoing climax sounded against his chest as her arms tightened around him.

"You've given me more than any woman has a right to hold." Her voice sounded filled with tears, emotion thickening it. "I love you, Sam."

He breathed in hard and deep. "And you've given me more than I dreamed possible," he countered. "I worship you, Heather. In ways you'll never know."

# Epilogue

"So what do you think?" Screams of pleasure echoed through the house, muffled by the door of the family room and the kitchen, as Marly begged, pleaded for release.

"Does it really matter?" Sarah yawned as she sipped at her coffee, then sighed tiredly as she propped her chin in her hand and stared at Heather across the table.

"But what do you think?"

"Explains the damned moodiness." Sarah said as she shook her head in amazement. "Would be kinda nice, though."

Heather blinked in surprise. She would have laughed in amazement, but over the last six months she had learned not to. The wedding had been strange enough, but the most beautiful experience of her life. Only the closest friends of the August family and the women had been in attendance. The controversy would have scandalized the community. Hell, the world. Three couples intermarrying. Heather was married to three men, as were Sarah and Marly. Not legally, of course, the legal ceremony had bound her to Sam for all time, but the less formal ceremony had bound her heart to all three men.

It was unconventional. It was scandalous. Heather was loving it.

"Those men will be grinning, strutting fools," Sarah smiled as she sipped from her coffee again.

Heather snorted. That wouldn't describe it.

"Sarah," she sighed. "Have you thought, they have no idea which of them is the father?"

Sarah shook her head. "It won't matter to them, Heather. That baby belongs to all of them. Just as ours will, no matter if the other two are there at the time or not."

Heather turned and stared out the wide picture window into the early spring morning. The last six months had been the happiest of her life. As Sam had explained, she held them all, though in different ways. Sex with the brothers wasn't an everyday thing, but it was often. The morning after the weddings, Cade had caught her stumbling into the kitchen for coffee. Before she had the first cup poured she had his cock filling her pussy.

Strong, driving strokes that had her crying out his name, spasming around his hard flesh as she climaxed in his arms. Later that evening, it had been Brock, straddling her prone body by the pool, his cock easing into her greased anus as the Rabbit vibrator had driven her cunt crazy. She still remembered that. The explosive, screaming climax had left her trembling as Brock shot his seed deep inside the hot depths of her ass.

And every night, several times through the day, Sam was there. Loving her, touching her, taking her with heat and joy. And now Marly was pregnant.

"Good God," she mumbled, dropping her head to the table. "Are you aware of the fact that as she gets further along, she'll be out of commission?"

Silence filled the room. She glanced up at Sarah and saw the concern on the other woman's face.

"Poor guys, I'm not taking up the slack." Sarah shook her head determinedly. "You can."

"Me?" Heather squeaked incredulously. "Do I look like a damned bunny to you? Those men have more testosterone than twenty just like them. I'm not taking the slack up."

"Now look, Heather, you're younger—"

"Don't you pull that younger crap on me, Sarah August," she sniped as she shook her head firmly. "No. No way. Not a chance in hell. I'll move to the damned bunkhouse."

"So?" Sarah blinked. "They would just follow you. Just like they did when you got pissed and stalked off to the barn that night."

Heather felt her face flush as her cunt clenched. A spanking shouldn't be so damned erotic, but she would be damned if that one hadn't driven her insane with arousal. Of course, the arousal had been taken care of in a more than satisfactory manner as each of the brothers had filled her body while the others touched, stroked and worshiped her.

"Those men are dangerous," she muttered.

"Not to mention potent," Sarah grunted. "She hasn't been off the pill two months yet."

Heather sighed. "We're sunk."

"Naw, we're fucked," Sarah laughed. "But how much you want to bet it will be an experience we don't want to miss?"

Heather could only shake her head. She had wondered if she would be jealous or angry when Marly's dream was realized. After the death of her mother, and the reports of her father and uncle's deaths, she had slipped into a moody, silent depression for weeks. When she came out of it, she announced her desire for a baby. She had gone off the pill that week. For a month, she insisted they would wear condoms, to allow the effects of the birth control to get out of her system. Amazingly enough, they hadn't bitched about it.

Then, four weeks later, at the height of her fertile days, she wanted them all together, one time, one chance to give her what she thought they all needed. She had wanted the child to be a part of all of them, she had announced, and this was her way of ensuring that.

Other than that one time, only Cade had been with her sexually until her announcement that morning. But Heather knew those three men didn't give a damn who the father was. That child would be loved, cherished and raised with a houseful of loving parents.

The sounds of passion slowly quieted in the other room. Long minutes later a door upstairs closed. Cade would be bathing Marly, soothing her, easing her, whispering his love to her, just as Sam and Brock did for Heather and Sarah.

"Hey, babe." Sam stepped into the room, followed closely by Brock. He dropped a quick kiss on Heather's cheek before heading for the coffee pot as Brock followed suit.

Heather watched the two men. Over the last six months the pain inside them all had eased. Bleak shadows and twisted nightmares were a rare occurrence, and when it happened…she smiled, remembering Sam's last nightmare. The women had taken him to the family room, and loved him as well as the brothers had ever loved one of them. She thought he was rather looking forward to his next nightmare now.

She watched him, her husband, her lover as he carried his coffee to the table and sat down beside her. He pulled his chair close to her, nuzzling her ear before turning to the caffeine. He smelled of sex and sweat and love.

"So we're having a baby?" she asked him softly.

His eyes lit with amusement as he leaned close to her. "I pulled out," he whispered softly, though loud enough for Sarah to hear as well.

For a second, shock held her still before laughter burst from her chest. She looked at him, seeing the smug male satisfaction on his face, the twinkle in his eye. "You are bad." She shook her head, glancing at Brock. "What about you?"

He leaned back in his chair, his fingers curling through Sarah's blonde hair as he shrugged, grinning like a fool. "Hell, do you think we're gonna let her carry anyone's baby but Cade's? She's loves us all, but I'll be damned if I'll take this from him. And he knows it."

They were too much alike, and yet so individual, so uniquely separate that sometimes it amazed her, these August men. As hot as the month they were named for, and yet so gentle, so deeply loving of each other, and their women, that they amazed her.

She leaned against Sam, content and at peace as she gazed up at him. "I love you, Sam August."

His smile was quick, and carefree. "I love you too, Heather August. Forever."

## About the author:

Lora Leigh is a thirty something wife and mother living in Kentucky. She dreams in bright, vivid images of the characters intent on taking over her writing life, and fights a constant battle to put them on the hard drive of her computer before they can disappear as fast as they appeared. Lora's family, and her writing life co-exist, if not in harmony, in relative peace with each other. An understanding husband is the key to late nights with difficult scenes, and stubborn characters. His insights into human nature, and the workings of the male psyche provide her hours of laughter, and innumerable romantic ideas that she works tirelessly to put into effect.

Lora welcomes mail from readers. You can write to her c/o Ellora's Cave Publishing at 1337 Commerce Drive, Suite 13, Stow OH 44224.

# Why an electronic book?

We live in the Information Age—an exciting time in the history of human civilization in which technology rules supreme and continues to progress in leaps and bounds every minute of every hour of every day. For a multitude of reasons, more and more avid literary fans are opting to purchase e-books instead of paperbacks. The question to those not yet initiated to the world of electronic reading is simply: *why?*

1.  *Price.* An electronic title at Ellora's Cave Publishing runs anywhere from 40-75% less than the cover price of the <u>exact same title</u> in paperback format. Why? Cold mathematics. It is less expensive to publish an e-book than it is to publish a paperback, so the savings are passed along to the consumer.

2.  *Space.* Running out of room to house your paperback books? That is one worry you will never have with electronic novels. For a low one-time cost, you can purchase a handheld computer designed specifically for e-reading purposes. Many e-readers are larger than the average handheld, giving you plenty of screen room. Better yet, hundreds of titles can be stored within your new library—a single microchip. (Please note that Ellora's Cave does not endorse any specific brands. You can check our website at www.ellorascave.com for customer recommendations we make available to new consumers.)

3. *Mobility.* Because your new library now consists of only a microchip, your entire cache of books can be taken with you wherever you go.

4. *Personal preferences are accounted for.* Are the words you are currently reading too small? Too large? Too...**ANNOYING**? Paperback books cannot be modified according to personal preferences, but e-books can.

5. *Innovation.* The way you read a book is not the only advancement the Information Age has gifted the literary community with. There is also the factor of what you can read. Ellora's Cave Publishing will be introducing a new line of interactive titles that are available in e-book format only.

6. *Instant gratification.* Is it the middle of the night and all the bookstores are closed? Are you tired of waiting days—sometimes weeks—for online and offline bookstores to ship the novels you bought? Ellora's Cave Publishing sells instantaneous downloads 24 hours a day, 7 days a week, 365 days a year. Our e-book delivery system is 100% automated, meaning your order is filled as soon as you pay for it.

Those are a few of the top reasons why electronic novels are displacing paperbacks for many an avid reader. As always, Ellora's Cave Publishing welcomes your questions and comments. We invite you to email us at service@ellorascave.com or write to us directly at: 1337 Commerce Drive, Suite 13, Stow OH 44224.

Discover for yourself why readers can't get enough of the multiple award-winning publisher Ellora's Cave. Whether you prefer e-books or paperbacks, be sure to visit EC on the web at www.ellorascave.com for an erotic reading experience that will leave you breathless.

WWW.ELLORASCAVE.COM